ART

A novel concerning Hoxton and Shoreditch

Also by Peter Carty

The Athenian Option: Radical Reform for the House of Lords
(with Anthony Barnett)

To Charmaine

Peter Carty

ART

A novel concerning Hoxton and Shoreditch

With Best Wishes

Peter Carty

Pegasus

A CIP catalogue record for this title is
available from the British Library.

ISBN 978-1-91090-388-9

Pegasus is an imprint of
Pegasus Elliot Mackenzie Publishers Ltd.
www.pegasuspublishers.com

This is a work of fiction. Names, characters, businesses, places, events and
incidents are either the products of the author's imagination or used in a
fictitious manner. Any resemblance to actual persons, living or dead, or actual
events is purely coincidental. And anyone looking for accuracy in the
chronology of background history and events within Hoxton and Shoreditch
during the 1990s will be disappointed.

First Published in 2024

Pegasus
Sheraton House Castle Park
Cambridge England

Printed & Bound in Great Britain

For Simon Worthington and Pauline van Mourik Broekman,
without whom this would never have happened

"Everyone can be an artist."
— Josef Beuys

Prologue

The Birth of Tragedy

Most of human existence is waiting. When I was a child I was told that everything I wanted from life would come to me in due course, if only I could be patient. As I entered my teens I was ever more doubtful, because it was becoming clear to me that my parents' advice was no more than supposition given the lives they led themselves. They were ordinary people and so were my friends, and so was everyone else I knew. What I wanted most of all from life, with all of the heart that I had in me (though I guarded this secret fiercely and would never have admitted it to anyone) was to meet people who were extraordinary.

Most of my childhood friends stayed in the Essex town where we grew up, reluctant to venture into the larger world outside. As soon as I was able I left, first temporarily and then for good, and when I returned for Christmas and other holidays it became tedious to ask them what they were doing and to hear the same responses once again. They were starting to live out frugal and monotonous adult lives, content to play their part in an endless replay of the prosaic. I wanted none of it.

I could not appreciate the town's charms back then, the appeal of a place where nothing much ever happened. The threadbare municipal park complete with dog walkers and loafers, the greasy comfort of the chip shop and café, the smoky democracy of the pubs and — above all — the infinite meditative complexities of the sea. I was blind to the consolations offered by the waves and by the sky above them. Instead I saw the rain-whipped sea front, the empty marina and the vandalised promenade shelters as confirmations that I was right to move on.

So I went to London and hung around the centre, working, drinking, dancing, partying. Now and then I tried to pluck up the courage to do some writing (because I had a vague, bruising awareness that I was an ordinary person too, and that writing couldn't really be for the likes of me). After a while I did meet the kind of people I wanted to meet and my life started to become different, sometimes in ways I had not anticipated. In the end, of course, it all got the better of me.

The passing of time has not brought a complete sense of proportion along with it, but I have learnt that to be ordinary means you own an innocence that is precious and that once it has gone you cannot get it back. I could claim that Alastair and the others stole away that innocence from me and yet that wouldn't be true, either for me or for them. The reality is that I had it ready and waiting for disposal and I could not have hung onto it indefinitely because, like almost everyone else's life, my life must be lived out in the realm of time and experience.

I do not know whether I paid a high price for my temporary seat in the front row. What I can say is that this part of my life is always with me, whether I want it to be there or not.

1

Human, All Too Human

You possessed all of the necessary mundane qualities for success: talent, initiative and persistence. As well as a couple of less run of the mill attributes, though they are still common enough: faith and luck. Then there is something which is not common at all. Genius. The feedback on your work suggests you might be a genius. It cannot be ruled out.

Most people do not know what they want to be. You always wanted to be an artist. What you were never completely sure about — though you have become good at pretending that you were never in any doubt — was whether you would be a successful artist. The most satisfying aspect of the way things have gone is the way aspiration has segued into reality. Your inner world has merged with the outer world in beauteous union.

You know that making the art is the only important part of it all. Sometimes you wonder whether you have an existence apart from your art. Without it you would not be you, and a life without it would be no life. Everything apart from the art is a detail. Though at times you revel in it all, and you catch yourself questioning what life would be like without it all.

*

'This is the end,' said Alastair.

It didn't seem like the end. It had been another storming private view and they were up in Alastair's studio doing big fat celebratory lines. Billy had no idea what Alastair was talking about but was chary of challenging him. Unlike Tom.

'Have you run out of charlie?' he asked.

'No, it's not that. I mean it's all over for us.'

'Then we might as well do a few more lines,' said Tom.

Undeflected, Alastair continued. 'They're killing the art with their bars and restaurants and loft conversions.'

'That's all shite.' Tom again.

Composed: Billy thought of Tom as a composition, music or poetry personified, a creation of Eton and the Royal College of Art. His motif was a large Roman nose, the concomitant of a sharp and assured intellect. He always wore tracksuits, but what would be hackneyed attire for anyone else in Hackney he managed to carry off with style.

'Forget all that,' he said. 'This is the best show you've ever curated.'

They knew Tom was right, not because they had been drinking and doing coke since late afternoon — or not just because they had — but because it was the simple truth.

The private view was a comet sweeping majestically across the night sky. The show at Idiot Savant, the after-show drinks upstairs in the Barley Mow and then a session in Alastair's studio up above the gallery. What was left was the core, molten and incandescent still. Billy poured himself another vodka as a siren cut through the urban surf below, shrieking and howling, and then wrenching out great tearing wails as proximity truncated and amplified the acoustic waves it set rolling. Tom leaned over to Erick, who was sitting slumped — a cigarette dangling from his hand the only vestige of consciousness — and whispered into his ear.

'Erick. This is the end.'

Uuuaaaarrrrgggggghhhhhh

Erick wailed in consonance with the siren but more deeply and briefly. He was bolt upright, wide eyed.

'Tom's winding you up,' said Alastair. 'Have a drink. You deserve a drink.'

Another undeniable truth, because it was Erick's show they were celebrating, the show for his latest and most challenging installation. It consisted of a series of books of different sizes, bound in fine calfskin and embossed with gold. All of their pages were blank and they were displayed on lecterns within a spacious vitrine. Billy thought it brilliant, everyone thought it brilliant.

A tumbler of Stoly was pressed into Erick's small white hands. 'Having a nap,' he said, looking round at them to reinforce his version of events. Erick's modest dimensions meant he looked neat and precise even in the final stages of dissolution. His glasses, his rosy complexion and his short back and sides made a mannikin of him. There was an extra flush to his cheeks tonight, but he wasn't completely fucked, not yet. Behind his spectacles his pale blue eyes were in focus and fixed the others with an intent gaze. His rimless lenses pulled in the edges of his face and shrank it, and Billy saw that behind them lived a yet smaller and neater version of Erick.

'Gentrification, development,' said Tom. 'New businesses, luxury flats — so what. Besides, you wanted people to move here, didn't you?'

'When it was cheap,' said Alastair. 'When it looked as if it was going to be different.'

Alastair's gallery, Idiot Savant, occupied the ground floor of the building. As well as Alastair's own studio living space up at the top, its other floors were occupied by artists and other friends and acquaintances. He had acted as intermediary to arrange very low rents for them all, and he organised shows for some of them in IS, as well as helping them buy materials and bailing them out in other ways. Where the funds came from for all this was never clear.

'We won't last into 1994,' continued Alastair.

'Your coke dealing won't last, if I can be excused for saying so,' said Tom. 'You're right there.'

'You want Idiot Savant to close even sooner? Didn't you see the bailiffs?'

'Was all that for real?' Billy asked.

An incident hours before, like a dream half remembered. Serious men, leading Alastair into a corner. Talking quietly, exiting loudly.

'They tried to collect the money for the catalogues,' he said.

'They do not look at any of my art at all,' said Erick.

'The council is bankrupting me over the business rates,' said Alastair. 'That is reality.'

'Reality.'

Tom waved his hand, but Billy knew that he recognised the realities of the art world. Alastair, by contrast, scorned all compromise and Billy looked over to his fearless idealism. He was in his mid-twenties, younger than the rest of them, but his was not the unsustainable vision of youth. His golden curls, his unmarked skin and his clear eyes made him into something else, outside of time altogether.

With Olympian detachment Billy's gaze shifted to the scene before him. Alastair's lifestyle was all one, in its mannered anarchy. Glasses, bottles of Stoly, ash trays, cigarettes, lighters, hash pipes, razor blades and CD cases littered the surface of an oak conference table, its French polish flayed with sandy scratches and patches of wear. On the floor around them newspapers and magazines rose up in long barrows, discarded bottles and cans winking from them with revenant sheen.

Beneath its inlay of rubbish the room was small, the most public part of Alastair's suite of accommodation right at the top of the building. He had painted its front door red but done nothing more. The bare brick of the walls around them was chipped, crumbling and dirty, and the stretches of wooden floor visible here and there beneath the detritus were a depthless grey, ingrained with more than a century and a half's worth of grot.

Billy wondered if Kevin Thorn would show up tonight. By this stage it was unlikely and his absence was not surprising. He was no longer, it appeared, at one with the rest of them now that he had started to pull away to become the front runner and was making a name for himself in the world outside Hoxton. Billy was hungry to encounter Thorn, because up to now he hadn't met him at all and he was determined to get to know him. At the very least he wanted to interview him and put together a decent feature article, but if given the chance he would have a go at writing a book about Thorn.

But right then Billy wanted more charlie. The CD case with the lines racked up on it reached him and he summoned his limited conjuring powers (this was his only trick) to make a couple more lines vanish, followed by another inch of Stoly. Substance abuse made it easier for him to believe that he was truly accepted by Alastair and the others. They were tight, they had all known each other since art school, except for Erick — but even so Erick was one of them, indisputably, in a way that Billy was not.

Alastair had been flinging charlie around for a few weeks and it had become impossible to imagine him apart from powder. His lifestyle had become linear. In galleries he divided lavatory cisterns, in bars he bifurcated counters, in the darker recesses of night clubs he segmented DJ's consoles, in lofts he blocked out desks and dinner tables and — on rarer occasions — he cut across surfaces in normal flats and houses. In the later stages of a session social geometry blurred, the lines became thicker scatterings, Bridget Riley and Sol Le Witt diffusing into Gerhard Richter, but soon after they would refocus and thin once again, to become a new template demarcating Hoxton alongside street plans, utility supply grids and transport routes.

Billy had an idea that what they got up here was the excess, the dealer's perk. Pristine snowdrifts of it. If this was the end then it might be for the best, he thought, since he wouldn't be able to return Alastair's largesse in any foreseeable future. Then he snorted another line and his guilt evaporated. Art was all very well for catharsis, but sometimes pharmaceuticals were better.

'I want Kevin to do another show in Idiot Savant,' said Alastair.

'Linda Bloom would never allow him to do that,' said Tom.

Billy recalled that Kevin Thorn was now signed up with Bloom's, a commercial gallery that had recently opened up in Hoxton, the first to do so. There were rumours that Tom was trying to follow Thorn and get himself a contract there too.

Erick stirred himself to speak again, skidded back through the discussion.

'It is not over,' he said. 'I will not be finishing.'

'That's right,' said Tom. 'Have a drink.'

'I am not drinking.'

Instead Erick took the dog-end from his mouth and used it to light a cigarette, the latest extension of an endless tube of tobacco stretching seamlessly from past into future. Erick smoked even more than the rest of them. Roused more fully, he took a drag, folded himself over, flared his nostrils above two lines and tracked them noisily and decisively without banknote or straw.

Sssssstttrewwwwwwuuuoooossssss

Sssssstttrewwwwwuooooossssssssss

Billy sniffed the air in front of his face once or twice, twitching the tip of his nose from side to side to manoeuvre any stray fragments of coke onto his septum. It was the cocaine that made him fully aware that he was drunk, and that his drunkenness had raised him to an exalted state. He was in communion with everyone who was drunk at this moment, all over the surface of the planet, as well as those who had been drunk throughout history, and those who would be drunk in ages to come. If he died this instant it would not matter, his spirit would be absorbed into the walls of this room to live on joyously with all of humanity for all time.

There could be no more to life than to be here at this moment with Alastair and with the others. On they came, a shining caravan of fine artists bearing rare gifts out of the creative desert of the early 1990s. This was not the end, it could not be the end.

Erick relapsed into slumber. His effluvia had gathered itself into dun cumuli which lowered over his end of the table, but smoke mantled everything in here. The coke made its grey and blue contours velvety, threw its folds and valleys of fumes into sharper relief. This peculiar, pastoral, effect was in contrast to the angular cityscape around them. The top of the building was not overlooked and Alastair disdained curtains or blinds.

'This has been our factory for art,' said Alastair, 'but it cannot survive much longer.'

During the years of empire the building had been a real factory, a furniture manufacturer. Several decades on it was manufacturing once more, producing quantities of art, much of it appearing for the first time on show in Idiot Savant. The CD case reached Billy again and, as he helped himself, Alastair addressed him.

'I'll help you place an article about the show,' he said.

Billy tried to hide his pleasure.

'Cheers.'

'Can you do me a small favour?'

'Sure, of course.'

'We'll talk tomorrow.'

Erick was upright and staring about wildly, his glasses heliographing panic.

'It is ending,' he shouted.

'Fuck's sake,' said Tom.

2

Found Object

'Why is this *hip* art scene developing in Hoxton?'

'It has the biggest concentration of talent in Europe. In the northern hemisphere.'

Alastair's face shone like a hero's shield, untarnished by excess and giving nothing away. A let down there, maybe, for an interviewer hungry to get on the inside of this new milieu of artists working and partying. Because so far as the arts strand of London Weekend Television was concerned the capital was swinging on, more than a quarter of a century after the advent of urban grooviness.

It was barely after eleven and early for Billy to be in his office space. This consisted of a desk in the tiny back room at Idiot Savant where he pursued his journalism, topping up his earnings by working in a housing department the rest of the time. The coke had counteracted the worst effects of the Stoly and negated the need for a full night's sleep, but his height and poor posture was a combination vulnerable to the after-effects of substance abuse. His back was aching, making it difficult to concentrate.

As was the television interview unfolding in front of him in the gallery's display area, visible through the back room's open door. The lighting was part of it. It turned everything inside out. What the lighting man had done, with all of his quartz lamps and umbrella reflectors and cables and meters, was to create illumination uncannily similar to the natural light outside. Billy had to keep reminding himself that he was in there inside his place of work, and not back outside on the street.

The surroundings didn't help his sense of displacement. Idiot Savant looked like a film or television set to start with, as an old industrial building reconfigured as an art gallery — or anti-art gallery. Now the television crew had created a set within a set, and in these regressions it was difficult to know where real life started and ended.

The interviewer was drowning out the London soundtrack outside. Most days traffic, building sites and sirens announced themselves. Millions of people frenziedly chasing each other around to emphasise their difference from Billy, marooned in the back room trying to jump on his work and catch them all up. This morning the muting of the urban noise was exacerbating the disorienting effects of the lighting.

'And the artists to watch?'

'Kevin Thorn is doing great things, obviously. I would also pay attention to Erick Heckendorf, Tania Russell-Smith and Tom Templeton.'

'So where is all of this going?'

'My dream is that artists will stay here and continue to create enduring art.'

It was the same interview Alastair had been doing with television people for the past few months. One started, the others followed, radio and print journalists too. If a media professional wanted something on Hoxton, they found their way to him. He gave good interview and they lacked the initiative to find other faces. Not that there was much chance of him becoming a celeb, since none of the interviews ever emerged on the small screen anywhere near peak time. A small number of insomniacs, a scattering of the unemployed and a few dozen nightshift workers might have had confused ideas of who Alastair Given was and what the nascent art scene in Hoxton might be about, but no one else gave it any thought. Art wasn't much of a story. With the exception of Kevin Thorn, that was. Because Thorn was already fodder for newspapers and magazines.

*

'Kevin doesn't do interviews,' said Ed Soames.

The television crew had packed up and gone and Alastair had vanished. Billy could make the calls he had delayed for fear that the noise would carry from the back room. Delayed also because the spectacle of the interview was impossible to close the door upon.

He was back in the workaday world, with its set procedures for processing time. One of his current routines involved ringing Ed Soames, Kevin Thorn's press representative. Soames was a route marker on the road of Billy's work, but he was stuck on a roundabout. His telephone encounters with Soames had started to loop round in repetitions that might eventually lead onwards to Thorn himself, or which might simply be rehearsals for a final halt without Thorn. Billy didn't know. Soames seemed more decided and he was not encouraging. He reiterated that his client was keen to minimise contact with journalists so that he could concentrate on putting together his next show.

'He'd like a spread in *The Herald*, wouldn't he?' Billy said.

'I'm afraid I have to go into a meeting. Sorry to disappoint you, mate.'

Billy's pursuit of Thorn was fanatical and that was because of his art, and because of art. Art: a word only three letters long but possessing of such affect and effect. Art had got to Billy through Alastair and the others. It had attached itself insistently to his thoughts and feelings, held him fast in its fever. He was starting to gain some understanding of art, beginning to look at some of these new works and now and again to get a sense of something, of a brilliance that was there flickering in and around them. Thorn had that, he thought, and sometimes some of the others, Erick and Tom especially, and he wanted to get as close to it as he was able.

British artists had been forced to wait until middle age before they were allowed any status and success, but suddenly that was changing, along with the whole notion of what an artist was and could be. Thorn was in his twenties, and his fame was starting to spread out of the art world and beyond. He had rock star or film star potential and he was in demand. Billy knew Thorn's gallerist, Linda Bloom, but unfortunately she had retained Soames to be

Thorn's press agent in the build up to his next show. She could refer all press enquiries on, hide behind Soames and dodge any obligations towards the likes of Billy. That wasn't going to stop him. He would just try harder and a frontal assault wasn't his sole strategy, because sooner or later he knew he would encounter Thorn around Hoxton. That was his ace. Alastair saw Thorn occasionally, for example, despite Thorn's departure from Idiot Savant for Bloom's — in an act Billy thought was disloyal, after all the help Alastair had given him, though Alastair didn't seem bothered.

Tania stormed into the office.

'Where is Alastair?'

'He was doing a television interview, but he's gone.'

'There's more fucking bills.'

Billy could not fathom the ins and outs of Idiot Savant's finances. Pointing out to Tania that he had given Alastair a couple of month's rent for his desk space the previous week would probably cause more strife and was not worth the risk. Tania ran the gallery with Alastair, as well as being an artist in her own right. She was tall, the same height as Billy, and broad in a fecund way. There was a suggestion of earth mother about her, and certainly she possessed elemental energy — though he had seen no displays of nurture. Her most distinctive feature was her hair, an orange hemisphere around the top of her head and a warning to steer clear. She leaned in towards him, a post-punk Wife of Bath.

'Were you at that session after Erick's private view?'

'Well, he—'

'If Alastair wants to deal drugs at least he could get some fucking money for them, instead of just giving them away to you wankers.'

'Doesn't he—'

'I heard Erick went loopy.'

'Not sure that's—'

'He thought there were people waiting to get him outside.'

Not for the first time, it occurred to Billy that an artist of lesser talent would not be humoured in the way that Erick was humoured.

'Don't pretend you weren't there, you lanky streak of piss.'

He never knew how Tania would be. Sometimes she instructed him about art and the art world in a manner which was offhand and impatient, but also helpful. Sadly, this might have been intended to keep him guessing, to render subsequent rebuffs more wounding. Abruptly, she dropped investigation of Erick's latest psychotic episode.

'Are you still trying to get an interview with Kevin Thorn?' she asked. 'Do you want to know what he's really like?'

'You know I do.'

'No you fucking don't. He was round his studio when his child was brought in to visit. Four-year-old boy. He piped up, "Daddy, what's an artist?", so Kevin stopped what he was doing and tried to tell him. Then his boy picked up some paint and brushes and said, "I'm an artist too" and started painting.'

'Sweet kid.'

'Real charmer.'

'So?'

'So that was the last time Kevin saw him. He said he couldn't have that going on alongside him, because he had enough difficulties making his art without his son standing there mimicking him.'

'He hasn't seen him since?'

'No. And then there were the body parts.'

Tania was talking to him at length not necessarily from amiability, he noted, more likely because this was an opportunity to denigrate Thorn.

'That show was wildly popular,' he said.

The show was entitled *Dead* and had taken place at Idiot Savant six months before. This was when Thorn had first begun to attract widespread interest.

'Hyped,' said Tania. 'He could have told the police beforehand that all the body parts had been donated by terminally ill people, but he schemed away with Alastair and they decided they preferred to be raided.'

Death. An ineluctable subject for any artist. Beckoning to them were the morgue and the funeral parlour. These were the places where they must venture to surpass their peers this late in the twentieth century.

'The work was exceptional,' he said.

Billy believed *Dead* was at the edge of art, the strangely rearward looking edge. What was it that Alastair had said? The great works gazed back with basilisk gazes, killing off the art that came before and tossing it all out and away into history.

'It was shite,' said Tania. 'Fuck knows why Alastair bothered with him.'

He wanted to ask Tania whether Becky was coming in, but he didn't dare. Tania seemed to be a mentor to Becky and he was starting to be fascinated by her, although it was a less abstract fascination than Thorn aroused within him. Soon Tania left as noisily as she had entered and he stared down at his desk while he considered his next move upon Thorn.

The desk was a miniature version of Alastair's living room, suggesting that some malignant spore had floated down to inaugurate another regime of accelerated entropy. Piles of paper were collapsed into each other, their strata deformed and shattered to expose dusty fillets of individual sheets, all testifying to long defunct projects. Bends of cable were engaged in serpentine searches for tape recorders, answerphones and fax machines. Mugs rimed with mould were chimneys from awful subterranean chambers, while a couple of defunct Anglepoise desk lamps craned over the tips and heaps, ichor oozing from their joints. His phone rang from the top of the ruins. It was Alastair.

'Tania isn't around is she?'

'She's gone.'

'There's nothing I can do with those invoices. Listen, can you pop up?'

He left Idiot Savant, went upstairs to the top of the building. Alastair beckoned him back inside his studio in conspiratorial fashion — unnecessary since no one else was around. By the light of day his accommodation was no more than a studio space with a couple of small adjoining rooms, so basic that it was hard not to imagine more extensive and sumptuous apartments concealed nearby.

The living room looked almost the same as it had five hours before. Slants of daylight diligently sorted motes from residual cigarette smoke hanging in pale tangles and skeins, a toxic dawn mist which refused to dissipate. The places around the table were palimpsests for the guests, the silence which had fallen after they left still lingering too. By narrowing his eyes Billy could catch their shades in carouse. For a moment he felt bilious, before he heard Alastair speaking to him.

'Has Tom told you yet?'

'What is it?'

'Linda Bloom's doesn't want him on her list. She doesn't think his work is sellable.'

Alastair wasn't crowing over Tom's rejection, he was simply interested, but Tom's casual disavowal of reality the previous evening had become a tempting of fate.

'Maybe he'll show some work in IS again,' said Billy.

Although it sounded as if Tom wanted a commercial gallery, which IS was not.

'Maybe. Take this.'

Alastair placed a package into his hands, releasing it fully when he was sure Billy wasn't going to drop it. It was oblong, shoebox-sized — perhaps it was a shoebox — with a white plastic bag clumsily taped around it. Billy turned it slightly, watched reflected light scattering and reforming around its ridges and folds.

'Can you mind it for a while? I can't keep it here.'

'Fine.'

Alastair gave a smile that was a celebration of human spirit.

'Is it charlie?' asked Billy.

'No, but here.'

Alastair reached into a pocket, pulled out a plastic bag full of wraps and handed it to him, before nodding at the package.

'Please don't mention this to anyone.'

3

Often Smiling

You move through Pauline Collard's private view at Bloom's, exit to a reception down at the Tate (they're interested in a show in the spring). Flip back to Hoxton for Peter Blacksmith's private view (you don't bother looking closely at the works, you're not that interested) and then on to a couple of parties. You have to arrive late at everything and once there you can never relax. You must move around and you can't stay long. Otherwise they start to collect. Never anyone you'd actually want to speak to. Gormless, needy or downright weird. They don't know you, so why would they want to talk to you unless they were lacking in something or other? That never occurs to them. You're available and they think that they know you because they've seen you around, caught your picture in newspapers and magazines. You're like a neighbour or workmate or friend — if they have any friends. You sense a lot of them don't.

Your height is a handicap because you are easy to spot in a crowd. You can see they're steeling themselves to come over, telling themselves to look normal, but it never works. They're always self-conscious. They never approach you in a straightforward way. Look at their faces. The way they walk. Really. Every time there's something: sidling, striding, mincing, marching. They can't even walk towards you properly.

You witness bizarre contortions of social relations. Sometimes they ask someone with you whether they can talk to you. Invariably, that someone is another unwanted new friend you've made moments before. That doesn't matter, because surprisingly often they assume the role of personal assistant. Nonentity A asks you if you'd mind having a few words with nonentity B, while you stand there looking at the pair of them shedding all dignity and self-respect.

It's vital to keep each encounter short. Then there's a chance of getting away with it. A handshake, a smile. A brief exchange of goodwill and move off while they're happy. They fade away safely into mediocrity and obscurity and you're onto the next. Pressing flesh. Smiling. You're not allowed to be unhappy, or preoccupied, or normal. They'd start thinking you were moody. It hurts your mouth, all that smiling, but it's better than getting it burst.

To talk to them for any length of time is always a mistake. They leave feeling wounded in some way. Your relationship with them can never be right because it's wrong from the start. They want to speak to you on equal terms but they know that they're not your equal, not really.

They all want something. Even if it's a simple conversational exchange. Because if they've talked to you they're on the same level as you. They ask questions about your work and supply the answers before you've had a chance to reply, to show that they know as much about how to go about it as you do. You can never point out that they're doing that. Whatever you say is wrong. If you're too friendly they think you're condescending. If you keep a little bit of distance, a portion of private space, they think you're aloof, snotty. You're a large corn plaster for a procession of crippled egos. Away they go, slagging you to all and sundry. 'Yes, I met him at a party. A right tosser. Up himself. I hope he gets what he deserves.'

Sometimes they're aggressive. They think that you're an embodiment of a problem with contemporary culture. There's usually some jealousy there, whether they're aware of it or not. Normally a lot of jealousy. They want to assert themselves over you in some way, verbally or physically. You can't go about with a minder. Everyone would say that was going too far. They'd slag you even more, assert that it had all gone to your head, that you believe your own PR. So you have to be careful, keep moving.

There are the ones seeking favours. They want you to look at their art, or to lend them some of yours for a worthy cause, or to give them an interview. Always you tell them to get in touch with your gallery, your press person. Let them deal with it all. Avoid giving outright rejections on the spot. Dangerous, and you'd be doing it half a dozen times at every event you ever went to. That alone would finish you.

*

Autumn was sharpening into winter, slashing the days back relentlessly so that the streets were cold and dark by late afternoon. Billy was hurrying across the junction of Curtain Road and Old Street, trying to get past a couple of motorcycle couriers before the lights changed. In daytime this stretch of Old Street was choked with traffic and he was dodging the stragglers, but it would be mostly empty of vehicles and pedestrians alike in an hour or two. His destination was a bar called Mother, which occupied a floor above the 333 nightclub.

The building which housed both of them occupied a whole block and was keep-like, with smooth sandstone walls devoid of ground floor windows. Formerly the 333 was the London Apprentice, a famous gay rendezvous. From twilight on men in leathers flitted down the deserted street and slipped into the entrance, like bats arriving at a nocturnal conference. Recently the club had been refurbished and renamed to lure in a wider clientele, the latest conversion of what was once a large and imposing Victorian public house.

Billy stopped short because the pavement was sticking out its tongue at him. He bent down cautiously. The tongue lay there, a pink slug glistening in a caul of translucent saliva, voluptuous in its obscenity. He looked at the strawberry pits of its uppers, at the velvety claret of its underside. It was ragged at the rear and encircled by bloody droplets.

He rushed the remaining few yards into 333, trying to escape the terrible truth of what he had seen. Maybe it was from a joke shop? The tongue was too realistic, not funny. Medical students on a spree? Too fresh. From a dog? Too short. He entered the club and saw a security man inside the doorway, sheathed in a long coat and leather gloves against the cold, his hair gelled back.

'Outside, there's—'

'Yeah, thanks, we know. It's being dealt with. Best go inside, sir.'

Billy wondered if this nonchalance was meant to be reassuring, but there was nothing more he could do. Whatever had happened, had happened.

Upstairs he seized a cocktail from a tray. He needed bolstering, largely because of what he had seen outside, but not entirely. This was Tania's birthday party and there were no formal invites as such, yet he was painfully aware that she hadn't mentioned the party to him or even in front of him in IS. He had decided to take the risk and come along, because a party was a party. Anyway, he had to be here because there was the chance Thorn might turn up.

He should have been able to avoid Tania for an hour or two until drink mellowed her to his presence, because she stood out, not so much like a sore thumb — more like a giant, inflamed middle digit. It was unfortunate she was standing right by the entrance and he walked directly into her sights, cocktail in hand.

'Happy birthday, Tania.'

'This is a surprise, seeing you here.'

She didn't look happy.

'I wish I'd hired the place exclusively,' she said. 'Who are all these fuckers?'

She waved a hand at a vista of indistinguishable youth in tracksuits and trainers, drinking and smoking for art amid flock wallpaper and 1970s office furniture. As she gestured her hair shone brightly, a testament to inexhaustible reserves of ire.

'Graphic designers, photographer's assistants?' he said.

He knew she knew who they were because they had started to materialise months before, but it was unwise to frustrate her wish to act up. It was her party.

'Where have they sprung from?'

'No one knows. They don't know.'

Tania's handbag was fashioned in the form of a small dog. As she hectored him it swung from her shoulder, its gleaming snout and glassy eyes lunging forward to second her words.

'Who's that guy in the Happy Mondays who just dances on stage?'

'Bez.'

'Go on then. Dance.'

She walked off. It could have been worse. There were more humiliating comparisons than Bez.

Billy raised his third cocktail to his lips, sipped carefully (the glass was over-full), and looked over its rim through the doorway of the club's chill-out room. The walls were decorated with blown-up reproductions of mid-western desert scenes, in grainy siennas and terracottas. On the room's far side he spotted Alastair, sheltering under an outsize image of a rocky outcrop, and walked towards him. First he was Bez, he thought, and now he was Tonto. On the way over he saw Tom among the throng, also in motion towards Alastair. In his own tracksuit and trainers he would not have stood out from the crowd, were it not for his prow of a nose and his unlikely accessory — a middle-aged man in a suit.

'This is Henry Lanchester,' said Tom. 'I'm assisting him with his art collection.'

Billy was surprised Tom had decided to advise a collector, because it was a big change of direction. So far as he knew Tom was looking for a new gallery and this new role was bound to leave him less time to make his own art. Lanchester nodded at them. He had a fringe of beard along his jaw which merged up into his sideburns, while the hair above was swept back from a receding hairline which completed a hirsute border around his large, open face.

'So what is it that you do, Mr Lanchester?' asked Alastair.

'I run the corporate finance department at Millhouse Durrant, for my sins.'

Lanchester was more ebullient than a man dealing with serious money had cause to be.

'Is sinning a *sine qua non* for your line of work?' said Alastair.

Lanchester continued to smile.

'Ah yes, very good. Well, naturally I'm an evil capitalist. Every night I dine in high style off the sweat and blood of the workers. Toast their babies over an open fire. Slap chutney on them and wolf them straight down. Delicious, can't get enough.'

Alastair started to laugh. Tom turned to Lanchester.

'Well maybe it's time we were—'

'Oh don't worry, Tom,' said Lanchester. 'I think I'm safe with your friends.'

Erick appeared with Becky in tow, a squat tug with smoke unfurling above it as it guided an elegant barque into port. Erick's gait was unsteady; he seemed drunk already. Billy scoped down to the potlet at his waistline. Perhaps after Erick's demise a skilled pathologist armed with his diary would peel back layers of adipose tissue and identify their origins: 'Yes, that's the Beck's promotion at the ICA' — scalpeling and forceping — 'Here's Waddington's last private view'.

Billy's gaze turned to Becky and he was struck once again by her charms. A rose in a zen rock garden: English mother, Japanese father. Hair of a black that was blackness itself, a bob framing her face in a teardrop of silk. Cheekbones that were delicate supplications, below eyes that were whole worlds, better worlds than this one. The scar set the seal, a hairline crack in rare porcelain. It was darker than the rest of her skin and wound round her left eye and past her mouth, segmenting her cheek like a river dividing a map. She never hid it with make-up.

When Becky came into Idiot Savant she gave the impression of knowing where she was going in life without giving any of it away, at least to him. He was interested in what lay behind her studiously remote face, scar and all. Her looks placed everyone at a distance and yet, he thought, they could not be there simply to intimidate. Her status as an artist, a status he did not share, was a more serious barrier, though he believed his journalism could forge a creative connection between them. Becky had mentioned it once or twice, and maybe beyond a selfish concern that he would write about her art.

This evening as he stood there observing Becky and Erick he realised that, like Tania, they looked unhappy. Though, unlike Tania, his presence was unrelated to their distress.

'I do not believe what I see outside,' Erick said.

'Revolting,' said Becky

'They are ripping it out,' he said.

'What do you mean?' Billy asked.

Then he understood they were talking about the tongue and felt the contents of his stomach straining to reappear. Erick pulled on his cigarette, oxygenating the tip and stretching it into a pyre.

'Apparently two men come up to this guy,' he said. 'One of them is forcing his mouth open while the other is ripping out his tongue with pliers.'

'He couldn't even scream properly,' said Becky.

'What did they do it for?' Billy asked.

'Must be drug related,' said Tania, who had reappeared, her hair a Belisha beacon glowing with hallucinogenic intensity.

'Such blood. Maroons and crimsons and burgundies,' said Eric. 'This scene, it is Goya.'

'I saw the tongue too,' said Billy.

'Do you not think it beautiful?' asked Erick.

'Let's not talk about it,' said Becky. There was silence for a few moments, broken by Erick.

'I have no present for you with me, Tania,' he said. 'Maybe you would like to select something from my studio tomorrow?'

'That's far too generous.'

'I have too much work. You are doing me a favour.'

'Are you sure you want to give it away?'

Erick waved his cigarette decisively.

'What I would like is to see you happy, so I am forgetting the crushing obligations I labour under.'

'Too few obligations,' said Tania, 'that's your problem. I should feed you up with obligations, strap you into a highchair and spoon them in.'

Billy imagined her towering over him as he protested weakly. A disturbing image.

'That would be interesting,' said Erick. 'Like a Paula Rego painting.'

'Don't get excited,' she said, as she left them for another group of guests.

'Billy, why are you not writing a piece about Becky's work?' said Erick.

Billy looked at Becky again. There she stood, one hand on her hip, the other terminating in a Marlboro Light, her neck, shoulders and arms in a long, sure line. She was an outline ready to be filled in, a story waiting to be written. Perhaps he could do a profile of an up-and-coming artist. Alastair would talk her into it, help him get it published.

'Must be cool, leaving Goldsmiths',' he said to her. 'Becoming autonomous.'

She lifted her chin fractionally.

'Goldsmiths' main benefit for me,' she said, 'was studio space.'

He had made an unwelcome reminder of her recent student status.

'Just studio space?' he asked.

She wrinkled her nose in a way that in other contexts could be adorable.

'Have you got another studio to work in yet?' he persisted.

'Studios are expensive.'

'What about the IS building?'

'Erick says the owner's trying to throw him out. Maybe you could give him some advice?'

Billy knew Erick often had trouble finding the money for his rent, but that wasn't the problem because Alastair stepped in to hand it over for him whenever necessary. The real difficulty was that Erick's lease was much longer than anyone else's in the building and the owners weren't happy about it, presumably because they wanted to sell up and cash in soon. Billy didn't see how he could help with any of that.

'I don't know anything about housing law. I just work in the housing department for ready cash.'

He was wondering whether her eyes were violet; the lighting in Mother was not good enough to decide. She watched as he winched his train of thought back onto the tracks of their conversation, wrote down her phone number so he could come and look at her art.

A couple of lines in the toilet put everything back into the correct perspective. The alkaline salt scrubbed at his nostrils satisfactorily, cleansing his brain and priming him for action. He needed the assistance of cocaine to summon the confidence to talk to Tania, Erick, Becky, Tom, Lanchester, all of them. On re-emerging he saw Alastair in the chill-out room again, under the same rocky outcrop and deep in conversation with another party goer. When Billy looked more closely he started. His quarry was in front of him. Kevin Thorn: recognisable from photographs in the press, gangling, emaciated, spavined. A meerkat gone wrong. He was rubbing his back as he talked to Alastair.

'Billy, darling.'

A voice behind him. Shit.

'Linda,' he said.

Linda Bloom, suited and booted and blond. Booting artists off her gallery list when it suited her. An upholder of the free market who wanted to sell expensive art, a camp follower of capitalism with a persona so irredeemably camp. He nodded at her attire.

'That's the second suit I've seen tonight,' he said.

'Jil Sander. Do you like it, sweetie?'

'Yeah, nice.'

'Thanks. Are you from the same part of the world as Kevin? Your accent is ever so similar.'

'Just an Essex accent isn't it?'

Her manicured home counties vowels were making him defensive, cocaine or not. They both knew he had a working-class accent.

'You don't know who that collector of Tom's is at all, do you?' she asked.

'The guy in the other suit? He's called Henry Lanchester.'

'It would be heavenly to meet him.'

'He was pretending to be from hell, but I expect Tom will introduce you.'

'Tom is being so naughty and avoiding me.'

He knew she was referring to her rejection of Tom's request to join her gallery, but he didn't want to discuss that. What he wanted to do was to talk to Thorn, who might not remain nearby for long. Linda placed a restraining hand on his arm, determined to pump him on Tom's new mentor.

'Is there any other way I can find out all about him, darling? You're a journalist aren't you? I expect you're brilliant at this sort of thing.'

'What about Tania?'

'She said she hasn't the remotest idea who I'm on about.'

'She didn't want any suits in here. Apart from you, obviously.'

'Obviously, darling.'

Much of Linda's working life was a hunt for the next Charles Saatchi. Without support from collectors most galleries could last a bare few months before they expired, like brightly coloured butterflies spiralling back down to earth. But he didn't care about any of that right now.

She paused, sensing his frustration.

'I'm sorry I couldn't arrange an interview with Kevin for you. You simply cannot imagine how many enquiries I've been getting about him. I've had to hire in a proper press person from a PR agency to deal with them all.'

'Couldn't you use an intern?'

'Has to be somebody who knows what they're doing.'

The coke was wearing off, his social skills with it. He could not extricate himself easily without offending her.

'Must cost a bit,' he said.

'I can't spend every waking instant dealing with journalists, sweetie. Present company excepted, obviously.'

He steeled himself to make his move.

'Thanks. Well, if you'll excuse me—'

He turned towards Alastair and Kevin Thorn, and by now, of course, neither was anywhere in sight.

4

When He Woke Up the Feeling Had Gone

The following afternoon Billy was in the lift in the Old Street tower block he inhabited. The compartment was descending slowly to the accompaniment of metallic groans, as though it was a stool the block was straining to expel from its bowels.

'What's up?' said Rick.

'Going down. That's what's up.'

Rick was smiling at Billy. Rick was solid and squat, with the slightly subtracted presence of someone who was at home in a group. Preferably a group with a cause. His sturdiness gave him an air of resolution, which was only a little betrayed by his smile. He had the right kind of mouth for smiling, with large and prominent lips, and he smiled a lot, a loose smile which appeared defensive as if to say: "Listen man, I've been doing my best. You can't blame me for all this."

Billy and Rick were mates. They had been better mates, but they remained mates. They knew each other from the squat party scene before moving in here, separately, a couple of years before. Billy lived on the ninth floor of the block, Rick was on the eleventh.

They were on nodding and greeting terms with a few of the other residents: some artists, a couple of actors, one or two out-gays and the odd goth or punk. Most of them thought they were passing through, that recognition of their talent by the tutelary spirits in charge of design or television or film or music was imminent. Sometimes they were right; someone on the twelfth floor got a part in *Neighbours*. A number of them resented and ridiculed Rick's attempts to involve them in politics. Billy attracted less attention.

The indigenous residents ignored all these sub-culture heroes in the same way that they ignored the refugees and migrants who dappled the block with blacks and browns. The indigenes were the working class of the inner city and mostly they shunned outsiders. Two or three generations of them were slotted away into the block's recesses, used up by work, worn out by welfare. Long term inmates, unable to change the views from their windows around, they disliked the interlopers. Silent dislike mostly, although their xenophobia gave them energy, reinforced their credo of keeping themselves to themselves. *Blankety Blank*. Rick tried to build bridges; he was a local so it wasn't so bad for him. Billy tried to ignore the fact that he was being ignored.

He wasn't smiling back at Rick because he was hungover again. An ill-matched couple — Billy, tall and gangling, Rick, stocky and smiley — they stood brushing arms. There was no avoiding it, in the narrow space left at the edge of the pool of piss lapping at their trainers. At times Billy found himself questioning whether the lift ran on urine, whether there was some sort of organic motor powered by human waste mounted beneath it. He wasn't suffering too much from the previous evening's excesses, he thought, as the lift shook itself down the shaft. His back ached, but mostly this was the rude health variety of hangover. The problem was remembering what had happened later on. The end of last night was blanking him big time; for all he knew, it was him who had pissed in the lift. Rick dragged on his roll-up.

'We've gotta do something about the gentrification, stop the hipsters before it's too late.'

'It is too late.'

'It's never too late,' said Rick.

The lift ricocheted around the shaft walls. They stared down at the piss pool, at the lift's neon lighting skating frantically over the surface, as if desperate to avoid immersion in the bacteria below. It was always going to be too late for parading around with banners, Billy thought, before clubbing policemen with the banner poles, anointing them with broken bottles, crowning them with pieces of paving stone. Anyway, gentrification was not a clear-cut issue. This wasn't the poll tax (what had been wrong with the poll tax? He couldn't remember). It was impossible to take a stand against a social trend and, besides, it was too late. Alastair was right about that much. He could only hope the gentrification didn't follow Alastair's prediction and snuff out the art before it got properly started.

'Those artists don't give a toss, it makes no difference to them,' said Rick.

'They complain to me enough about it.'

'What do they care? They're all posh, public schools, family money and all the rest of it.'

'You have got a point there. ''The art world is elitist and discriminatory.'

Rick brightened, lips starting to gather into a loose smile.

'You must have seen all that come on top,' he said.

'It sucks.'

'I can imagine, yeah.'

'Yeah. There is blatant discrimination in favour of the artists with the most talent.'

Rick centred the lenses of his little round glasses on him.

'You never used to be like this Billy.'

It wasn't very long ago at all that they were united by pills and music. They wanted to be friends with everyone, and their psyches had loosened and sparkled, had overflowed cramped bodies and narrow egos to merge with hundreds upon hundreds of others into a massive compound organism which danced all night and was always very happy. That was when Billy started writing his first articles, for music mags and fanzines, while Rick got himself involved in organising the raves.

The E massaged their hearts, tugged spiritual yearnings up and out of their chests onto the dance floor. Pumped them up with inexpressible love and set them sailing over racing seas of sound, full of breakers and rollers for their emotions to rise and float over, always set to climb and descend, and to climb again once more and for evermore. It was a period when Billy had no difficulty believing the world could change for the better, and he knew that even now he could tell Rick anything, and that he would understand and would not judge.

'That last squat party was great, wasn't it?' said Billy.

'Storming, man.'

Billy's spirit inclined towards Rick once more, drawn by memories of an evening of surging techno and chemical beneficence. Rick was grinning again with his inner-tube lips, inflated and saliva-sheened, and Billy pushed away a momentary image of the tongue on the pavement outside Mother.

'Gonna be another this weekend,' said Rick. 'It's in an old printing works off Kingsland Road.'

'I'm well up for that.'

'Cool. And there's a Criminal Justice Bill meeting on Wednesday.'

'I'll see if I can make it.'

He didn't want to go to that event but refrained from saying so outright. They were about two-thirds of the way down and he was thinking that the blobs in lava lamps shifted faster than this when Rick pulled out his surprise.

'You're mates with Alastair Given aren't you? I'd like to meet him.'

Billy didn't say anything. As he looked at Rick properly for the first time during their ride, at his combats (why was he so wedded to trousers from the military-industrial complex?), at his glasses and his big sloppy smile, he tried not to feel the way he felt when he was a kid, when an old, used-up best friend wanted to play with him and his new friends.

'And the Japanese-looking woman who's knocking around with him,' Rick said, 'what's her name?'

'Becky.'

It was impossible to meet Becky and then not recall her name, and so Rick was dissimulating for some reason. Most likely he was finding it hard to cope with his lust for her.

'She came into the housing office.'

Billy did not want to discuss Becky with Rick, but this couldn't be ignored.

'Come on, she's not signing?'

The beautiful people didn't claim benefits, not unless they were given to making eccentric lifestyle statements, but it sounded like Rick really had encountered Becky visiting his workplace. Their workplace. They had part-time jobs in the local housing department, in the housing benefit section. Rick got in first and then sorted Billy. Few paper qualifications were needed for a clerical job, but neither of them had any at all. What the fuck, they just made them up — and it worked, because employers like theirs never checked applications properly. All the same, Billy hated it. It was just money while he got going with his art writing.

'She's very politicised,' Rick said.

'You mean she nodded a lot while you talked?'

'Alastair Given too. I have a lot in common with him.'

'Yeah?'

Perhaps they did, in their denial of reality. Alastair wanted Hoxton for art and for the artists, while what Rick wanted (some longer lasting variant of the Paris Commune of 1871, probably) was equally unrealistic. Billy was glad that at least he had stopped talking about Becky.

'We're outlaws, man.'

Billy said nothing. Rick worked in a housing department, for the government. The raves he organised were no more than a hobby and not up to now an illegal hobby. Billy hoped he knew nothing of Alastair's more illicit activities, but Rick was in there ahead of him.

'Where does Alastair get his wedge?' said Rick.

'Fucked if I know.'

'I hear he's hanging with some lairy people.'

Billy spread his arms wide.

'News to me, mate.'

So that was it, always the way on the left. The workers, united. But preferably united behind Rick. He wanted dirt on Alastair and the others so that any campaign against gentrification that got underway remained in his hands. Billy bit his lower lip to stop himself coming out with this and for a moment he felt ashamed, as so often he did these days with Rick. Rick meant well, a movement was all that he wanted, and he'd be happy to be a foot soldier in it. He wasn't a mad dictator in the making, any more than Alastair. Nevertheless Billy wasn't about to tell him anything.

The lift allowed itself a spurt, and the acceleration made them brace themselves against the walls. They stared at each other again, this time with concern, wondering if the cable had snapped. There came a *crump*, accompanied by a prolonged, shuddering rattle. Ground level.

'Sorry, Rick. Got to do one.'

Billy shivered in the chill wind busy tossing litter around the street, stared back at the block. Concrete exterior discoloured, as if a passing giant had emptied his bladder over it. Blackened cladding and boarded windows, where fires had gutted individual flats. Atolls of refuse around the rubbish chutes, weeping bin bags grouting the slimy fridges, purulent cookers and disembowelled mattresses. What was the solution? He did not know the solution.

South of the roundabout he entered Shoreditch proper. Narrow streets with warehouses and workshops hanging over them, Alastair's citadel for art. Into French Place, normally a reassuring constant. The building containing Idiot Savant was here long before he was around and it would endure long after he was gone. Warm Victorian brick, those jibs up above reminders of a bustling mercantile past, and all of it now part of a dazzling present.

Alastair's talk of the end of all this was beyond Billy's comprehension, because each element of this life he had started to lead was so precious to him. In the cigar box that was the back office at Idiot Savant he would raise and lower the phone to try to gain work and then, when he had it, attack the keyboard and get it done as best he could. In between times he glimpsed Alastair about mysterious business and observed a traffic of artists through the gallery which was too numerous ever to retain more than a fraction of names and faces.

Less precious was the housing department for earning regular money, with its magnolia walls and scouring strip lighting, where he endured keening infants and minatory drunks, and legions of accusing claimants, forever sending him after their lost forms and files. Sometimes he hid away for an hour or two writing up a diary, because he thought he might be able to put something together about Idiot Savant, maybe after his book on Thorn.

Even so the housing office was like the gallery and the dying termite mound of his tower block. They reached out to him with the spare appeal of the inner city, sparks of affect kindled from the human mass wedged into all that cracking brickwork and mouldering concrete.

Renewed forebodings about last night intruded into his reverie. His last complete memory was of Alastair and Kevin Thorn vanishing almost before his eyes, and after that a few snatches, impressions which wouldn't cohere. It was a question of discipline, he knew. The charlie was a tool which stopped him getting too out of it, helped him to drink all night and ameliorated his hangovers the next day. He needed to stick with the coke, avoid memory loss and stay out of trouble. A couple of lines now would help get rid of the legacy of last night's excesses — but he realised that was a bad idea, because his heart was beating rapidly as it was, trying to pump away toxins.

He needed to see Alastair, chase him to fix up the piece on Becky. Alastair hadn't come down into the gallery yet, so Billy tramped upstairs to see if he was in his studio, noticing it wasn't as much trouble as it could have been, his tachycardia notwithstanding. Perhaps he would have a line or two, after all, when he had tackled Alastair.

Alastair's front door looked different. It remained as red as usual but seemed to extend out into the passageway. Then Billy realised that he was looking at a man wearing a red tracksuit standing next to it. The visitor spoke first.

'Detective Inspector Harkness,' he said. 'I'm looking for an Alastair Given.'

Billy tried not to think about the wraps of charlie on him. The policeman must not detect agitation and decide to search him. If he was a policeman. Harkness looked nothing like his idea of a detective (gained from television crime dramas: angry middle-aged men, wearing rumpled suits). Harkness was younger, his face unlined. He wore white trainers (Jordans, Billy thought, or maybe Reeboks, he wasn't great on labels) below his tracksuit (Ellesse: the logo was clearly visible). There were sweatbands on his wrists and he had a number two crop, augmented by small gold earrings. As if in answer to Billy's doubts he flashed a small wallet bearing a silver badge at him.

'I'm after him myself,' Billy said.

'If you get hold of him, could you tell him I'd like to see him?'

'Can I let him know what it's about?'

'You don't need to worry about that.'

In the Idiot Savant office Tania was not a calming presence. She raged about the gate crashers and hangers on at her party.

'I should have thrown Kevin Thorn out straight away. Bastard. And the state you were in. Why the fuck were you trying to set the club on fire?'

A memory formed, a miasma gathering and coalescing into a vivid and horrible sequence. He had seen Kevin Thorn a second time, walked up to him and attempted conversation. The responses were strange, off putting. Piqued, he persisted more assertively. Thorn had a cigarette in his hand. Billy offered him a light but couldn't ignite the tip of his cigarette. He tried again before realising that Thorn was mocking him, jerking his cigarette away from the flame. Billy spoke sharply to him and then, when he continued his horseplay, began shouting. People stopped their conversations and stared at them. After an indeterminate period Billy understood that he was standing in front of a large mirror, yelling at a reflection of himself into which he had been trying to thrust lighted matches.

'Fucking performance art, was it?' said Tania.

'That's right.'

'You arse. You were nearly as bad as Erick.'

A memory of splintered wood all over the floor, of many falling leaves of glass.

'It's a good thing he's such a little shit,' she said. 'He could really damage someone, otherwise. Speaking of which, you know that guy's dead?'

'What guy?'

'The one outside whose tongue was ripped out,' she said. 'Died of shock by the time he reached hospital.'

He felt sick.

'I don't know what all that was about.'

'I didn't say you did, did I, fuckwit?'

'Well, I—'

'And you, you should watch yourself.'

'That was the problem, I—'

She was staring straight into his face, hands on hips.

'You need to be very fucking careful, Billy.'

5

In and Out of Affection

You have never thought you were at the epicentre. You live in a provincial capital. A satellite city. London has never truly been swinging. London has never really been happening. London has never ever been a twenty-four-hour city. For the whole of the twentieth century London has remained twenty years behind New York. Less money. Less vitality. Less.

London never recovered from two world wars. Everyone knows this and everyone spends their lives acting as if it is not so. Everyone pretends that the present does not consist of the crumbling grandeur of yesteryear. You know that London can never rise above the monochrome, that it can never forsake the legacy of rationing and austerity. And you are part of London's pretence, whether you like it or not. London dissembles by trying to substitute cultural capital for material capital. Mostly it does this badly, and for long stretches of time it remains stupefyingly dull.

Occasionally — only very occasionally — something seems to happen. You know that this is part of the pretence. Whatever it is feels revolutionary, because so little takes place otherwise. The rest of the world is taken in, it takes an interest. The Beatles, then punk, and now art. Baroque fragments, hangovers from an imperial past. Glimmerings in the twilight. You are a glimmer before the fade back to grey.

*

Each party offered up the story of Hoxton in microcosm. A fiction of unified consciousness steadily, relentlessly descending into collective unconsciousness and chaos. Each was a temporary autonomous zone which fought to become a permanent status quo, even as it degraded and collapsed. The parties were stories with similar beginnings and endings, but in between was an infinity of happenings and revelations and mishaps and coincidences and episodes and reversals. So many encounters, all the interactions of a lifetime, folded and compressed into such short durations, which were then mutated and deformed and expanded by chemicals to become all of the time there had ever been, before disjointed exits and abrupt endings.

This. A black cab grinding its way slowly through Hoxton, for a quarter of a mile or thereabouts. Billy didn't know why they hadn't walked. The headlights did no more than light up the fog outside, which was suffocating the streets, sulphurous smoke from some underworld pit. Tania's hair a burning busby up above. Talking about her work in progress.

'Wood is fucking expensive,' she said.

'So it's wooden,' said Tom, his nose angled towards her, 'but what is it?'

'It's a box.'

A box — or a package. Tania and Alastair, thought Billy, were fucking with his head in an elaborate piss-take.

'Stop winding me up,' he said.

'What's your problem?' Tania said.

She was serious, he realised. She was talking about something else.

'Fucking loop,' she said. She turned to the others.

'It's going to be more than thirty cubic metres in volume.'

'This is a size,' said Erick. He was smoking next to a rolled down window, exhaling into the cab's slipstream in discreet defiance of the prohibition sign in front of him. Billy saw that Erick's exhalations were coinciding with surges in the cab's engine, as if he was part of the exhaust. Perhaps he was under some synaesthetic delusion that the increases in noise would conceal the smoke.

Billy gazed from the cab window at the scene outside again. He saw that the drink, spliff and coke had joined forces to propel him into a virtual world. The streets and the buildings were no longer Hoxton. They were paradigmatic representations, he could see, of streets and buildings in a run-down inner-city area in the throes of redevelopment. It was a model, a theme park, a future sociologist's simulation of the inner London of the late twentieth century.

The streetlamps slathered themselves over the window, then separated out. The cab had swayed and lurched to a stop. They were getting out. He needed this, he thought, he needed to be taken out of himself. Alastair's insouciance when he spoke to him about his encounter with the policeman had not set his mind at rest. He had brushed over it quickly, started talking instead about the possibility of Billy going to art school. He was very enthusiastic, so that it became clear that he wasn't simply making a convenient change of subject. The plan was that Billy could support himself while he studied by working as the gallery's press officer. It sounded great, except for the omission of the detail of where the money for his salary was going to come from and given this oversight he didn't pay too much heed.

A low block hung over them in the gloom, an enormous book end abandoned by the roadside. Fluorescent lights whined in the deserted foyer. They passed on the crepuscular lift and walked up. Another vertical street leading nowhere, another broken machine for living in. The stairwell was tattooed in tags. Tom lauded Basquiat, Erick belittled Basquiat, Tom drew attention to Erick's littleness and Erick sighed. Tom was alone in his regular teasing of Erick over his size. Erick ignored it because challenging Tom was beneath his dignity, and this impasse lent a surreal quality to many of their exchanges.

The party was on the top of the block. When the door opened noise slammed into them. They stepped inside and Billy looked round. Space, a term that was one of the art world's more irritating pretensions: either something was a studio, an office, a living room or a gallery — it was never just a space. It was ridiculous to say, for example after a private view, 'I liked the space'. Space was something between books on a bookshelf, or an interplanetary medium, or a mathematical or philosophical concept, or where you parked your car, or something between someone's teeth.

Nonetheless, there was no other handy term to describe the area they were in. It wasn't an art studio, not completely, because there were signs of habitation: screens at one end sectioned off a kitchen area and presumably the doors on the far side led into areas used for bedrooms and other living annexes. The whole wasn't precisely residential, either; it was an undefined unit of the block which had been subdivided in a minimal way, nothing more. A kissing cousin of the spaces in the French Place building that housed IS.

This space was spacious, there was that. Becky's place at the back end of Dalston had been cramped and would have been impossibly claustrophobic, if not for the fact that Becky was in it. The poky bedsit, with its psoriatic wallpaper and linoleum, was a skin to be shed, a setting to establish the impecunious circumstances of a young artist at the outset of her career. A setting for a scene in a drama, not a documentary, because Becky was too conventionally attractive, notwithstanding her scar, to be credible in a documentary. To Billy's mind the art itself fitted the setting. Her installation, with its signature video looping smoothly on its monitor, was a mere prop.

*

The piece is called *Walking* and consists of a filmed sequence showing Becky walking down a street carrying a large paper bag. The bag hangs down awkwardly from one of her hands, which grips it at the top, scrunching its open sides together. Becky is dressed conservatively in a mackintosh and court shoes, with a scarf tied round her hair above a pair of dark glasses. As she proceeds the camera begins to zoom in on the paper bag dangling from her fist and it becomes apparent that the bottom is soggy, so that the contents are at risk. The paper begins to give way and a white shape starts to emerge, resolving itself into an egg which, as she walks on apparently oblivious, slowly frees itself before falling from the bag to smash on the pavement. This sequence is superimposed onto another piece of film, which shows a fainter image of Becky's face, scar prominent, gazing impassively into the camera. The composite result lasts for about ten minutes and plays in a continuous loop. Becky's technical expertise is clear, the result of her determination to master camera work and editing, and there is none of the jerky cutting and variable focussing that features in Tania's videos.

Critics have talked about the way in which *Walking* deals with complex, messy conceptual issues in a neat and witty way — they have been struck by what they see as its sharp, ironic humour. As for Becky herself, it is a work that features heavily in her recent autobiography, though she remains unforthcoming on the question of how much it might have been inspired by her personal history.

*

Billy was not impressed. He thought he knew what Becky had done and he thought he knew how it differed from what she thought she had done, and he was not going along with any of it. If finally the good art — the great art — was enigmatic, he believed the bad art presented no problems. It was easy to say why it was bad. It was too similar to what had come before, imitation, pastiche, the result of insufficient imagination.

Most work by students was flaky, he reasoned, as flaky as the plaster on Becky's bedsit ceiling, as flaky as the remaining wraps of Alastair's cocaine in his pocket. He was polite, he dissembled, so that Becky could have had no intimation of his real opinion. She talked about another installation she was making, which she thought would be better. Billy saw her excitement as she spoke about the new work. He couldn't have failed to notice; she became very animated, with a flush discolouring her pale features, where usually she was reserved, aloof even. She was undecided about what to call her new work and asked him if he thought *In Between* would be a good name. Billy agreed that it would. He thought something less succinct would work better (there was a vogue for lengthy ironic titles for works, after all), but he kept that to himself.

Normally she would have been out of his reach, but what happened in the environs of Hoxton was not normal at all. True, there had been no overt signs that she was attracted towards him. No touches on the arm, no minor collisions, no prolonged eye contact in the damp and cramp of her home.

On the other hand: he had been on what could be construed as a date. She had invited him to her home and paid attention to his statements and drank a little of the bottle of wine he brought with him (though she declined the coke) while he looked at her art respectfully. They met the others at the Lux and, several cocktails later, everyone left together to travel the short distance to the party. As she talked in the bar and in the taxi he watched her scar's slight ripples and waves, and started to think that perhaps, rather than hallmarking her perfection, her disfigurement reduced her to the same level as everyone else.

In the party he moved towards the space's bar area where he found himself talking to Tom, taking in the cultivated cut of his jib, topped by the yard arm of his nose.

'Your triptych is amazing,' said Billy. 'I've never seen anything like that, ever.'

'Thanks,' said Tom. 'I love urban blight.'

Billy had seen Tom's latest work when he brought it into Idiot Savant as part of the preparation for the upcoming group show, which he gathered was also to feature work by Tania, Erick and Becky. Tom had photographed a tower block (not Billy's) from three different angles after dark. Under rinsings of street lighting, the block's component flats threw out myriad radiances into the night. The flats with no one at home and the black smears from burnt out dwellings became lineaments of a numinous whole, enhanced by Tom's triple perspective. Billy groped for a formula to describe this achievement.

'You've made squalor beautiful.'

'Thanks. Well, I've never pretended to be interested in social realism.'

'Maybe it is social realism too.'

'No, it isn't. It's not. You know, I'm not very different to those eighteenth and nineteenth century artists who painted landscapes out in the countryside. They weren't concerned about the rural poverty in and around these settings, because it was the art that mattered to them, and it's the same with me.'

Billy considered the triptych, its majestic camouflage.

'I'm glad it's going into the group show,' he said.

'Afraid not, sadly. It's not right for IS, it doesn't lend itself to that space. I've had to remove it from the gallery. It's a shame because Alastair helped me out with the hire fees for the large-format cameras and the lab time for developing the film and so on, but there it is. It can't be helped.'

A repetitive high-pitched noise stilettoed into Billy's mind, puncturing the output from the sound system. It seemed to be coming from one of the sectioned off areas, a bedroom, whipping across the surface of the alcohol which was swamping everything. After careful thought he concluded that it was a screaming woman, and wandered over to investigate to find Tania, a Fury in full spate tearing into Alastair. Billy considered what to do. He brought out a wrap, in his eagerness untucking its folds to make the contents more readily available and enticing and offered it to her.

'This is exactly the fucking problem,' she shouted.

She swept it from his hand and it slipped and slid to the ground, to become a tiny white sand painting lost in the infinity of the space's vinyl flooring. He wandered away again.

The hours sped through him and around him, halting at random tableaux: the partygoers helping themselves to cocktails at the makeshift bar, the fog pressing threateningly at the windows, the revellers chopping out lines on the window ledges, and the dancers, at once serpentine and marionette-like, pulled and twisted by the drugs, moulded and smoothed by the music.

He would come back into himself, bring his mind down into the space and the people in it again, and then resent these episodes outside of the passage of time, because he wanted every one of these instants to be his forever. Then he would merge into his environment once more, absorbed into the fabric of the party, until the next time his mind clambered out from beneath rising tides of pure sensation.

Alastair was talking to Becky. Alastair's golden curls set off the blackness of Becky's hair, the fineness of her features. Billy saw Alastair hold out a CD case, a CD case with four large lines laid out on it. Becky did one of them, and Becky was dancing with Alastair.

Fewer cocktails, more vodka. Viscous alcohol, denser than the glass that contained it. He saw Erick's cigarette hand smudging vaporous hedgerows into the air.

'The man whose tongue is ripped away,' said Erick. 'This is good art.'

Billy thought it was as if Erick had a small catch securing the top of his skull he could flip back at will, so he could thrust his hands inside and rummage around after diverting material to pull out for inspection.

'The man is dead, Erick.'

'He dies for art.'

Billy wanted to change the subject.

'What are you working on now?' he asked.

'I work on nothing.'

'You're having a break?'

'No, I am so busy.'

'How do you mean?'

'I work with the spaces between matter, between thoughts. Everyone neglects them. Everyone is thinking they do not exist.'

'I suppose they are easy to overlook.'

'It gets me into trouble,' said Erick.

Smoke overflowed his lips, a grey scurf draining from his interior. Billy looked down enquiringly.

'I go to my bank manager to try and get my overdraft extended to finance the project. We sit down together and I detail the basic concept to him most carefully.'

'So?'

'He locks me in his office and calls the police. He tells them I must be put away.'

Billy nodded. This sort of thing was always happening to Erick.

Billy was listening to Pulp, lost in velvet reverie. Like a raver alone in a crowd. A moment of evanescent clarity. It was as if, in the length of time that a twisted strand of Stoly sparkles and twinkles from bottle to glass, he had been left all on his own. Becky hadn't spoken to him since they left the Lux. His memories of his encounter with her earlier that evening, were becoming starker, as their backlighting intensified. He remembered her refusal of his coke (or Alastair's coke) in her bedsit and the way the coke had enlarged him, made him too big for her modest home. He remembered her unwillingness to discuss any subjects other than her art, her perfunctory replies to his questions and her reluctance to linger.

When Billy left the party later, how much later it was he could not know, he was distracted by the sight of a door that was vertically split, half of it curling away like a lettuce leaf, with Erick next to it vomiting with exuberance. This visual detail did not engage Billy's attention for long because he was preoccupied, thinking that he should have given the same spiritual respect to Becky's video installation that evening as he had given to Jarvis Cocker's music, and that maybe there were other things he could have done to try to alter the course the evening had taken, and whether any of that could have made any difference.

6

Fractured English

Becky stretches herself, leaves the embrace of Alastair's bedding and begins to dress. She knows Alastair will be her first fully adult relationship, because everything before him now seems no more than a few adolescent flings. Momentarily she thinks of Billy and the comparison elevates Alastair further. Alastair said that Billy could write a feature about the group show and its preparations, enthusing about the appeal of an account of young artists getting a show ready in a Hoxton gallery, the benefits from the publicity. Tania objected and so did Becky, but Alastair prevailed and said he would help Billy place it in one of the broadsheet supplements. That means he will be hanging around them even more often, but if Becky is not keen on this she has no real cause for complaint.

Alastair is giving her prodigious help, more than she has any right to expect at this stage of her career. He respects her talent and she hopes the others will follow, although there is no reason why they should. Her transition from academia to art has been seamless and much swifter than theirs. All of them have CVs gilded with postgraduate qualifications: Tom from the Royal College of Art, Tania and Erick from the Slade. All of them have had gallery shows before, too. Mainly at Idiot Savant, it has to be said, but there's no denying the cachet that Hoxton's most alternative, avant garde, underground (take your pick) gallery has bestowed on them all. Then there is her, the remaining member of this quartet, her sole achievement to date the Goldsmiths' end of year show, that fest of student earnestness.

A group show with established artists is a radical departure and it is hard to resist a sense of unreality. A dream which comes to be never ceases, entirely, to be a dream. Kevin Thorn isn't in the show and she is grateful for that, since then she would be truly dwarfed, not by his talent — she knows she is capable of making work as good as his — but by the tempest of media attention that is steadily gathering around him. Fortunately he refused Alastair's entreaties to participate.

The rest of them will have to lump her. If they protested to Alastair, it hasn't worked. He has prevailed, and rightly. He is holding everything together, keeping the gallery running and shielding everyone from all the money problems.

Her thoughts turn to her new video installation, completed the day before and entitled *In Between*. It will bring her first sliver of fame (though *Walking* will be exhibited in due course and widely praised too). Critics and commentators will return and re-engage with the new work many times. The consensus will be that the agency evident in this second video represents a significant advance in Becky's art. Many of them will focus on the playful use of signifiers of domesticity to mediate its feminist sub-text of empowerment.

The video opens with her entering an archetypal suburban living room with a swirly red and orange carpet, antimacassars on the armchairs and settee, a tasselled lamp stand in one corner and the blank eye of a television in another. Above an old-fashioned gas fire is a row of kitsch china ducks flying across the wall. Becky takes the ducks down from the wall, one by one, and smashes them to pieces with a hammer. This part of the video is in slow motion. The hammer comes down, fragments of pottery flowing out smoothly from it in all directions.

She looks blissful as she wields the hammer and this, together with the decelerated violence, makes the scene mesmeric. Like the earlier work this one is looped too and, once again, the sequence is superimposed over another one, this time of a fainter, larger image of Becky's face. She is wearing another headscarf and is in profile, her scar prominent as she gazes serenely upwards at a flock of geese which is heading across the sky in classic wedge formation.

When Becky thinks about *In Between* she gets a tight feeling in her stomach. It is almost the same sensation she gets when she thinks of Alastair, but sharper and more intense. She experienced this feeling for the first time when she was five, at an age which lends reality plasticity and weightlessness. Her parents had separated, her father was back in Tokyo and she moved into a commune in the countryside with her mother. It was the mid-1970s and the old manor house that was her new home contained a rag-taggle band, some of the remnants of the tribes of hippies which had flourished and appeared ready to take over the world half a dozen or so summers before.

That was now an age ago and the love generation was busy falling out of love with itself. There were factions, bickering between anarchists and Trotskyites, acrimony between vegans and agnostic vegetarians, and antagonism between the rest of the commune and a contingent of women who wanted their own separatist feminist community — and who, indeed, moved to a couple of big, refurbished barns a short distance away a few months after Becky and her mother arrived. The continual conflict might, in retrospect, have been a group displacement, a collective denial of the wider social traumas which would end in Thatcherism and the final dissolution of the commune, leaving the buildings to resume their interrupted decay.

Fortunately the strife was literally over Becky's head. This was where she fell in love with art. She could splash paint around for as long as she wanted in the roomy, draughty nursery that had once been a stable. There was usually an adult or two around to admire her work and fetch her fresh paper and materials and, except for mummy, none of them ever bothered making her tidy up afterwards.

Jethro (thus called after the rock band he listened to incessantly) was her favourite. He had the longest and frizziest hair of anyone she had met, then or since, a huge mass of it hanging most of the way down the back of his faded and patched dungarees; it was as if he had a couple of sheepskin rugs attached to his head. A woolly mammoth or giant hairy bear, he was always ready for play. Jethro and Becky spent hours together, painting, modelling with plasticine, messing around with sand and water and all of it was fun. Lots and lots of fun, almost too much fun for her to cope with.

One day Jethro wasn't around — perhaps he had gone into town to go shopping or to sign on — and in his absence she set about painting a picture she was determined would be a masterpiece. She worked on it long and hard, and when he returned in the afternoon she showed it to him proudly.

'That's mummy and me, and that's daddy in his house in Japan, and here's everyone who lives here. And there's the sun in the sky and the trees.'

Jethro took the picture off her, held it out at the end of his arms and admired it while she stared up at him eagerly. His breath smelt like medicine, but what he said next dispelled everything else from her mind.

'This is fantabulous, Becky. You are a clever little chicky aren't you?'

'Yes.'

He looked at her gravely.

'Did you know that I am a wizard?'

'No,' she said solemnly, adjusting her tone and expression to his.

'Yes, I'm a wizard and I'm going to show you some magic which will make you feel good as a reward for painting this super-duper picture. Now you mustn't tell mummy or any of the others about it because it's secret magic. If you do an evil wicked witch will come at night and take you away.

' 'Kay?'

' 'Kay.'

Becky remembered staring at her picture laid out flat on the table and then through the barn door at the intense colours of the trees, the grass and the sky. The sky in particular was saturated in what she would think of from then on as the only real blue there could ever be. Lying full length on the ground and propping himself up on his elbows, Jethro busied himself licking her wee-

wee place. It was tickly and it made her tummy squirmy and nice. Ever since then, whenever she sees an artwork that she finds exceptional, this feeling has returned to her.

The scar followed soon after. The memory of what had taken place was already ineradicable, but Becky was to receive her disfiguring memento regardless. Despite scaring her into silence Jethro decided he thought licking her hairless private parts was cool, and that he should have no inhibitions over telling other residents of the commune about it. His deed was a breach of a rule that was there to be derided, one laid down by the pigs in the straight world they were all there to radicalise.

Becky recollects being in a van with her mother, driving at speed, unsecured possessions crashing around behind them as they accelerated down country lanes which high hedgerows turned into long green tunnels. The milk float appearing in front of them, the rising whine of its electric motor the only noise she heard as she flew through glass and then, triumphantly up and out into the air, to out-Pan Peter Pan at long last, to become a bird in flight in an instant of freedom that stretched right out for ever and ever.

When her mother reached her she was completely coated in milk. Much later, in her autobiography, Becky will write that for at least a minute or two she was indisputably white, free of racial baggage for the first and only time in her life, and that she regrets having been unconscious and unable to enjoy her fleeting transformation.

Becky has nearly the same intensity of feeling towards Alastair as she has about her new installation, nearly but not quite. She was hoping, somewhere towards the edge of herself, fuelled chaotically by all that cocaine and by images from the manga comics she reads occasionally, that her encounter with him would be mythical. That they might make love for night upon night, until their bodies created earthquakes and thunder, and their breath became clouds hanging over the earth as they merged into a single indissoluble soul.

His bedroom was small and airless, barely wide enough to contain a double bed. Its walls were made of pine and an absence of windows made it like a wooden crate or — she could not stop herself thinking — a coffin. She saw, with relief, that the bed linen was clean and then Alastair was naked in front of her, blond curls crowning his cleanly knit physique.

To start with when they embraced it was awkward, a reminder of the dancing. For long minutes on the dance floor they had become enmeshed, each of them lost in the other, but they could never come fully together and move as one with the fusillades erupting from the sound system. Their smiles were rueful acknowledgments that sharing the same rhythm was beyond them.

She moved from his arms and started to undress. He helped her gently and when she was naked and sitting on the end of the bed he stood in front of her, the pale wand of his cock level with her face and placed a pinch of cocaine on its head. She laughed and cuffed his tip away so that the powder scattered, superfine confetti, and then as he started to laugh in turn, put her hand round the swinging member and pulled him down on top of her.

He was over her, a new outer layer of flesh and bone laid upon her frame. They kissed, let their tongues hang pregnant together for seconds at a time as their lips sealed and resealed themselves. He gripped her shoulders, cupping them in his palms as if creating extra joints to yoke their limbs together. His hands took the weight of her breasts, his tongue drew teasing circles around her nipples and eased them out into soft brown nuggets.

He looked up at her shyly. Becky had sought him and found him and yet, even now, she did not know if he was here for her, or she for him. She brushed her hair from her eyes to see him move further down, his tongue dabbling round in her belly button and then flicking its way between her thighs. He was so fair and unblemished and, as she gazed at his curls (she cannot help being fascinated by blond hair, because her own hair is so black) and felt his lips and tongue working upon her, she thought again of her soul, a bird circling, the slow flaps of its wings like heartbeats, and whether it would stay watching from up above or descend to play a part in all this.

His hands were still on her breasts but she took hold of them and held them, linking her fingers between his to weave twin caskets from pliant digits. His tongue was moistening her lips, moving up and down the neat ruche of her perineum, returning to find her clit and to circle and re-circle until all of the energy in her body started to loosen and to flow to his tongue, and she pulled him back up and onto her again.

Becky looked into his eyes and, as he smiled, saw faint, questioning reflections of herself, her scar for once diminished into invisibility. He began to kiss her anew, this time holding her to him with one arm round her waist, slowly moving the other hand over her breasts and nipples, and then downwards to her moist cunt.

When finally he entered her she released one of his buttocks to wet the middle finger of her right hand with saliva before working it quickly into the delicate folds of his anus, as if piercing a peach. He gasped, but they were gathering speed, moving together faster and faster until it was no longer clear who was penetrating who, who was cock and who was cunt, who was moaning and who was crying out.

She looked at his face before they came, fixed in a rictus of painful effort, turmoil fixed in marble. They climaxed together quietly with no more than plaintive, wounded sighs, as the traffic in the streets outside offered up an ironic fanfare of horns. They came, and they went, retreating away into themselves once again. As she lay there she saw a remoteness in him and much later on she wondered whether the same remoteness, less open and unguarded, had been there all along.

Now Becky ventures cautiously from the bedroom into the small corridor beyond. She has an idea she can recall where the bathroom is and its door has been left open, assisting her orientation. Through it she can see a lozenge of pale sunshine fastening onto the porcelain of the basin and bath.

As she performs a hasty toilet she is thinking that staying over regularly at Alastair's place would not be a great idea, because she values her own space and independence. She realises she can hear

Alastair's voice coming from the living room. He sounds subdued, his customary brio muted, though it is difficult to be sure because there is a corridor and a door between them. Puzzled, she ventures after him.

She doesn't know why Alastair allows his home to stay in this condition. Making a stand against bourgeois conformity is one thing, she thinks, ignoring housework altogether is another. In her father's culture everything has its pre-ordained place, so that a space can present a harmonious whole. Sometimes she finds herself imagining that Alastair's space has a stylised disharmony, a spatial discordance to match the aleatory music of say, John Cage — and yet that cannot explain the dirt. Now and again she thinks Alastair has chosen this background as a contrast for his lustrous skin and his shining hair. Mostly she finds it all an unpleasant, dirty mess.

The other side of the building is receiving what watery winter sun there is, so that the living room is in shade and this might be why she does not recognise Alastair immediately. Or it could be his posture. He is hunched over the telephone receiver like an infantry man sheltering from sniper fire. She hadn't been wrong about his voice. He is defensive, and if it had been anyone else she would have described his tone as craven.

'I'm sorry,' Alastair is saying.

Becky can't hear the person at the other end of the phone, but the receiver is buzzing slowly and deeply, like an under-powered electric razor. Alastair is bowing, she thinks, or learning to bow. He is like a performing animal, a chimp perhaps, forced to mimic human rituals. Satisfactory obeisance will come with practice because his willingness to please is so evident.

'What do you expect me to do?' he says.

This behaviour is baffling. Usually Alastair is careless with his debtors: the printers, the council, the utility companies and the other organisations he offers disinterest in lieu of funds. It is surprising the phone remains connected; maybe it will be one of the last things to go.

'If I don't have it I can't give it to you, can I?'

Becky has heard Alastair respond in this fashion before, though this time there is none of his customary dismissiveness. The receiver buzzes slowly. Alastair holds the receiver with an expression of pain as though it is a piece of scorching metal straight from the forge. He replies quickly.

'Yes, I know what happened to him,' he says.

When he hangs up he stands there over the phone in the shadows, ghostly in his white linen shirt.

7

Industrial
(Part I)

Another warehouse, another very large shed built of brick, this one sited near the Bethnal Green Road border of Hoxton. Tonight it was a venue for industrial music. Raw machine code, punching itself directly into the body in preparation for a future where man and machine are one. Android and cyborgs united, willing slaves of robot masters, all of them dancing until they break down.

Rick's combats and T-shirt were blotched and streaked with dirt, some of the final contents of the building behind them. In its last incarnation he thought it had been used to store white goods – he had shown Billy a couple of filthy, barely legible copy invoices from the 1970s he found in a boxed-in office space in one corner.

They were outside, leaning against the main door, a flimsy barricade for the bass lines which loped remorselessly on through it and into their chests. A fillet of freezing sky was visible above them, sliced off by the roof line of the office building across the street. Some of the office interiors were visible, their lights left on as a security safeguard. With their desks and chairs empty they looked calm and ordered, and Billy thought about how pleasant it would be to relax in one of them for a few hours, sit there reading a book maybe, free of all human contact.

He looked down and saw Rick dragging on his roll-up, its tip the same red as the rear lights passing in the distance. It reminded him that they were different, that Rick was born and bred round here, part of the urban fauna of Hoxton, and that for all of his own working-class antecedents and his flat in the tower block, that he was not. He had his nose pressed up against an invisible window, like the plexiglass screens in the reception area of the housing office where they worked, and he would never have full access to Rick's world.

Rick was talking to him about how hard it was getting to find venues, how empty warehouses were being bought and refurbished, and about the Criminal Justice Act on the way which would make organising raves much harder.

'They're legal for now, though, aren't they?' said Billy.

'Yeah, they're fine tonight.'

'Good to know,' he said.

They grinned at each other. Billy always found Rick's grins formidable. You had to fight hard not to feel good when a smile that size was directed at you.

'But we might have to jack all this soon.'

Billy said nothing but he knew that the raves Rick helped to organise, resurrecting derelict buildings and dancing their sombre histories away, were becoming history themselves. They were poor relations of other gatherings in Hoxton, the private views and parties which were merging into one ongoing celebration of an astonishing new world in which everything was fresh and young once more, a world in which Rick in his turn, would never have a place. He told Rick about Alastair's idea that he should go to art school, and Rick shrugged.

'Why go running after that lot? Look at the shit they're causing round here.'

He began to take issue with the artists again and in a way it was true, thought Billy, it could be argued they were to blame for a wider decline in Hoxton, unwittingly or otherwise. They needed somewhere cheap to live and work, but they had made this area intensely desirable for the hipsters who were starting to appear en masse, desperate to clothe themselves in boho chic.

'I'm not so into politics as you,' said Billy.

'Everyone's political.'

You couldn't be apolitical, not according to Rick; if you weren't actively opposed to the status quo, you helped support it. They fell silent and the goodwill that existed between them came back, caught and catapulted by glissandos of synthesized sound lancing out into the night. Behind them the warehouse and its occupants continued to hurtle off into uncharted regions of inner space. Fuse, Cybersonik, LFO, Xon, SL2, Joey Beltram. Techno. Repetitive beats, self-generated layers of sound. The synthesizers and their aural panoramas, their satin smooth alterations of mood, the rhythms — the accelerating rhythms.

Billy took a swig from his can, but alcohol couldn't keep the cold out tonight. Flecks of bluey white were drifting across his vision. Snow was falling, and then he realised it wasn't snow, despite the iron sky and the sapping cold. A police van was on the corner, and the spinning lamp on its roof was sending specks and splinters of light arcing out towards them.

'The fuck,' he screamed.

The rear door opened and policemen started piling out. The police sirens were now faintly audible behind the music. Another van slalomed round the corner, suspension wobbling, and slid to a halt behind the first.

'Don't worry,' said Rick. 'They can't come in.'

By now Billy was running down the street, his can discarded.

'Come back,' Rick shouted, 'what the fuck are you afraid of?'

8

A Tremendous Force of Nature

You want some time for yourself for a change. You slip into John Rowntree's show at Makin's over in the West End. You were at the private view last night (Liam Sheehan's Staffordshire bull terrier went for Mary Carmichael) but today you want to look at the work properly, alone. In your peripheral vision you see the assistant get on the phone and the gallerist emerges from his office a minute or so later. He sees you massage your lower back (you really need to get it seen to) and enquires after your health as the overture to a full schmoozing. You are a prize marrow being painstakingly anointed with liquid manure. East London beckons. You think about checking out Idiot Savant, realise that if you do Alastair Given will start requesting favours. At Mother someone asks if you are that artist in the papers and you deny it as a matter of course, vehemently and repeatedly. He pulls out a magazine and shows you your picture. He is bigger than you, so you laugh it off and buy him a drink.

In the Bricklayers your former assistant Max Pirbright is paralytic. He screams his accusations of plagiarism at you again. You can feel flecks of spittle on your face and you can't be bothered with it all. He is smaller than you, and when you land a couple of right-handers on him his friends are too drunk to do anything except stand there rooted, gazing on in wonder. After you are thrown out you are relieved and can't think why, before remembering that you wanted to glass him. You're not sure you can face the private view after all this, but you are obliged to go and see your old friends because you haven't seen them much at all lately.

You're meeting ten times the number of new people you used to, plus you're always being hassled by your gallery, your assistants, your accountant, your lawyer and the media. Always the media. Your old friends think you're distancing yourself from them. You explain everything. You can see that they don't believe you.

Why should they? You're all in the same profession and of course they're envious. They're looking for excuses not to like you much any more. You know that every last one of them thinks that their work is better than yours. You can't blame them because they couldn't carry on making art otherwise. You're the same, with the difference that the art world agrees that your work is better than any of theirs. Some of them make a point of omitting to praise your work any more although you know it hasn't fallen off (not yet). Some of them overpraise it, and you are sure that behind your back they're saying it's shit.

There are these difficulties but they are your old friends. You can't be sure of your shiny new friends. Partying with your homies is better, more comfortable. Like slipping into old trainers. You can let yourself go, have more Stoly than usual. You're not in public.

After a while no one talks about work. You were relieved that most of them had the tact not to talk about it much to start with. Instead everyone talks shit. For long moments you can pretend that nothing's changed. Their charlie is as good as yours. Later on, simultaneously, you all realise it's the same charlie. You're all in this together, all united against the world and all having a humongous time. You can never completely forget that in reality you're on your own, but at least you know you're on your own in good company.

*

Billy fortified himself for the private view for the group show with several pints of Stella and a clutch of lines in the Bricklayers and he felt extra fine as he strode through IS's gallery display space.

This was most of the unreconstructed ground floor of the French Place building. The deal panelling around the walls was dirty and splintered, the windows were shuttered loading bays and the lighting came from naked bulbs set into metal sockets ducted along the ceiling. An uncompromising environment for uncompromising art, or so he'd heard Alastair claim. For the time being he ignored the works on display, instead zeroing into Alastair and the others in the bar area. It was at the rear of the main gallery and consisted of a battered trestle table supporting serried ranks of Kirin and a gunmetal cash box.

The group show had materialised as a joint show. Tania had withdrawn, complaining that her work wasn't finished and that Alastair's solution of showing a video of her work in progress was ridiculous. Tom, also and as he had told Billy, was not participating. This had caused problems with the feature Billy had written for *The Bugle* about the preparations for the group show. Fortunately Alastair had intervened and charmed the arts editor there into agreeing to go along with a piece about a joint show. Billy was forced to do a fair amount of re-writing, but the feature was now finalised and he was looking forward to some celebration.

Billy glanced at Becky's latest installation, newly hatched from its monitor, video recorder and nest of cabling, confirmed that he didn't think there was anything special about *In Between*, no more than *Walking*. Apparently Becky had not known which installation to choose for the show. She had been horribly conflicted, Alastair said, but he had reassured her she was making the right choice with the new video, because it marked a big step forward for her work. Billy looked over at Erick's work. It was a series of monitors, each much the same as Becky's, but he saw that the screens were blank. Alastair turned to him.

'What do you think of Erick's latest work?' he asked.

'It raises interesting questions.'

'It's brilliant isn't it? His ongoing work with nothing is so inspirational.'

'A broad subject.'

'Visionary,' said Alastair. 'Where we all come from, and where we're all going.'

Erick wandered up.

'This is a work in progress,' he said, 'and so I am not happy with certain aspects of it. It is not possible to reduce the flicker on a cathode ray tube in order that it can show fully nothing.'

They looked at the screens closely and saw that he was right, the blank pixels were not completely static.

'None of the technical solutions I am trying is effective and they are all most expensive,' he said. 'You know, it is enough to make me start drinking heavily.'

'Start?' Billy said, as Erick handed out more beers, a joyous homunculus dispensing good cheer despite his complaints. He liked to construct his life around impossible creative challenges and this was his best yet.

Billy looked at Erick's work again, and he thought of the art he had seen in the past few months, the ironies of all those works saying they were what they weren't, or not saying they were what they weren't, or professing not to make statements of any kind. Their unending regressions, subversions of reality, subversions of those subversions, resolute underminings of what it meant to be anything at all.

Private view goers met and merged into fragile groupings, bubbles forming and bursting. He saw Dennis Smythe being rude to Angela Flaxman, and Stewart MacKenzie tripping over some of Erick's cabling. He knew a lot of people here, too many. Peter Wallington, Robyn Blackman, John Rowntree and Joshua Elam. To acknowledge one was to overlook another, and he was becoming overwhelmed. His attention returned to Alastair and the others and he was reassured, they were the cynosure, a court exacting due homage. A wrap was passing from hand to hand between trips to the toilets, and drink was sluicing away. Every so often someone new approached, effusing congratulations: Fleur Debries, Raj Jaffrey, Veronica Greenwood. Excitement was rising up steadily within him and he knew he needed more drink and charlie to contain it.

He started to cough and couldn't stop. Each convulsion of his upper body launched droplets of saliva into the air, tiny kamikazes diving through mauve strands of cigarette smoke, some landing on the people around Billy, others crashing down to earth. The coughing was on the cusp of turning to retching. Everyone fell back except Erick, who took hold of him, reaching up and slapping his back with surprising strength. A dull pain began to register between his shoulder blades and he gave one last violent splutter, some of which found its way onto one of Erick's monitors. Erick stood by, expressionless, as the others averted their eyes, before he shrugged and turned to Becky.

'Your work is promising so much for the future.'

Becky was staring fixedly at Erick's work, her eyes wide and her cheeks flushed once more. She didn't respond to Erick immediately, then started and turned to him, thanking him politely with a small smile. Billy couldn't understand what Erick saw in her art, and then he asked himself whether all was lost with her. A short time ago she was impressed by him and she was by his side, and she could be there again. He took another swig of Stoly; he knew probably he had reached his limit, but it was impossible to stop. Cocaine was not a reliable panacea, snorting enough to dam the torrent of alcohol flooding into him wasn't easy. After the first few sessions up at Alastair's, that halcyon time when he was able to drink what seemed like unlimited quantities of vodka with impunity, he was starting to find that the coke merely postponed an inevitable descent into oblivion.

They were in a private party in a café on Hoxton Square. The café's windows overlooked the square where a couple of mini-cabs stalked the drunks straggling home through the cold from pubs and clubs, all of them oblivious to a shaggy rat burrowing its way into a kebab in the gutter, tail trembling this way and that. Up above the moon was a shimmering discus frozen high in mid-throw, and when Billy looked at the freezing air closely he thought he could see it sparkling.

They were high up in Alastair's studio, and it was that point in a binge when body and mind adjust themselves to the flow of chemicals and a second wind kicks in, imparting a precarious equilibrium. In consequence the atmosphere was oddly formal and Billy understood they were cultural arbiters, sitting round a table to settle matters of note.

'We are a new movement,' said Erick. 'What must we be called? How about the neo-situationists?'

His spectacle lenses gleamed. He had revelled in the praise for his blank (or almost blank) monitors, Alastair had locked up the gallery and now it was time to play.

'Or the neo-geo-situationists?' suggested Tom, looking down his nose towards Erick.

'No, I don't think we should be an art movement as such,' said Alastair. 'I want to found a new kind of transnational corporation to harness creative flux.'

'You sound like the villain in a James Bond film,' said Billy.

'That's it. That's exactly the aesthetic I'm looking for.'

Billy was sure that was the charlie talking. It was interesting, sometimes, he thought, the way you could separate out the effects of different components in a compound intoxication. The gallery was bankrupt, everyone knew that, and Alastair wasn't about to found anything, regardless of rhetorical flourishes.

'You need a white pussy to stroke, Alastair,' said Becky. 'Where's your pussy?'

'We must stage marches with banners,' said Alastair. 'We will wear armbands.'

'I am never marching,' said Erick, 'and I am never wearing an armband.'

'I've something special for you all,' said Tom.

He produced a joint.

'It's laced with opium,' he said. 'A *digestif* for the cannabis.'

'So exotic,' said Erick, the joint an unwieldy baton in his delicate hands.

'Pity Kevin's not here,' said Alastair. 'He would appreciate this.'

Kevin Thorn hadn't appeared, that was another blow, and clouds were gathering over Billy's head as he continued his night voyage across this chemical sea, knowing that at all costs he must avoid shipwreck.

'He's not a stoner,' said Tom.

'Liking very much his charlie,' said Erick.

'Who doesn't?' said Tom.

'And his brown,' said Erick. 'Half this time he is strung out.'

Billy pondered whether they were exaggerating. It was a shame if they couldn't accept Thorn's burgeoning reputation without doing him down. Brown wasn't much of a taboo, and if Thorn found it necessary for his work then it was necessary. Maybe this was his brown period.

He felt a sense of solidarity with Thorn. Thorn was one of his own people: they were from the same part of the world, from the same kind of background. They knew how fucking awful it was to try and get anywhere in a country so wedded to social exclusion, and Thorn had gone out there and he'd taken them all on and he was winning. With help from Alastair, admittedly, but that didn't detract from his audacity, or from his sheer talent. He was unpopular, of course he was. Someone like him moving up was guaranteed to produce lorry-loads of insecurity, especially from his fellow artists, who were never willing to give each other credit for anything. Maybe there was hope for him too. Perhaps he really could go to art school. Why not? Thorn had, and Alastair thought it would work for him as well, help to boost his art writing and get him started as a fully-fledged critic.

Reality descended and started kicking his euphoria apart. He was too old to hang about with students, he didn't have the money or the right bits of paper and, anyway, his face wouldn't fit. He wanted another drink. He didn't want to think about any of this any more. Each time his glass emptied he was reaching over to the Stoly and refilling it. He had set up a small, efficient vodka drinking production line. As he leant over again, the image of a table lamp was caught in the bottle's shoulder and it became a shape thrown from solid light.

'Why don't you take it easy, Billy?' said Erick. 'When I am seeing you drink it is like watching an old speeded-up black and white comedy film.'

'Pot and kettle,' said Tom.

'Please shut up and roll another joint,' said Erick. 'I would like pot.'

Napoleon exhorting his troops, Erick poured himself another drink and sorted himself out with a line, the hologram on his credit card shimmering as he separated and chopped, before performing his party trick of leaning right over the charlie and hoovering it up without a banknote.

*

Is Hoxton the world? It is. Created by a god who does not exist and who is like the Toymaker in the film *Blade Runner*. The private view was taking place in an old warehouse the size of a miniscule dolls house. Through its windows a microscopic cluster of artists was visible. Nearby were other tiny warehouses with different private views taking place inside them too. In between the buildings cars like grains of pilau rice clogged the streets. A toothpick railway bridge waited for a centipede train. A 747 in a holding pattern was a matchstick pulling a dental floss contrail across the moon. Below it a police helicopter was buzzing around like a gnat. Everything that has happened and will happen here has taken a couple of hours of the Toymaker's afternoon. The Toymaker eats a chocolate digestive biscuit, looks on and knows that it is all good. He thinks of creating other worlds, worlds that will be entirely inassimilable to the inhabitants of this one, with the rows of tiny tools that are waiting, neatly stored in his scuffed leather bag.

*

Becky was sitting side-on to the table and Billy noticed her footwear. Large and clompy, platform trainers which emphasised the neat perfection of her feet. She could walk around with a couple of plastic bags on her feet and look fantastic, he thought. That was fashion, it mimicked fine art by commandeering ugliness, confident in the knowledge that it couldn't fail if it allied itself to the imperialism of youth and beauty. An imperialism he had a stake in still, and once more he debated whether his chances with her had diminished to zero, as she began telling everyone about a squat party she'd been to with Alastair earlier in the week.

'It was in a warehouse off Commercial Street,' she said, in the clipped, respectful tones familiar from voice-overs for wildlife documentaries. 'The sound system was awesome, but the police arrived mob-handed and started arresting everyone.'

Billy started. She was talking about the rave he attended a couple of days before. He found time to feel irritation that she accompanied Alastair there. He hadn't spotted them in the crowd inside. She wanted Alastair all for herself and he had been excluded, and then he shrugged the irritation off because it was no more than childish jealousy.

'We saw your friend there, Billy,' said Alastair. 'What was his name?'

'Rick, that was it,' said Becky. 'He's a lovely guy isn't he? I've never met anyone so smiley.'

Billy said nothing.

'Rick pointed out how much we all have in common,' said Alastair. 'He says squat parties are a way of bringing people together outside of commercial premises and events, much like Idiot Savant.'

'Yeah, he's keen on building a broad movement—' said Billy.

Becky spoke over him, effortlessly seized everyone's attention.

'The police were very systematic,' she said. 'They even brought a desk in with them, made us all queue and give our details, before letting us go — I mean, we weren't breaking the law.'

Billy decided to have another hit of coke, it might counteract some of the Stoly, for a while anyway. He examined the line before consuming it. There it lay before him, each of its granules a thing unto itself, and all of them united into one perfect strand of whiteness.

He didn't know why he had been so exercised about the package, the police, everything; all his concerns had dwindled down to the size of one of these grains, a speck lost beside the monument of Alastair's friendship. He looked at himself as clearly as he had ever looked at himself, and he realised none of this rancour swirling around in his head was any good, and that there could be only one cure for it. Love. He needed to feel love, the same love he used to feel for everyone on the dance floor.

'The police claimed they were cracking down on organised crime,' said Becky.

This time she sounded subdued.

'We should found a new race here,' said Alastair.

'The overmen, I suppose,' said Erick. 'Please, no more of this.'

'You might be more of an underman,' said Tom.

'I am a new kind of man,' Alastair continued. 'All of you, too.'

'Me included?' says Becky.

Everyone must have been completely drunk by now, Billy thought, but the charlie was keeping paralysis at bay. The progress of his own intoxication was elegiac. What he understood of the conversation was stupendous, and he sensed through his cocoon of chemicals that whatever was obscured from him was also stupendous. Any time he wanted to bring himself back to full awareness he knew he could have another couple of lines. It was pleasant to be able to switch in and out like this, spiralling down into a dark, comforting vortex and then rising back up from it again.

The next time consciousness returned he decided that it might be fun to ask Becky, in an ironic manner, if she would like to have an affair with him. Drugs created a reality in which experiments and meta-discourses like this were acceptable, in which he could become a sociologist or anthropologist carrying out a field exercise, gauging reactions and testing emotions. He pursued his researches, and the last thing he remembered was that he couldn't interpret Becky's responses properly.

9

You Mustn't Touch This

'It sounds like Billy was such a shit,' says Tania. 'There's something sordid going on there.'

'Let Alastair deal with it,' says Becky.

Becky doesn't want to think about it. The sooner Billy's behaviour recedes into distant memory the better. He is a stray dog nosing in and baring its fangs when it is shooed away, but she has more important matters to deal with. Thankfully Linda Bloom wishes to leave this distasteful subject behind. She is regarding Becky with exaggerated surprise.

'Just look at *you*,' she says. 'All young and talented.'

'Why thank you,' says Becky.

Southern belle might be the best response, she thinks. Linda must have seen the two or three rave reviews Becky has received for her installation in the group show, though she has said nothing about them directly. Last night Erick had praised her work and she hadn't known what to say, excited as she was by his installation. Fortunately she had managed to collect herself and thank him politely. It was a surprise to gain validation from an artist she respects, someone she had no reason to believe respected her work. And if Linda is being patronising then that is fine: artists need patrons. She looks back at Linda. Blond, not as blond as Alastair but nevertheless interestingly blond, her hair cropped into a short bob that manages to be both gamine and business-like.

Nowadays when journalists talk to Linda Bloom she says that she recognised the quality of Becky's work immediately, but if that was so she did not sign her up straight away. Events intervened which nobody involved wishes to hold up for close inspection, and which are not included in Becky's autobiography.

Linda is in another suit. Joseph. There has been discussion about how she cannot afford to wear Joseph and cannot afford not to wear it, either, what with the need to avoid being under-dressed when meeting clients. Tania is wearing a sundress with spaghetti straps over a white T-shirt. Ordinarily Becky would think it very late in the year for an outfit like this. It is a high street look and they are on a high street, that much is indisputable, yet it is Shoreditch High Street and this, together with the cold, makes Tania's outfit assertively alternative.

In Japan there is a tradition of cooperation between *kōhai* and *senpai* — junior and senior, or learner and teacher. For the time being Becky does not mind being *kōhai* to Tania's *senpai*, eager to help and to progress. After all, Tania was the first to take up her cause, when she came to see her end of year show at Goldsmiths' and then returned with Alastair. Becky has expressed interest in Bloom's and here Tania is again, selflessly taking Becky with her to meet Linda for coffee.

Three cappuccinos arrive. The waitress deposits them carefully, smiles, retreats briskly to the counter. Becky watches Tania and Linda as they teaspoon chocolate sprinkles off the froth and lick them neatly away. Tania gestures with her spoon towards the waitress's back.

'Did you see those?' she asks in an undertone.

'I don't know why,' says Linda, taking a considered sip, 'you put so much energy into re-appropriating sexist behaviour.'

'Well someone has to, don't they?'

'No, not really, sweetie. But I suppose it is a divine embonpoint if you're inclined that way.'

Becky also thinks Tania's baseness must be at least partly put on. Like Alastair's squalor, if it has a place in the politics of her art surely it is unnecessary outside of it. As for the waitress, Becky wonders momentarily what it would be like to have such an attention-grabbing torso. It might be interesting for a day, say, but not any longer than that.

'Once in a while you should forget your spreadsheets,' says Tania. 'Spread your legs.'

Linda sighs.

'How many men was it in that film, sweetie?' she asks. 'Thirty?'

'Thirty-five,' says Tania.

Becky knows they are talking about the art video Tania made a year back. It was called *Fucking Men*. Rather than a critique of patriarchy, it consisted of Tania enjoying sex with thirty-five men in succession. She recruited her participants through small ads, and the city's libidinal currents threw up more than two hundred applicants. Propelled to Hoxton by urgent lust, most were tossed back out after swift and brutal casting sessions. It was obvious that Tania's final selection was to her taste. She stripped each participant rapidly, peeling off shirts and tugging down trousers, before fucking them one after the other in an extended frenzy of thrusting and bucking and screaming and moaning and clawing.

Some of the men were in uniform: British Telecom repairman, milkman, gas man and so on. Others were casually dressed. One or two might have been dykes; it was difficult for viewers to judge because the film jumped in and out of focus so persistently. Whether that was a deliberate alienation effect or due to technical problems — or both — was also hard to ascertain. No one dared ask Tania. Becky gets excited about outstanding artworks, sometimes very excited, but this one does little for her. She admires the film's anarchic exuberance and satirical honesty, its position on the boundary of what art is and what it can be, but it is not the kind of work she can get involved in. Not least because she thinks that Tania's actions towards a couple of her participants on screen are aggressive, not to say violent and abusive.

'You should have had yourself looked at,' says Linda.

'The whole point was to have myself looked at.'

'Instead of Tania, we might have to call you Chlamydia.'

A loud hiss from behind them masks Tania's sweary response. Becky starts, turns to see the Gaggia emitting flares of steam. There are beads of condensation on the window in front of them, and thin sunlight is half-heartedly burnishing the spindly aluminium table they're circled around, each woman with her bag nested securely between splayed feet, wrists comfortably floppy, a white china cup set before her — Tania's matches her T-shirt, Becky sees — to be raised or lowered, or suspended in mid-air, according to the need to underline particular utterances in particular ways. She observes the intensity of Tania and Linda's interactions. Their mouths. They look as if they are biting and chewing upon opposite sides of a large, invisible loaf of bread. Their arms. Constantly shoving aside long, invisible beaded curtains.

Becky set herself the task beforehand of finding out a few things about Linda. Her father was the artist, Leon Bloom — a figurative painter, and a contemporary and friend of Frank Auerbach and Leon Kossoff. Outside of the art world he was more famous for his spectacularly dissolute and eccentric private life than his art, though his works did win critical acclaim. Some of his closest relationships were with animals and at one point he was looking after so many pets in chaotic conditions, mainly dogs, that the RSPCA raided his house and prosecuted him.

His practice of keeping several dead family pets, including a Great Dane, in leather bags under his bed gained him widespread notoriety. Alongside his pets, he had numerous wives and girlfriends, many of them society ladies, which also fuelled coverage in gossip columns. He had ten different children by four partners, of whom Linda was the youngest, and when he died a few months ago, they commenced feuding over his estate in a series of acrimonious disputes that show no signs of resolution. Linda never talks of this or about any other aspect of her family history, and not even, Becky has heard, to Tania. The only tangible thing Linda has in common with her father is a love of animals, but she has taken a different approach and restricted herself to one pet only, albeit a slightly exotic one: an African grey parrot. Becky is enthralled by the idea of a parrot and hopes she will get to see this one.

There is no sign that Linda has reacted against her background in any significant way; if she had she would have nothing to do with the art world at all. As it is her life is conspicuously ordered, perhaps in reaction to her father but more likely, Becky thinks, because she knows that in business it is necessary to be conservative and uncontroversial. To exude probity as well as modest amounts of Chanel No 19. Yet there are limits to rectitude and Linda can't help being arch in her manner. Perhaps this is her last line of defence against spreadsheets and cash flow. Or maybe she just likes camping it up.

Tania and Linda's friendship is handy for Becky, but she finds it puzzling. They went to art school together; at one point they were in a band together, even, but they have ended up inhabiting different continents of the art world.

'Anyway, I prefer admiring my sales figures,' says Linda.

'You know, I am starting to wish I could say that,' says Tania.

'You said you never wanted Idiot Savant to be a money thingy.'

The gargantuan match head that is Tania grimaces, as if trying to strike itself.

' "Thing". I would never say "thingy",' she says.

'Well, excuse me.'

'I can't even put together a show for my own fucking gallery. Dealing with the creditors has got so bad it takes up almost all of my time.'

Becky feels awkward because she is gaining so much from the group show, but Tania is only gathering momentum.

'A lot of what money there was went on things like paying Erick's rent for him and hiring equipment for Tom, and the amounts that Kevin Thorn grabbed were obscene. Honestly, Alastair is so fucking naïve. I don't think any of these wankers has ever been really skint, but if they asked him for the shirt off his back he'd tear it off and gift wrap it for them. Then when it comes to supporting me with my art, suddenly there's nothing left, just all these fucking bills and endless phone calls from creditors.'

'Well I must stay I actually like taking the reins of the gallery into my capable hands,' says Linda. 'Getting on the phone and sorting things out, dealing with my backers, dealing with the talent.'

Becky is surprised that Linda isn't being more tactful, but Tania doesn't seem to mind.

'I expect you're good at making them offers they can't refuse,' she says.

'Don't tempt me,' says Linda. 'But I do so wish I had a better grounding in business and finance.'

It is Tania's turn to sigh.

'You're as about as ungrounded in business and finance,' she says, 'as Bill Gates or Warren Buffett.'

Linda raises a forefinger to Tania, coral nail prominent. 'That's enough commercial chat for today. What I'd like you to talk about at length instead is this box of yours. When are you going to stop being so sphinx-like about it?'

'You know all about my box.'

Linda gives an operatic tut.

'You know I mean your work in progress.'

Becky was not surprised to hear a day or two back that Tania plans to enter her new work for the Shiraz, even given her vocal hatred (up until a few moments ago) of the art world. The Shiraz is mainstream, a prestigious annual award for artists under thirty, but Becky understands Tania's ambivalence. Artists will say they despise the art establishment but they continue to court it, because there isn't anywhere else to go with their work.

'You won't like it,' says Tania. 'I will enter it for the Shiraz but it's completely uncommercial.'

Linda raises her finger once more.

'There you go again. Sales revenue isn't a great indication of quality, but it's all you really have to go on.'

'So there is accounting for taste,' says Tania.

'That's exactly the kind of smarty pants remark Tom would come out with. I'm so glad I didn't sign him up,' says Linda. 'Oh my, did I say that?'

Becky considers whether Linda's repartee disguises a deficit of compassion. Through the window she sees a pair of crows on the pavement feeding off the remains of a Chinese take-away. The sun gives their feathers a petroleum sheen as they tug and toss around noodles that look like shiny white worms. Disgusted, she turns back to Tania and Linda.

'Not that running a normal gallery is easy,' says Linda. 'Have you any idea how much fire escapes cost?'

'A lot?' says Tania.

'Absolute fucking fortune, darling.'

Apparently Tom has told the council that Linda's gallery is in breach of fire regulations, a vindictive revenge for rejecting him. It doesn't fit what Becky knows of Tom, and yet she has to admit to herself that she doesn't know him all that well.

'Haven't you got the money?' asks Becky. If everyone else is being blunt she might as well join in.

'Kevin Thorn's the only one earning me decent wonga. The angel.'

Tania snorts.

'He's selling out on all cylinders.'

'Imagine if Tom's work had sales potential,' Linda continues. 'He'd adore me, be my most devoted supporter.'

'Are you sure he grassed you up to the council?' says Tania.

'Who else could it have been?' says Linda.

'Let me know if he does anything else,' says Tania.

Tania's fiery coiffure has become a martial head dress, and Becky imagines Boudicca ascending into her chariot.

10
Away from the Herd

When Billy turned the corner back into French Place that afternoon he felt as if he was walking on the bottom of the ocean, although his mouth was dry, as dry as it had ever been. His head was a single throb, a massive zit poised to burst, and his heart was racing up through all its gears and threatening infarction. He was avoiding eye contact with other pedestrians so rigorously that he walked into a nun in the Old Street tube station underpass, a collision that was both painful and disturbing (her wimple askew, her pinched, angry face).

Some of what happened the previous evening was lost to him forever, other events were rising to the surface of consciousness, momentarily confused before surging into horrible, sharp-edged clarity. Love. After asking Becky for an affair or for sex — he couldn't remember which — he had asked all the men around the table if they wanted an affair, or sex, too, to see if there would be any gender-related differences. As if he was a mad psychologist. There was variation in the responses, he could recollect that much, but not what had actually been said. Except for Tom, Billy recalled Tom declining gracefully before handing him another large spliff. After that there was a dim memory — tragically, with a feeling of veracity about it — that he had taken off all of his clothes. Then nothing. He had no idea what happened subsequently, except that it couldn't possibly have been good.

Why had everything gone wrong? His failure to seduce Becky at the party after visiting her studio, that was a terrible moment of truth. She had rejected him decisively in favour of Alastair, seen through his pretensions to the wretch beneath. But he couldn't leave it at that.

It wasn't Becky alone, it was everything. He could not understand what had happened to the Billy McCrory of a few months before. Dependable, liked his lager: vanished. He had no idea what the others thought as they saw him floundering. They never showed any signs that he was plummeting in their esteem. They were like the American presidents carved into Mount Rushmore. Without rope or crampons he was sliding down their stony faces into oblivion, while they gazed on, implacable.

The building stood there looking the same as ever, as if in mute reproach. Alastair had summoned him by phone and he dreaded the confrontation to come, yet he had to try to defend himself. He tottered up the stairs and knocked at the crimson door to Alastair's studio. Memories came back, of standing in front of other doors after other transgressions, of headmasters opening them and of the ineluctable odours of justice: floor wax, furniture polish and eau de cologne.

Alastair appeared in a spotless white linen shirt, serene and clear eyed, looking as if he had enjoyed the restorative effects of a full night's sleep. He gazed at Billy impassively, before ushering him into the living room. While Billy was thinking of what to say, he rubbed his lower back and stared from the window. Down below a row of workmen in hard hats and grimy polo shirts sat at the kerb with their boots in the gutter, chugging cans of energy drinks, heedless of the temperature. A British Asian couple in workwear stopped to talk to a fat man in a tracksuit wearing white trainers, before they all laughed together. To one side he saw a road sweeper with an Elvis quiff leaning against his trolley and smoking. As Billy watched the fluorescent strips on his jerkin became rips and slashes, apertures into a more colourful world behind this one. He looked away hastily.

'Are you all right?' asked Alastair.

'Could be worse.'

Although he didn't see how.

'I'm sorry,' he said.

'It's too late for apologies.'

'What do you mean?'

'What's the last thing you remember?'

'Taking all my clothes off.'

'I've been trying to defend you to the others, but it hasn't been easy.'

It was odd to be admonished by Alastair because he was younger than Billy, yet he possessed unchallengeable authority.

'Thanks.'

'It's a good thing Becky isn't around.'

Becky. What had he done to her? Whatever it had been, it couldn't be undone. He summoned the power of speech again.

'Where is she?'

'That's not your concern.'

'I'm sorry,' he repeated.

'I'm sorry that Kevin had to restrain you.'

'Kevin?'

'Kevin Thorn. You're lucky he was here.'

Kevin Thorn had been there. He could have talked to him properly, softened him up for an interview, talked about the book he wanted to write about him. Instead of being restrained by him — how had he been restrained? Billy wondered what Thorn had said to him, what his replies had been. Did Thorn ever feel the same quickening desperation Billy was feeling now? Thorn was a heavy drinker too; he knew that much. He tried to bring his full attention back to what Alastair was saying.

'You've been helping the gallery out. There is that.'

'You mean my rent for the desk space?'

'Can you deal with the other matter for a little longer, do you think?'

'Don't see why not.'

'You've got it safe?'

'Yeah, no problem there.'

Alastair handed him a clear plastic bag full of wraps.

'Here, take this.'

As soon as his hand closed on them the hangover began to dissipate. Relief flooded through him. He hadn't fallen out with

Alastair. In a few months, a year or two tops, what had happened last night might be the stuff of jokes, even.

He knew that the scene had played out to Alastair's advantage as well as his own, but that wasn't a dampener. Instead he felt some of the glow shared by a director and his leading actor after a successful scene had been shot. He gazed out of the window again and saw the road sweeper moving off, before noticing two large men striding down French Place. There was no leeway for anyone else on the pavement, and all the way along the street they left a wake of pedestrians slipping and sliding through the frost into the gutter. They powered on out of sight with unsettling indifference. He thought of the package, couldn't see any harm in asking the obvious.

'It's charlie I'm minding for you, isn't it?'

'No, it isn't. Definitely not.'

Probably Alastair felt he had to make a token denial for form's sake, because it couldn't be anything other than charlie. In his unstated way, Alastair trusted him a lot.

'Your article on the show is out in *The Bugle*. Looks great.'

'Cheers.'

'It's definitely coming along, your art writing. I meant it when I said you should go to art school.'

'Yeah, I know.'

Billy hoped he wasn't going to start up with all that again.

'You know, it's odd, but you sound like Kevin.'

'Someone else mentioned that. Linda Bloom, I think.'

'You're both from somewhere near the south coast, aren't you?'

'Yeah, that's right, Essex.'

'I guess you're kindred spirits. You know, you could be as brilliant as writing about art as Kevin is at making it.'

Billy felt proud and shy, but mostly surprised.

'Anyway, *The Bugle* piece is fab, but you're not looking so great yourself.'

'Yeah, I am in a state.'

'But even a hangover is an alternative state of consciousness.'

'Not a fantastic one.'

Talking about it was making him feel its full force again and he felt like collapsing onto the floor, giving into it.

Alastair gestured towards the window.

'We don't have much choice over going right over to the edge, do we? We have to rebel against a world that judges some of us to be different from the rest, and then rips us apart. You know, not far from here was one of the East End's biggest gallows, at the crossroads between Old Street, Hackney Road, Kingsland Road and Shoreditch High Street.'

'That can't have been recently.'

Billy was having difficulty concentrating and he couldn't see what Alastair was getting at, but it sounded ominous, whatever it was.

'Not that long ago really, in the scheme of things. The gallows were directly opposite the church.'

'The Hawksmoor church?'

'Looks like it could be a Hawksmoor, I grant you, with that hypodermic syringe of a spire, but it's George Dance the Elder. He's more obscure. Kevin Thorn told me that Alastair Crowley was obsessed by him.'

Thorn's interest in Crowley had to be ironic; Billy didn't want to think about it.

'You know what the locals did whenever there was an execution?'

'Got drunk, watched?'

'They tore the body apart and carried pieces away to use for necromancy. Because once you condemn a man, you give him power.'

11

Love Poetry

Becky likes the Lux. It is one of London's first European bars, a piece of Kreuzberg or Ravel in the middle of Shoreditch. Patrons descend a short flight of steps from the street and enter a long room without any traditional pub trappings. It looks industrial, with its low ceiling, walls of bare render and exposed pipes. There are no hidden corners and no clutter. If it wasn't a bar it could be a gallery or a studio.

The ambiguities extend to the decor. Becky enjoys especially the signs for male and female on the toilet doors: crude genitalia scratched into the wood. She is partial to their provisionality, the undecidable question of whether they are permanent and official, or temporary gougings by a drunken patron.

Most of the time when she visits there are few customers and she is fond of the disengaged ambience. One or two artists she knows say they don't like the scene that is developing around the Lux and its neighbour, the Electricity Showrooms, and that instead they prefer to spend time in the area's pubs. She thinks this is inverted snobbery, but she sees that today is busier than usual and she does hope the bar won't start to get overcrowded.

Becky is fascinated by the huge window that fills the Lux's back wall. The glass is always very clean and when she gazes through at the passers-by and cars outside she imagines it is a film screen, and she is watching a documentary about inner London life. Or maybe a thriller. The window looks onto a street corner and from inside this creates an illusion that vehicles are driving straight at the glass, poised to crash through and crush the patrons underneath. Invariably, at what seems like the last instant, they turn away as they negotiate the corner. Becky finds these teasing preludes to catastrophe compulsive viewing, though she never sits anywhere near the window.

Today she is drinking with Tom at the other end of the bar, near the entrance. Becky retains hopes of a future with Alastair, but also she is drawn to Tom. This is rooted in a strange affinity she possesses, despite herself, with Britain and Britishness. It goes back to her childhood, but it causes her adult self a nagging discontent, alienated as she is from nationalism. Her upbringing meant her identity got lost somewhere between England and Japan. Against her mother's protests Becky re-established contact with her father in her teens. He is an artist based in Tokyo, where he was born and grew up. As a teenager she had only a few fleeing visits over to see him and her grandparents, but she believes they have had long-lasting effects, these small but powerful injections of a radically different culture. They pulled her sense of self away from Britain, made her feel that she is not really British at all and that, perhaps, she belongs nowhere.

So her adult self is lost in space, but even so some of her psyche remains inhabited by her infant self, and her infant self has a very different stance on who and what Becky is. Because, in spite of herself, Becky is drawn to people who are very British. She knows it is the five-year-old Becky, the Becky before the fateful encounter with Jethro and the catastrophe that followed, who is calling her back to the seemingly stable world she inhabited all the way back then. Later on she will have many therapy sessions to assist her with this troubling predicament. She will choose therapists with art world connections. They will not be cheap, even given the monumental amounts her works will fetch, but they will offer fresh insights.

In the meantime her infant self remains at hand, rejecting her disorienting cultural deficit, pulling her back into the timeless Britain of children's stories and films, of *Mary Poppins*, *The Railway Children* and *Sherlock Holmes*. And this is why, she believes, she is drawn towards people who are much more British than she is.

Alastair is not one of them. He intensifies her adult estrangement, if anything, because he too belongs to no country. He inhabits the beating heart of the avant garde, a vector in a creative network that abhors frontiers. His linen shirts and jackets and his neutral accent place him as readily in Kreuzberg or Brooklyn as Hoxton. Becky must look elsewhere for Britishness, so often she finds herself with Tom.

Listening to his accent and his elegant wit, observing his public school posh. Tom is looking straight at her, nose to the fore. A flying buttress brought over by the Normans, bequeathed by the Romans, it should be acquired by the National Trust. She will never give into her childish temptation to ask Tom what it feels like to be so utterly British. What could he say, anyway? Only that he doesn't feel British, that he feels like Tom.

She looks at his navy Adidas tracksuit. Does Tom look stylish whatever he wears, or because he would never wear anything that wasn't stylish? His tracksuits are not new, but their wear is always in the right places. With anyone else she would suspect they had been deliberately distressed to their best advantage, but Tom has no need for such ruses. In her fantasies he has a retinue of devoted servants to press his tracksuits and perform other vital household tasks. Her infant self, offers daydreams which run to Tom's being measured up for Savile Row suits, Tom grouse shooting in plus fours, the high teas served each afternoon in Tom's drawing room.

Sometimes she thinks, in this fetishisation of Britishness thrust onto her from her long-lost infant self, she is like the Japanese tourists who buy Burberry macs and troop round the Tower of London. The difference is that she can tell herself, and almost convince herself, that her imaginary scenarios for Tom are her own private joke. It must remain private, because all her friends religiously reject British tradition, tainted as it is by colonialism and class. Despite almost all of them being white and most of them privately educated and possessing family money.

Tourist or not, she can't stop the fantasies. Besides, there are compensations because Tom's charm is considerable. He has taken care to arrive earlier than her, complimented her on her appearance and attire and fetched a bar stool for her to perch upon. He has enquired what she wants to drink (Becks) with the gravity a prime minister devotes to pressing matters of state, and now he is making solicitous enquiries about her career. The latter is an important bonus, given his new agency in the art world.

'I wonder when exactly Idiot Savant will close,' she says.

'It's been closing since the moment it opened,' says Tom.

She smiles a small, careful smile and Tom smiles back. In a decade or so, she expects, he will be good at displaying the concern of a favourite uncle.

'It's not as if Alastair wants to represent any of us, as such, anyway,' she says. 'Which is fine, but I have to try and sell my art.'

For a moment she is distracted by thoughts of Alastair (can aesthetic purity be lovable, as opposed to the art itself?) before collecting herself and asking Tom if he thinks Linda Bloom might be interested in her work. She watches Tom's features reflect more light as they tighten and stretch, then darken as blood rushes into them.

'Don't expect Linda Bloom to support you in a genuine way.'

'Why wouldn't she?'

'You're kidding? Linda wants to be a big noise in the art world like her father but she's chosen the easy route, by exploiting other people's talent.'

'That's a bit harsh, isn't it?'

'Harsh? She says she isn't here to nurture anyone, as if she's proud of it — you'd think "nurture" was a term of abuse, the way she uses it. Don't be taken in by all those "darlings" and "sweeties" of hers, either. She's a complete nutter like that father of hers. I wouldn't be at all surprised if she keeps dead bodies under her bed like he did.'

'It was only his pets. Don't exaggerate.'

'And be careful of that bloody parrot. Someone should report her to the RSPCA too.'

'What sort of parrot is it?'

'How should I know? All that squawking, and then it shat down one of my prints.'

Becky can't wait to meet Linda's parrot. Although the bird's fouling of Tom's work was an ill omen. She wonders whether it presaged Linda's rejection of him. Which prompts, in turn, the question of his revenge. His mention of denunciations to the RSPCA is worrying. When, the last time they met, Becky raised the subject of who shopped Linda to the local council over fire regulation breaches, he declined to speculate as he looked at her with a widening of the eyes, which either conveyed innocence, or was intended to.

She has not leapt to a categorical conclusion of his guilt, like Linda and Tania, but she is no wiser. Becky has to admit to herself, not for the first time, that she doesn't know Tom all that well; her private fantasies probably haven't helped her much there, distracting her from the reality. Although, in truth, Tom's charm, wit and impeccable manners do seem to be armour-plating for an impenetrable British reserve.

As Becky muses she listens to the music (Massive Attack's *Unfinished Sympathy*), wandering around inside its sonic landscapes. Round Tom's shoulder she watches a cheery man wearing a kind of Mao jacket and a beret of felt-like fabric working his way along the bar towards them, talking briefly to each customer before handing some of them what looks like a pamphlet. He taps Tom's arm.

'Slag?'

'Excuse me?'

'Do you want a copy of the *Shoreditch Slag*? All the juice in the 'hood. Quid to you, squire.'

'No thanks.'

'Anything else? Pills? Charlie?'

'Not today thank you.'

The *Slag* vendor moves down the bar.

'I know businesses are flocking to the area,' says Tom, 'but this is ridiculous.'

Becky sees herself staring out from the mirror behind the bar and shifts her gaze from her face and its scar to see the reflection of the vendor talking to a thin woman in a black tracksuit sipping a latte, before an unusually solid-looking man (a brick would surely bounce off him) crosses Becky's line of vision and eclipses both of them. He is moving with a decisiveness that makes her uneasy, and then there is a commotion. Becky can't see clearly what is happening and it is over quickly. Tom remains facing the other direction, oblivious. She pays no further heed and decides to try and buy a *Slag* later, to see if it contains any art reviews. There is another matter she wishes to raise with Tom and this time he responds more equably, with his customary kindness and consideration, if not in the way she had hoped.

'Lanchester pays me for impartial advice,' he says, 'and he knows I'm associated with Idiot Savant so it might be hard to bring him to the show.'

'I can see that poses problems.'

'Mind you, it would be more of a problem if my work was going into the show — it's a shame the space wasn't right for it.'

Becky doesn't buy what Tom is saying about impartiality, not completely, because she knows lots of his artist friends think it worth their while to approach him, hopeful he will interest Lanchester in their work. Becky knows that probably she isn't the first artist today, even, to ask him to get Lanchester to take a look at some of their work. Tom jokes about people he doesn't recognise materialising in front of him at private views and reminding him they were at art school together. Becky finds this humour unkind. She feels sorry for Tom, too, since taking this role as Lanchester's adviser means he must be desperate for money, and she doesn't see how his powers of patronage can compensate for giving up a large chunk of his own art practice. These are sensitive issues she can't broach, not after riling him over Linda Bloom.

'Have you thought about tapping into the Tokyo art scene?' he asks.

Later on Becky will indeed mount shows in Japan, which are extremely well received, but right now Tom is scratching at her insecurity around her tenuous connections with her father's country.

'I've decided to base myself in London for the time being,' she says.

'There's nowhere else to be right now. That's a given isn't it — if you'll excuse the pun?'

She considers Alastair momentarily, and then wonders once more what might lie behind Tom's reserve. She examines the thought from different angles, folds and refolds it into an origami flower which she allows to float up and away from her, before turning to look into the mirror again. The vendor and his alarming interceptor have disappeared, and the thin woman is sipping a fresh coffee.

When she leaves Becky sees the *Slags* which are slewed all over the pavement outside the bar. They fan contrarily this way and that across the frost, their psychedelic covers making them resemble cross-sections from a mound of vomit. Attracted by the colours, a blackbird is pecking at one of them. It reminds Becky of a frock-coated undertaker. She claps the bird away, stoops to pick up an undamaged magazine from the heap.

12

Beyond Blind Faith

After his encounter with Alastair the temptation was to go back home and climb back into bed, but Billy knew that way lay disaster — or more disaster. Besides, work was a distraction from whatever had set him off last night.

It must be the stress of looking after all that charlie for Alastair. But that couldn't be why he'd got so overexcited. Why couldn't he keep his cool like the others? Maybe they were to blame. It was as if he was attuned to all their mishaps and angst, so they could channel all their negative stuff through him. They were like that 1970s executive desk toy, lately resurrected in the craze for all things retro. It was a row of steel balls hanging from strings along a beam set into a small rectangular frame (like a gallows, he couldn't help thinking). When the first ball was pulled back and released it swung into the others to set each of them oscillating back and forth with the same rhythm. He was the ball at the end of the row, and his string was frayed and liable to snap.

The depressing determinism of this weighed on him as he limped down to IS, sat at his desk, lit a Silk Cut, turned on his computer. As much as he would have liked to forget about Becky and about whatever had happened, that was impossible since she was now in his face every time he was in IS, constantly and massively. Instead of running on a video monitor as it had been initially, her video was now being projected up onto a large screen. He rated Erick's *Nothing* installation highly, but even so it posed existential questions which he did not wish to confront all day long in his work space. Yet at least it was on a modest scale (like its creator). Now whenever he entered or left the office Becky's film reared up at him, eight foot tall and inescapable, and that didn't help with anything. Especially today, a day when circumstances had crushed him and forced him to make a choice that was no choice. He would have to give up drink and drugs, at least for the time being. The knowledge depressed him further. His phone rang.

'Billy, please can you come up and help me?'

He walked to the stairs and ascended a level. The whole of this floor was divided into artists' studios, crudely boxed off with plasterboard walls either side of a long, dim corridor. Grey daylight was trickling out from Erick's studio and framed him as he stood in his doorway, an incensed cherub confronting a bearded man in a brown jacket.

'Ah Billy, thank you. Can you please be a witness to this trespass?'

'Mr Heckendorf, there is no need for this. I have completed my inspection of the premises.'

'Why are you interrupting me while I am working? How would you like it if I walked into your office in such a way?'

'Our offices have a reception area for the public, Mr Heckendorf. We wrote to you several times to arrange an appointment and you had notice of this visit, but you did not respond.'

'You have not the right to enter of the studio without my permission.'

In lieu of pausing for breath, Erick took another drag of his cigarette. His ability to smoke and remonstrate simultaneously was interesting, Billy thought.

'I am empowered to investigate breaches of planning regulations Mr Heckendorf, and I did knock—'

'You are here to spy over me, are you not?'

The bureaucrat was called Jeevons and his beard was fuller than Lanchester's and came complete with a moustache. Where Lanchester's facial hair was a statement of difference, Jeevons's was more about indifference towards shaving of a morning, a signifier for employment in which sloth and officiousness stood in for stimulus. The man in beige continued in a monotone.

'...and I have seen evidence that this workspace is being used for residential purposes, in breach of your licence.'

Erick's pale eyes fixed themselves on his tormentor.

'Am I correct that the owner in the building has persuaded you to do this? I know he is not liking my lease, that it is too cheap and too long.'

A lesser man would be shouting and swearing, but when sober Erick handled his affairs with clinical precision. He had the self-possession of someone with no need to account for himself, because he was engaged in work of greater importance than any issue flourished by an official. This poise unnerved the bureaucrat, who took an involuntary pace back from the doorway before retreating down the corridor with a dignified gait and a parting shot.

'The planning regulations must be upheld, Mr Heckendorf.'

'Why didn't you make an appointment with him and dump your bed and cooker in Alastair's place?' asked Billy.

'They would not give up, because this is something about money. They tried to raise my rent by ten times, and because I have refused this craziness they are getting me out.'

It crossed Billy's mind that it was Alastair who mostly paid Erick's rent for him, but then a massive rent increase remained a problem whoever wrote the cheques. He looked down doubtfully at the small artist in front of him, fumes streaming from his nostrils. Surely Alastair could intervene, he thought, as he passed the giant image of Becky on his way back into the IS office.

He stared at the Sisyphean boulder of his phone, levered it up, rang *The Herald* to chase the ideas he'd sent them the previous week. Nothing. He rang *The Bugle*, then more newspapers and magazines. Nothing. Work was scarce, editors made the salaried staff write most of the features, got their regular freelances to do the rest and he was on the outside.

If he hadn't obliterated himself so disastrously last night he could have been introduced to Kevin Thorn properly, maybe schmoozed him into agreeing to an interview. All it had needed was half an hour of relative sobriety. More charlie, less vodka. If only he could adjust his consumption of charlie retrospectively, take out some lines here, insert them there, create a more productive narrative for himself. Thank god Alastair had defended him. He saw the best in everyone. Admirable of him too, to insist on continuing his friendship with Thorn after the others turned against him. Sitting there, he wondered if Thorn felt the same way as he did about Alastair.

At least he wasn't stuck in the housing department any more. He hadn't turned up for a few mornings. He was only up and about by late afternoon when it was already dark and the day was over. So that was that. He could have involved the union and tried to hang on but there was no point. That work was shit. If he stayed on soon enough he would turn out like Jeevons, or worse. The only satisfying part of that job had been sneaking off and hiding himself away to write up his diary, and he could do that in the flat or in IS. Losing the money wasn't good, but he didn't want to think about that side of it all now.

Now. It was difficult to live in the moment all the time, without heed to past or future. The rave scene had all been in the present, but only when he was raving. Like any sub-culture it had a natural lifespan of a few years, and after that the best part was all played out. The pills wore off, the love fell away, the music became no more than music, and he was back in normal time again. For a while he carried on half-heartedly, before bailing out and looking for something else. He noticed that London was in a recession, and that it was as cold and grey as it had ever been.

Billy collided with art, and it was becoming obvious that art was more than a sub-culture because there was something bigger about it all. The rave music had kick-started the body to reach the mind, and good sounds and goodwill gave physical and mental release. Yet in the end it was inward looking; they had all been preoccupied by their music, their drugs, their scene.

Whereas art looked out, and it could take to itself anything that there was out there, it was something everyone wanted to grab hold of, but no one could say what art was or attach it directly to anything, including the artists who made it. It could expand to include the world, the universe and everything that there had ever been, and then it might be nothing, too, a colossal escape hatch that led everyone into a series of nowheres. Whatever it was, it was creating an energy around here that was mounting, streaming out, starting to become overwhelming. That was what set him off last night. It wasn't the stress of minding the charlie for Alastair, or the others offloading through him. He was floundering in the ripe-tide the art was creating, he couldn't surf forward on it the way the others did.

He lit another cigarette, fought back a gagging reflex, and reflected on his dearth of writing commissions. It wasn't looking as if he would meet Thorn, get the interview, or do the book. He asked himself whether all his achievements might be behind him, such as they were. The sole large stroke of luck he'd enjoyed had come a couple of years back. His only journalism experience up to then, had been writing a few articles on dance music and he was struggling to branch out from that. Then he encountered Francis Bacon in the Colony Room early one evening and managed to persuade him to give him an interview.

Although not even Bacon could say what art was or what it was about.

13

Some Traces of Living

Bacon, Billy surmised, had been drinking all afternoon. He was visible in glimpses by the bar, surrounded by a thicket of rent boys and Soho-trash. As Billy prised his way through to get himself a beer Bacon was shouting at a pretty young man.

'Get away from me you annoying little queen.'

The recipient of this abuse flounced off, leaving a gap for Billy.

'Oh hello,' said Bacon, 'who's this?' A smile chased the scowl from his face. Billy introduced himself, but Bacon was already gesturing to the barman.

'Give him a glass. Have a glass of champagne.'

Billy was handed a bubbling flute and stood facing his benefactor. Bacon's face was an old man's, he saw, though his cheeks remained faintly rosy and his hair was a strange glossy black (later he discovered that Bacon applied boot polish to it). The bar's dark green walls made it into an aquarium — this was not Billy's first drink that day — and he was among strange fish at its bottom. They drank, Bacon held forth.

'I love cities and I hate the countryside,' he said. 'There are enough animals in Soho to keep anyone more than satisfied. My instincts tell me consistently that I am essentially urban.'

'But not always urbane,' shouted a heckler, a stunted-looking man whose ruddy face appeared to Billy to consist, by this mildly hallucinatory stage of the proceedings, of one enormous broken vein.

'I think it's time she went home to bed,' interrupted the barman.

The heckler exited. Two down. Bacon continued, unperturbed, to talk about his approach to life and art.

'Instinct, that's the thing. You must follow your instincts.'

Billy decided to take a risk and ask him for an interview. Bacon was puzzled, stared him up and down.

'You aren't trade? I thought you were trade.'

'I'm trying to be a writer.'

He was making a fool of himself but it was too late. Bacon looked round the others enquiringly, and then he turned back and appraised him again.

'A writer.'

He laughed shortly and thoughtfully.

'Well, why not? Yes indeed. Just this once you shall go to the ball.'

Soon they were in a taxi, heading off to Kensington. When Bacon was alone he often travelled by tube, Billy heard later, but this time he took a cab, possibly from solicitude for his young companion or perhaps from a desire to impress. He was making an effort with Billy, that was apparent. It was a rare privilege for a stranger to be invited to the studio, though it must be said that by now Bacon was ancient, in his eighties, and erratic.

Billy did not recognise the area. After the uproar of the Colony Room there was quiet, the hush of affluence, in this quarter of consulates and pieds-à-terre. Bacon's studio and home was down a mews, and it was modest and rather squalid, with none of the opulence conjured by Billy's imagination. He looked into a large mirror in a rococo gilt frame which had been starred by a missile, saw himself fracture into a dozen images of diffident tipsiness. Bacon led him into the studio, which was surprisingly small, with curtainless windows and illuminated by a naked bulb. It was made smaller still by an ankle-deep mulch of dismembered books and magazines, paint cans and brushes, as well as less identifiable debris, all strung together with coagulations of paint. In less frequented areas of floorspace this undergrowth was lush and verdant, frosted with fluff and dust, but there were pathways and clearings — the most prominent in front of the easel — where it was compacted into springy uniformity.

At first Billy found the havoc affected before he realised that, instead, it was a template for the assumed squalor of the shoals of lesser artists following in Bacon's wake, hoping that the determined addition of disorder to garret could yield genius. The walls were coated in paint streaks, blacks and reds in daubings upon daubings. The red splashes were gore-like and he tried not to look at them too closely. Nimbly, Bacon seated himself, an ageless sprite in a timeless setting.

'I'll have to throw you out soon because I want to start work. But do your interview. Go on, ask me any questions you like.'

This last sentence was delivered archly, yet Billy sensed no predatory intentions. He pulled out pen and paper and launched himself into faltering enquiries.

'Why don't you have a bigger studio?'

'I don't know. I used to have a very big one near here, then I gave it up. It doesn't matter because I don't like to work upon more than one canvas at a time.'

He waved an arm.

'Pay no attention to all of this. It's all artifice. Like me. I'm probably the most artificial person there is.'

'I'm sorry?'

'Artifice is concealment. And yet artifice sometimes also reveals truth. All of art is artifice. '

'What are your paintings about?'

'I don't know. I've no idea. Once an image can be explained it's worthless. Isn't it?'

The interview as it was written up would have been interesting but unremarkable, except that Bacon died a few months later, giving the piece a weight it would otherwise have lacked, with the result that it was anthologised in a couple of books and reproduced in several magazines. Even so, within a short time hardly anyone would remember it.

For Billy the article would be almost incidental compared to the encounter itself. Even as they talked Billy knew that a stark social asymmetry was at work. To Bacon, he was no more than one of a legion of his fans, perhaps more youthful and proletarian than some. The banality of most of his questions made him cringe when he tried to decipher his notes afterwards, yet Bacon rose above them to offer majestic responses.

'Why are you so obsessed with the pope?'

Bacon grimaced.

'Those fucking paintings. I could have done them so much better.' Then he chortled. '*Well*' — he drew the word out, expelling a long breath that became a wheeze — 'that's hilarious. They've got nothing to do with the pope.'

'What were you trying to achieve?'

'I tried to capture the beauty of the human scream and I failed. Change the subject quickly, or you'll have to leave.'

'Sorry.'

'No, no. Don't be embarrassed. Carry on. You carry on. You're doing very well.'

'Do you see any connection between your gambling and your art?'

'No, none at all. The gambling is something I do for fun when I'm not working.'

'Why do you gamble on such a scale do you think?'

'Ordinary life is so meaningless, we might as well be extraordinary if we can.'

'Do you think life itself is a gamble?'

'I don't know what life is or isn't. Maybe gambling is a good enough metaphor for it, I wouldn't know. What do you think?'

'What do you want to do next?'

'I don't know. Nothing. We come from nothing and we go to nothing. All this' — he waved around the studio again — 'is a brief interlude between birth and the grave. Nada. Nada to nada.'

After a while Bacon tired of Billy's tremulous interrogation, wished him the best of luck and ushered him out, saying that it was time he began painting.

14

Sell-out of the Image

He was at his desk in Idiot Savant's back office, painfully sober and watching what he could see of the scene in the main gallery through the half-open office door. Tom had arrived with Lanchester a few minutes before and was conducting him around the show.

As they talked they moved back and forth across his field of vision through the door. He looked at the door itself. The unvarnished deal, the dents and pocks, the whorls and knots in its surface, the fissures in the planking, all of it part of the infinity of matter the gallery had captured and imprisoned in time. He was eavesdropping on the conversation beyond but he had no choice, since Lanchester was addressing Tom loudly in his bullish fashion.

'I have it on good authority that Saatchi is due to visit later on today.'

'Are you sure, Henry?'

'Alastair Given told me.'

'I see.'

'Straight from the mouth of golden boy himself. He's very entertaining, isn't he? A little down on financiers, but I expect his dad's an accountant or something.'

Lanchester's remarks about Alastair gave Billy pause. Alastair hadn't sprung into being fully formed, but questions of his parentage and background always seemed peculiarly meaningless. Tom came into view, led by his wedge of nose. It struck Billy he was not standing as vertically as his employer, that there might have been a deferential inclination.

'We're lucky we've been able to get over here before him,' continued Lanchester.

"We" — there was no need for his plural because Tom was already familiar with the show and Lanchester knew that. It was corporate self-importance, although Billy thought Lanchester seemed relaxed for a financier. Perhaps he was simply being nice, going out of his way to refer to Tom and himself as a team. Yet if they were a team there was no doubt who was the key player.

It sounded as if Lanchester would buy Erick's installation; he deserved the patronage of a wealthy collector. He didn't see how Becky's work could find favour. That hammer-wielding vandalism. He was becoming convinced that slow motion should be confined to sports action replays. Worse, that gigantic image of her face with that seraphic expression, the headscarf making her look like a Soviet heroine of labour who had stepped down from a constructivist poster. He had started to detect a certain dismissiveness in her gaze as she looked down at him.

'This is amazing,' said Lanchester.

It sounded as if Erick's work was harvesting due approbation. If Lanchester bought it Erick might be able to afford the increased rent for his studio, or to move to a better space altogether.

'To be perfectly honest with you—'

'I am so glad that I insisted on coming.'

Lanchester moved across Billy's line of sight, shading in areas of the gallery with his pinstripes as he strode around. In profile the oval of brown hair round his face looked like a mane — fitting, Billy thought, for someone with a mania for collecting art.

'I love this determined lack of concession to anything resembling a normal commercial gallery.'

'I'm not sure it's a deliberate strategy exactly. You see—'

'I'm so bored with these white boxes you keep taking me around, all exactly the same, like an extended exercise in sensory deprivation.'

'I hadn't realised you liked post-industrial decay. If I'd—'

'An interesting change of scenery. I have to say I feel out of place in my suit. Maybe I should have borrowed a tracksuit from you.'

They moved off further away into the gallery space.

When Billy heard them leave, he picked up *The Herald* again, because it contained an article about Kevin Thorn he wanted to see. He scanned it: nothing new about any of it, lots of second-hand information and uninformed speculation about his next show. Thorn could be right to refuse more interviews, given all the shite written about him.

The media coverage of artists round here was starting to build, but that didn't mean much of it was worth reading. Billy knew the artists, he knew their work and he tried to do better pieces of writing about them. If there was any justice (a forlorn hope, he knew) he should be getting more feature commissions. He gave the rest of the paper a desultory scan, leafing through the style sections. Crap, all crap.

He started. Becky was staring up at him from the page. He looked more closely and saw that she was the subject of a "Day in the Life" feature about a young artist in Hoxton. A couple of months ago she had been no more than a student (though he had to admit Becky had not been the normal callow student, a-buzz with enthusiasm and non-sequiturs). Now she was edging her way into the national media.

Her typical day did not strike him as believable, and as he read on he felt transported to a parallel universe. Each morning she had a glass of freshly squeezed wheat grass juice before setting off for the gym. The last book she had read was Michel Foucault's *Madness and Civilization*. She enjoyed rollerblading and was thinking of taking up kickboxing. Her favourite newspapers were *The Herald* and the *Financial Times*. She was keen on the latter for its arts coverage, she said.

Alastair knew one or two of the commissioning editors on the arts desk of *The Herald*; that must be behind it. Billy was stung that he hadn't been asked to write the piece, but then he remembered what had happened in Alastair's living room — or remembered the gaps in his memory of it.

Her favourite place to eat and drink was Soho House. She said she liked meeting talented people from other creative disciplines there. The best thing about living in London was the wide variety of bird life to be seen around its streets and buildings. He tossed *The Herald* aside.

*

In her autobiography, Becky will describe what this period of her life meant to her. With each of her two installations she was beginning to make her mark, but beyond these prosaic facts this was the end of her youth and it was a time characterised by hope and faith. Her body, her mind, her life, her art, all merging into an invocation from her that everything happening, the incoherent daily rounds of stops and starts with all their diversions and dead ends, would come together to shape a life which could take wing.

Tania raises her coffee cup, and as she sips stares at Becky over its rim.

'Your work is stunning, it really is.'

'You make me sound like I'm making cattle prods.'

Linda and Tania are fulsome with their compliments, but in Tania's case now and again Becky has apprehensions about her flattery, wondering whether it might have unwelcome sub-texts. She recalls that some of the participants in *Fucking Men* could have been women. Becky is completely open to gay relations, but some of the savage sex on display in Tania's film is off-putting. A dildo should be a toy and not a weapon and Becky can see that Tania is forcing herself on some of her participants who — as her pushes turned to shoves — have decided too late that they do not wish to participate after all.

They are in the Bean café again but this time Linda is absent. Becky puts her apple juice down, runs a finger over the luscious exterior of her newly acquired Mila Schön handbag. It is actually second-hand, but even so she went into the shop knowing she couldn't afford it. She decided she needed it to cheer herself up because she thought the reviews of her work were not going to lead anywhere. That was before she heard the news about Lanchester's visit to IS.

106

'You can look at yourself in the mirror and know everyone thinks you and your art are fabulous,' says Tania. 'The worship. The power.'

'Now you're confusing me with Kylie.'

Becky thinks of the Bean café and how it is special, not because it is different, like the Lux bar — this is just a normal commercial space, after all — but because it is here in Hoxton. The Bean is a kind of workspace for her, because whenever she comes here it is to discuss issues around her art. She is starting to realise that there is no boundary between work and play for an artist. It is sometimes fun, though mostly serious; either way there is no escape. Although Tania and Linda seem to be plotting something and that might make a change.

As Tania talks Becky watches pedestrians scissoring past the window behind her. One of the scissors closes into a vertical, then foreshortens abruptly. The café door opens with a blast of glacial air and a moon face stippled with lesions grows in her field of vision.

' 'Scuse me. Can you—'

Tania wrenches her purse open, thrusts coins into the beggar's hands.

'Now fuck off and get a job,' she says.

She gives him a shove back towards the door to initiate his quest for gainful employment. A rush of steam from the Gaggia, like a crowd drawing breath. Tania continues to talk as if nothing has happened, while Becky looks at her and considers her volatile contradictions.

Tania dislikes beggars and gives them money, slags off men and shags them in quantity (sometimes singling out the ugly and hopeless, making her the only woman Becky knows who does charity fucks), tells everyone off and won't take any criticism herself, hates violence and relishes breaking up fights in pubs and clubs, dislikes women talking about their children and wants one herself, despises drunks and drinks like a steam engine, bad mouths materialism and loves shopping, is resolutely independent and remains best friends with Linda Bloom.

Tania's compliments, she decides, are at least partly genuine, regardless of any base motives. She thinks that probably Lanchester won't pay her much if he makes an offer at all. Still, he is likely to give her something and a sale would be a major coup. First the reviews, now this.

Her sudden success means her *senpai* and *kōhai* relationship with Tania is looking fragile, which in one way she thinks a shame because there must be a lot more Tania can teach her, if so minded. From another perspective it has run its course. Tania found out about Lanchester's interest in *In Between* from Tom, who rang her an hour ago. She told Becky straight away but, at least momentarily, Becky was resentful Tom hadn't contacted her directly. It seems that, in Tom's eyes, she remains Tania's protégé.

'How is the work on your box going?' asks Becky.

'I don't fucking know. It's a big project.'

Tania falls silent for a moment. If anyone is stunning, Becky thinks, it is Tania. In her white Issey Miyake dress she is ethereal. She is more than a style pioneer; she is the high priestess of a new religion set to save the world and everyone in it. Becky looks at her hair, that hemisphere of orange, ignores the awareness that to many eyes it is ridiculous. It is exactly right and could be no other way.

'It's time Tom stopped causing problems,' says Tania.

Becky does not recognise this Tom, the Tom who exists in Tania's and Linda's minds, an explosive mix of rancour and revenge.

'Linda's had a letter from the Inland Revenue and they're asking her all sorts of questions.'

Becky puts down her cup and leans forwards because it is hard to make out what Tania is saying. Pulp is playing through the café's sound system at high volume. Becky is not really sure that things do go better with razzamatazz, catches the eye of the waitress whose bosom Tania commented upon so inappropriately, and mimes turning the dial down. She receives an eye roll in return before the noise level falls.

'Isn't that normal?'

'They're investigating her. Whether she's declared all her sales revenue, whether she's paid the tax and national insurance for the gallery assistant. I think Tom's stirred them up.'

'I bet they won't get her on anything.'

'The gallery would go out of business if she paid them everything.'

Tania appraises Becky again.

'You know, you are a work of art.'

For an instant Becky fears that Tania knows of her unusually visceral aesthetic sensibilities. Tania continues to gaze at her.

'You might be able to help us,' she says.

15

Journey into the Soul

You don't like talking to artists who are above you in the hierarchy, or notionally above you. People like Lucian Freud. It would be better for you if they were dead, or if they had never existed at all. You are glad Francis Bacon is dead; recently you were pleased to hear of Leon Bloom's death. You don't like talking to artists who are below you, either. There is no reason why you would want to do that, to let them drag you down to their level. To let them pretend that their concerns are your concerns. You don't have a peer group. There are worrying signs that other artists of your generation are beginning to receive similar amounts of publicity to you, but so far these are only signs.

You don't like talking to artists at all. The people you have realised you like meeting are postmen, plumbers, builders. People you encounter in clubs and bars, people without cultural baggage. It was a delight to spend hours talking to a black cab driver in the Colony Room, for example, though of course you can't remember any of what was actually said. You tell yourself that you've got more in common with these people than anyone else. That you are a straightforward person doing a regular job of work just like them. Although for all you know they have vast, labyrinthine secret lives dripping with intellectual and creative conceits. Some of them might have. If they do, you're grateful that they keep all of that to themselves. Still, nowadays it's their opinions that you claim you value. About everything including and, perhaps especially, art.

You know that there is pretence in this unpretentiousness. Tradesmen, artisans and the like do not talk to you on the basis that there is no difference between you and them. You are such a fucking snob, but you can smile about it to yourself. One of your best memories is of a policeman coming up to you in the street. You thought he was about to arrest you, then he asked you for your autograph. You tell people about this, often.

*

A British Asian girl walked towards them through the punters who were standing in front of the stage. She had long raven hair and was clad in a crimson basque edged with black lace. Lamb dressed as mutton. It was a garment which a wife might don to titillate a bored husband, thought Billy, or into which a transvestite might clamber for solitary relief. Tom tossed a couple of pound coins into the beer mug she held out.

'They collect before each dance,' he explained.

They were in Browns. An address for undress, the strippers' pub frequented by city workers and other misfits. Grey wallpaper, mirrors in silver frames, a marble fireplace, rococo cornicing up above. The pub's interior could be a set for a skin mag photoshoot. A gentleman's study or an expensive hotel room in which, by happenstance, women were disrobing and cavorting about.

'We're not eating here, are we?' said Billy.

'Erick told me about this place. He says he comes here all the time. They do a good lasagne and chips.'

Tom was on the defensive, Billy sensed, otherwise he wouldn't have invoked Erick. He hadn't thought Tom inclined towards sleaze, but it was possible, of course, that his choice of venue was ironic. They ordered at the bar. Billy accepted a drink and asked for Pepsi (Pepsi, dismal Pepsi, no Stella) and declined Tom's offer of food.

'Did you see Lanchester in action at IS?' he asked.

'Caught some of it through the door.'

'He'd read one of the reviews. No stopping him.'

Billy stirred from his torpor as Tom recounted the tale of how wealthy new collector Henry Lanchester was going to pay fifty thousand pounds for a work by unknown new artist Rebecca Edge.

'How's that for a scoop?'

'Thanks, it's fantastic. Surely he could have paid far less?''

He couldn't understand why Lanchester had latched onto Becky's work instead of Erick's. Tom didn't take umbrage at the implied slur on Becky. She was a competitor of his, after all.

'Correct. Becky hasn't sold anything else yet and she hasn't even got a proper gallery.'

It struck Billy that Tom himself was without a gallery.

'When I told Lanchester that,' Tom continued, 'he wasn't interested at all. It's hard to get anything across to him, hard to even finish a fucking sentence when you're talking to him, and besides, he has a strategy.'

'What's he up to?'

'He says that the money will fund Becky while she makes more work, and he'll have first option on all of that.'

'He might not make anything out of any of it.'

'He's banking on other collectors taking notice, so that the value of her work rises. Give a dog a good name if you like.'

'Isn't he hurling all his eggs into the one basket?'

'He's collecting lots of other artists' stuff. He reckons making deals like this means new artists with anything decent to sell will start approaching him instead of Saatchi.'

'So do you think it will all work?'

'It's all a gamble, obviously, but it isn't much outlay for him. He's riding high in the City — look at that beard of his. Only someone hideously important could get away with looking like that over there.'

'At least it isn't a goatee.'

'He's so alpha, that guy. He's just donated more than he's paying Becky to the Tate, simply so he can be on their list of fucking patrons.'

Billy considered Lanchester's incontinent largesse.

'He must be paying you well.'

'Not that well. I wouldn't be advising him if I had any decent alternative. And every nutter in town with any art to sell is starting to stalk me. I'm like some medieval lord chamberlain, mobbed by hordes of crazed petitioners, all desperate for an audience with the king.'

'He's the new Arts Council.'

'Everyone thinks I'm the new Arts Council.'

'Can I interview Lanchester for my piece?'

The stripper executed a pirouette, before twining herself round a stainless-steel pole. The stage was lit by coloured spotlights and there were two square pillars to the front to frame her, making her jerky, stop-start movements into a Muybridge sequence. Her movements were more aerobic or athletic than abandoned. She was just paying for her kids' school uniforms, Billy supposed. This area would never rise above poverty, gentrification or not. The only trickle down from hipsters was the bodily wastes swamping the decrepit sewers under their overpriced lofts.

'You see,' said Tom. 'You want to get to Lanchester through me. You're exactly the same as all of the others, aren't you? Well, you'll be pleased to hear that the next step in his grand strategy is indeed to do some press interviews.'

'Cheers.'

'You owe me. I'm sure Lanchester will be delighted to talk to you. I mean, however well he does in the City in the end he's just another corporate hamster racing round his wheel alongside the rest of them. Over here he can throw his loose change about and be a real king of the jungle.'

Loose change. Billy was considering if there could be any justification for Lanchester placing such a huge value upon Becky's work. He tried to be fair to her, to discount the oppressive affect her oversize installation in Idiot Savant was having on him.

Strictly speaking it was impossible to reach any firm conclusion. Wrong, even. Art lost its horizons after Duchamp, anything could be art, and once Warhol had done his worst that included unapologetic self-promotion, and it was all much later on from that now. There were no boundaries, no objective criteria, and all of that self-reflexivity and irony in all of the contemporary works on display in the galleries was circling around a void. Yet there was that flicker some works had, and that most did not, and he was unconvinced Becky's work possessed it.

'I'd love to see Linda Bloom's face when she reads the interview,' said Tom. 'She hasn't managed to get her hooks into Lanchester yet.'

Billy had heard the rumours that Tom had shopped Linda Bloom to the council and to the Inland Revenue but thought better of asking him about it.

The stripper's act ended and a screen behind the stage began showing football. There wasn't that much difference, he thought. The players' movements were elaborately choreographed and their clothing was designed to be noticed. Although mostly they did keep it on.

'Alastair will be pleased,' he said. Lanchester's purchase had to mean a reprieve for IS.

'I can't imagine why. He's not interested in money, he's never wanted to be a commercial art dealer.'

The football disappeared and a white woman, in her mid-thirties by the look of her and with badly bleached hair, mounted the stage. 'Give it up for Chanelle!' cried a compere. Tom aimed his gaze at Chanelle in between disposing of his lasagne, which had arrived promptly.

Billy watched the fruit machine opposite. Its display steadily expanded, segment by segment, into an oval, which would then melt away, before slowly starting up again. Banks of icons around this central design flickered round in Mexican waves, an audience to the repeating sequence in the middle. He did his best to ignore this reminder of his enslavement to the bright lights. Tom ate his last chip before shoving his plate away.

'I've had a shit morning, quite apart from Lanchester,' he said. 'When I got back home I found graffiti sprayed over the outside wall of my flat.'

'You said you liked Basquiat.'

'Fuck Basquiat.'

'What did it say?'

' "Die hipster scum." '

'It'll take ages to clean off. They mis-spelt "hipster" too, gave it two "p"s.'

'They'll have to come back and spray it on correctly ten times.'

'Thanks for the moral support.'

They left Chanelle to it and departed. He knew Tom had done him a handsome favour. The tale of Becky's sale was eminently sellable. Unknown young British artist, mysterious new collector, outlandishly high price, evidence of feeding frenzy developing — he would do well with it.

On the way back to IS he walked up Shoreditch High Street and paused at the crossroads, staring at St Leonard's, the church opposite with its priapic spire, his breath hanging in front of him like ectoplasm. He remembered what Alastair had told him about the gibbet sited there, but even Alastair would have to acknowledge that was all a very long time ago.

16

Blimey! How Cheap is That!

The atmosphere is strained. Becky is starting to abandon her efforts to remain light-hearted and is falling back on a question that is often fundamental for her — of whether what they are doing together is art. For Becky art consists of experiments to illuminate feeling, and feeling, obviously, is part of life. So life can be heavily implicated in art. But that goes only so far, she thinks, because so many artistic experiments fail. A life full of failures wouldn't be much of a life. She thinks of Erick and his obsessive projects. She doesn't want to become like him.

Alastair's life is his art, yet she can see that he is different in this to everyone else. Even this early in their relationship, she suspects he is engaged in a gloriously erroneous crusade. Although he cannot be other than the person that he is, she understands that too. Nevertheless, mostly life is not art.

None of that helps her with this. Is this scenario an art experiment she wants to enter into? She isn't clear what she is for Tom right here and now: lover, nurse, prostitute or psychiatric social worker. All of them, probably. There's an intensity of feeling about all this that is interesting, exciting even, yet she remains doubtful.

The issue of fidelity to Alastair is tapping her on the shoulder, but she believes he would be tolerant. He is faithful only to aesthetic sensibility, because for him there is nothing else. Still, Becky wonders whether she is being unfaithful to her own values around honesty and trust. This is very intimate, even if it is not a direct sexual act. Most likely it is a betrayal.

Tom wants to put her to a lot of trouble. The honest directness with which he made his request won her over, a hair's breadth away from abject entreaty. For an uncomfortable moment she thinks of Tania and her charity fucks. But she was won over, too, by the prospect of discovering more about what lies beneath Tom's supposedly impermeable reserve (even if, maybe, it is impermeable only in her fantasies of him). There is also the democracy of fantasy to consider. She has her fantasies about him, and it seems that he has his too, in which — whether flatteringly or not —she has a starring role.

Now she is finding out more about Tom than maybe she wants to know. They are in Becky's studio flat. Tom wanted that, presumably to help him foster the illusion that she is as interested in this as he is. How can she be without sharing his compulsion for it? The walls are flimsy, their fragility in inverse proportion to the substantial rent she pays. Everything is audible. Flushing the toilet is embarrassing. It is fortunate Tom is so quiet.

'Is this really what you want to do?' she asks.

Muted assent. Becky notices that Tom's voice is strangely thickened, that his ironic wit is absent. She tries again not to feel disappointed, because this should all be fun and Tom's seriousness is a dampener. He seems guilty and ashamed, but not sufficiently guilty and ashamed to abstain. Just enough, she guesses, to spice his forbidden pleasure.

Tom undresses slowly, perhaps trying to not appear too eager. His carapace of style and charm falls away, and here he is. A sheath of supple skin, an angular physique with well-defined musculature, an assertive jaw with the nose above it like a beak. Becky thinks he is a bird of prey stripped of its plumage. He lies on the bed and as she picks up the rope Becky looks down at him, in all of his awkward extremis.

*

Billy decided to reward himself with a drink. No point abstaining from alcohol and drugs altogether. There was no harm in a single beer. Like popping into the garage for petrol: onto the forecourt, a quick fill-up, and out. It would not be quite as routine as that, however, because the exercise would provide him with a bonus of valuable data. It would be interesting, after the one beer, to see how strong his need for more alcohol might be. It made sense to monitor his response directly, so that he could start to control it more effectively.

Could the part of his brain which supervised his general wellbeing, which controlled awareness of alcoholic wear and tear, generate better connections with the part that induced the cravings for more and more alcohol? Could superego and id communicate more positively? There was no harm in carrying out practical research. He had brought the charlie with him, too. Silly to throw it away when friends and acquaintances could benefit from it.

As he took his first sip he regretted his choice of beer. His bitter was sour and lukewarm, yeasty consommé. More disappointingly, it lacked the cleaving force of strong lager. If he was going to have one drink and one drink only then it needed to be a good one. He debated whether to order again, or to claim that he had actually asked for Stella and that the barmaid had misheard. But he was short of funds, and the pub was too quiet, with few other patrons and the music — The Cure's *A Night Like This* — too muted to support any assertions of error. Besides, the barmaid was a formidable goth: tall, black-clad, and armoured in steel piercings and martial armlets and bracelets.

After making a few calls the piece had taken no more than a couple of hours to complete, although there were a couple of tricky aspects to the research and writing. Lanchester chundered on a bit, would-be king of the jungle and all, but cutting him short hadn't been that much of a problem. Then he had been at a loss how to deal with Becky's new installation. Finally, he decided to fall back mostly on straight description. It was an approach many critics were adopting, faced with the impossibility of arriving at any set of standards for judging contemporary art. He didn't desert his critical responsibilities altogether because he wanted the piece to have some relation to reality (especially his reality) so he added that the art world was divided over Becky's work, that not everyone could appreciate its ironic homage to the video installation work of the preceding decade.

His choice of hostelry was the Red Lion, tucked down a side street off Hoxton Square, not too far to walk against the polar wind whipping in with evening. The pub was small, sited on a corner, with an L-shaped bar giving views onto two thoroughfares. Its oak fittings were worn and their polish uneven, the walls stained with nicotine, the wooden floor faded and scurfy. It all looked original, although you could never tell — perhaps a few hundred grand had gone into making it so modishly down at heel. In the escapist mood that possessed him, he had ordered the bitter. It was a good idea to vary his choice of beverage, he thought, especially when drink was incidental (almost irrelevant) to his reason for being in the pub, which was to provide a respite from work and a short break before he went home for the evening to tidy his flat energetically and thoroughly, and to cook himself a simple, nutritious and economical meal.

He sampled the beer once more. Disgusting. He wanted strong lager. To be precise, the pint after the pint after the next pint of it. When he stared down at the bar top he saw the ring the glass had left glistening on the wooden surface. The wood was more cared for than the door to the back office in Idiot Savant; it was heavily varnished and someone had cleaned and polished it recently. And yet despite this there was a whole universe here also, under the protective sealant, in the spirallings of the grain and all of the nicks and pockings. These times, the times when he had a drink in his hand, were the only occasions when he could relax, absorb himself in the details of his environment, scope right down to its component pixels.

He scanned the rest of the pub. At this comparatively early hour, a few minutes after six, he didn't expect to see anyone he knew. Then he looked back down at the bar quickly because, even before fully apprehending what he saw, he knew that it was trouble. The plainclothes policeman who had called on Alastair was feeding the fruit machine, pulling out a fugue from the *ker-clunks* of his coins and the chirrups from the speakers. Billy looked at the illuminated display, a lesser version of the fruit machine in Brown's, then looked at the copper again. This time he wore a grey T-shirt, neat and ironed-looking (perhaps an involuntary slip of disguise), and black Levis with his white trainers. Billy could see rings on the fingers channelling silver into the slots. Maybe he had entered while Billy was communing with the bar top, or perhaps he had been here all the time. Whichever, there he was.

Billy's instinct was to remove himself from the immediate awareness of the invading enemy, abandon his beer and walk out. He decided that would be too obvious. Better to finish his drink and try to depart more discreetly. If he could avoid prompting recognition he might get away with getting away. There again he hadn't got away with giving up on giving up drinking. Was the copper's appearance his punishment for piss poor will power? But maybe he would be okay. The received wisdom was that the Bill were witless. Look at this one, shovelling away his silver into an insentient automaton.

'Shit.'

As he cursed the gambling detective slapped the machine, its plastic veneer responding dully to the impact. He looked over at Billy, contorted his features in mock chagrin and walked round to stand next to him at the bar.

'Wish I could stop feeding these fuckers.'

Billy said nothing, locked into rigid immobility, then arranged his face into a polite, if distant, smile. Suddenly the barmaid and other customers were a long way away. He knew they wouldn't intervene to save him if he was slapped about, cuffed, dragged off.

'You're a friend of Alastair Given's aren't you?'

Porky recognised him. Not good, not good at all. That was the problem with pubs, no face control. He would not come here again.

'I know him slightly, yes.'

'Remember me?'

'Detective Harkness, is it?'

Confirming that he knew who Harkness was ceded power to him, but it was unavoidable.

'You're Billy McCrory.'

'So they tell me.'

'I've read some of your pieces. Great.'

'Thanks.'

Praise for Billy's work was rare. He accepted his lot as a journalist, that his work disappeared into a void the day after it appeared. This was a bit of a turn up, congratulations from a stranger who had read more than one of his articles. A policeman, granted, but still more or less a person. Nevertheless Porky was up to something. The encounter did not feel coincidental; Porky's comment appeared premeditated and based on research. Billy had bolted the dregs of his tawny soup and was darting longing glances at the frosted glass of the street door.

'Can I get you a pint?' asked Harkness.

'Stella.'

Three pints later a fragile kinship had developed, though in Billy's case at least this owed much to the chemical goodwill generated by Stella Artois. Bonhomie or no, he knew there was a private view nearby and was working out how to shake off Harkness and exit. Harkness confused him. He was a policeman, a hired thug, someone in an occupation that was first choice for the school bully. And yet filth or not, he was well informed about art to an extent which challenged Billy's own pretensions. It made him think again about Alastair's enthusiasm for his going to art school, how perhaps it made sense. Harkness was also well informed about Alastair.

'Gifted bloke,' he said.

'Yeah.'

Billy looked at Harkness, appraising the conversation's directed quality once more. Its destination was unclear, but his instinct told him it was undesirable. He wondered whether he could risk venturing to the toilet for a line of coke. It was legitimate. It would help him with the stress of the situation and Harkness might not notice.

'Why does he quote Nietzsche and Heidegger so often in the gallery literature?' asked Harkness.

'Everyone's doing that. They're fashionable.'

'I haven't seen it much elsewhere. And he's got some odd friends.'

Billy shrugged. He was refusing to feed Harkness cues, simply grunting or offering politely rude responses, yet the cultured detective inspector persisted.

'There's a couple of them I'd like to know more about.'

Billy began to sober up rapidly, but not rapidly enough. He thought about going to the toilet, sticking a finger down his throat and regurgitating the beer, but there was no time for any of that.

'Don't know what you're on about.'

Harkness gripped him by a shoulder and pulled him round in the same decisive manner with which he had chastised the gaming machine.

'You know you're in trouble.'

'Can you let go of me please?'

Harkness relaxed his grip. From the start, Billy knew, he had been on the brink of being manhandled and it was some relief that it had happened and was no longer about to happen. If Harkness was frustrated there was no sign of it. His professional impassivity was back in place as he pulled a card from a back pocket of his Levis and handed it to Billy.

'Ring me when you decide to get yourself out of trouble.'

After Harkness left Billy decided that it was safe to look at the card. It bore Harkness's name and rank, as well as his phone number. While Billy breasted successive waves of shock and outrage, a small but significant part of his attention remained devoted to the bar top in front of him. Harkness had left half his last pint on it, the upper interior of the glass laced with froth. He debated whether to swap it for his empty one. It would be a pity to waste it, now the stress of his predicament was forcing him, at least for the time being, to resort to alcohol once more. There was another thought impressing itself upon him, too. There was no question he deserved a couple of therapeutic lines.

*

Tom is pretending to pay great attention to the Helen Chadwick print on the wall to his right. This is irritating Becky. When he arrived he made one or two cordial observations about the print, enough for her to know it is of no real interest to him. She acquired it because it excited her, in the way that outstanding art always excites her. Becky has not told him about any of that, because she wants to keep her own predilections a secret, especially since he hasn't asked her about them. What he is really doing by staring at the print, she perceives, is trying to give the impression he is not here, that he is not actually involved in any of this. That his immobility, tethered as he is to the bed with orange plastic washing line, is all her doing. Inside his bonds Tom has retreated, moved another step back.

She looks at him and he looks away. It is hard not to laugh, and it is comical that she did not guess. He is not so distant from stereotypes of Britishness after all. The English vice, the masochism and flagellation that goes along with nannies and boarding school. The power of empire to discipline and punish from childhood on. It captured Tom's infant libido, a forbidden stimulation strengthened by being hidden and repressed, only to reappear in adulthood.

He is bound and abject, and for a moment she feels powerful although she knows this is all a fiction. This is his story because he has pulled the strings, arranged the ropes. She is simply an element of the set he has created to stage his drama. A mere prop. Becky is tempted to throw open the door to her bedsit, knock on the neighbours' doors, invite them in to view her diffident captive. That would end everything quickly.

Her displeasure eases. They have unusual orientations, each of them, and Becky feels that she should help him if she can. He is knowledgeable and enthusiastic about Japanese rope bondage, assumed she would know of it or be willing to learn. Wrongly, because much, if not most, of her father's culture remains closed to her. And apart from all of that, taking up *shibari* is not like reading manga comics. It is an esoteric discipline that would take her years to master, even if she didn't have her own art to deal with. Becky felt guilty about using washing line to tie Tom up with, rather than nylon rope (although it is funny, to resort to washing line for this), and about her crude bows and knots. Until he was trussed and gagged because, oddly, now the guilt has dissipated. She does enjoy his company ordinarily, but nonetheless it is also pleasant to be with him when he is silent and when he avoids her eye.

In the bedroom there is only the sound of their breathing. Becky rouses herself, lights a couple of cigarettes and places them in an ashtray, picks up a belt and swings it experimentally. She considers where to place the first cigarette tip upon the expanse of flesh before her. Shadows are thrown up from the bedside lamp and move round the ceiling; for a second or two she thinks she sees the silhouette of a bird with spread wings. Tom continues to stare up at the print on the wall.

17

Don't Ever Take My Breath Away

I listen to the *tinktinktink* of the boat rigging (Essex people have boats, not yachts). I'm coming out the other side of my meagre career. Why not say it? I'm on benefits. Sometimes I write an art review, not often enough to shout about. The Bacon interview was the high point as it turned out and as I suspected it might be at the time, although there were a few good pieces that came after that.

Today is one of the days I go and sit in a shelter out on the promenade. I've brought a quarter bottle of Bell's to nurse while I'm about it. Nowadays I am more careful about my substance abuse, but there's no harm in a drink now and again. I have the *Fincham Gazette* with me, reassuringly parochial. Then in the arts section I see an article about a travelling exhibition of drawings by leading British artists which is due to pitch up in Colchester in a fortnight's time. Some of Becky's work is in it. At the end of her autobiography she says she is starting to draw again, so more than likely part of her recent output is in the show. The Indian summer of the Young British Artists (all middle aged now) rolls on and on, not least because ongoing global asset inflation propels prices for their work ever higher and higher.

So there's the mystery of why she's bothering to show in the provinces. That's not something the arts pages of the *Gazette* are concerned about. There's a picture of Becky, three decades older but looking much the same as ever in a badly reproduced black and white image. Smiling that small, careful smile of hers. I wonder whether she ever smiled broadly after her childhood accident. My theory is that when she was very young she got into the habit of being careful with her smiles so that her wound wouldn't split open again. But it could simply be that she doesn't like smiling much.

I've finished with London. The others all pretended to be classless, disguised themselves in boho versions of street culture before moving up and out and away from the edginess, leaving me back there mired in the shite where my mental health deteriorated. Stuck alongside all the other trapped people, all of us busy chewing our tails day and night, every day and night. The helicopters, the planes, the electricity seething from all those lights, the traffic always snarling away at me, the suffocating weight of the streets and buildings, the absent horizon.

There is still the art and I go up to town to see shows sometimes. Although I do think about how good an art critic I am, or I could have become. Going to art school might have improved my writing, given it more depth and assurance. I can't help wondering whether I could have been as talented in my field as the artists Alastair brought together were in theirs.

Thorn, Tom and Erick were unarguably gifted. As for Tania, Tania never gave a toss what anyone thought of her work or anything else, and maybe that is just as well. The public and the critics, most of them, say loudly and clearly that Becky is almost as stellar as Thorn, and I have come to agree with them. There was what could have become a downturn in Becky's fortunes a few years back when she was sued for passing off someone else's work as her own. That didn't mean much one way or the other about her art, in fairness. It was all played out through the media as another episode in the ongoing drama that is her life (I won't label it a soap). Nothing can strip Becky's reputation from her, excepting the broader history of art, in which the YBAs are set to be not much more than a footnote in the chapter of the twentieth century. But that's not going to be a problem for her in her own lifetime.

Even back when I first met her, Becky was securing her particular vantage point like a gold prospector staking out a claim. Her tangential take on Britishness, in particular, has brought her international acclaim, has been deconstructed by myriad commentators and critics. Her latest work has returned to images of birds, this time blackbirds and crows, and she has explained in interviews — with her polite reserve, those small smiles for her interviewers — that she has drawn upon the Japanese myths and legends surrounding these birds, to which she feels spiritually connected.

It doesn't surprise me that I do not feature anywhere within Becky's autobiography, but then Alastair is not mentioned much at all either, regardless of Becky's career kicking off in Idiot Savant. Despite the help of a Halloween's worth of ghost writers, her book is not much more than a list of awards, residencies, works, commissions, shows and other matters of public record.

What I've set out here is the truth of what happened back then. Of all the people around her that early in her career, I was most interested in what she was doing from one day to the next. The rest of them were dedicated to placing themselves at the centre of everything, to use it all to lend their art significance. I was watching from the sidelines, for much of the time with my eyes upon Becky.

Becky and all of the rest of them are firmly wedded to the art establishment nowadays, though I don't see how they can be criticised for that. Becky, Thorn, all of the others, would say their art was entirely about aesthetics, not at all about producing commodities for financial speculation. That is the denial forced upon all artists, though dealers and curators pay less lip service to it.

Yet nobody could have lived up to Alastair's ideals for art — nobody mortal. At the time I thought they had betrayed Alastair and I was angry with them all. Maybe I should have been angry with Alastair instead, like Tania. But that wouldn't have changed anything, let's face it.

Not that any of that matters much any more. It's fine to coast along back home here in Essex, the county without irony, where I can be myself and there aren't any problems with that from anyone else, in this hub for limited aspirations. Or so I tell myself, since of course Essex is much the same as anywhere else in the provinces. I look out at the white caps, smiling teeth on a blowy day like this, a minatory reminder of what would happen if I was out there trying to swim for it.

There is this ugly paradox lurking there, which is that if I was an artist it might be fine for me to be me: common, uncouth. For a long while I thought it was an asset for Thorn, but it's no good for an art critic. I can never be more than a ventriloquist's dummy for a media that excludes people like me from high culture.

You could argue that my shortage of commissions has more to do with my lack of a solid background in my field. Yet if I had gone to art school or university and lost the accent, then I would have no longer been me, I would be no more than a ghost in my own society. Either way, I could never have won.

Yes, it is handy to have the class system there to hide behind. Being drunk a lot of the time hasn't helped either. I take a sip of salt air with my whisky. It's beginning to drizzle and I am glad of the shelter, the windows smashed, the wood graffitied and scorched into charcoal in many places. I can gaze on at the others and what they're doing from a long way away, like Becky today. I don't see much of any of them any more. Why I ever believed I stood a chance with Becky I don't know, because from the start that was ridiculous, the idea that I could have had a relationship on an equal footing with her, even before she became an art world superstar.

Another sip of the Bell's, there's a seagull wheeling above the shelter eyeing me and crying away, those red eyes giving the lie to whiter-than-white plumage, banking, sliding down sideways through the drizzle, a small fighter bomber dodging flak, locking onto the target, before reascending abruptly when it registers the bottle isn't food. It's lucky I wasn't shat upon. Then I look up above it to the sky, up and out over the estuary. Past the rain into a cerulean blue that is both a final something and nothing, a sky that curves up into a limitless arc, stretching all the way over the silvery water which comes up to meet it far out there on the horizon, where sea and air almost become one and where anything at all can slip away over that faintest of edges lying between them.

Billy stared at the bag of wraps Alastair had given him, the nearly empty bag of wraps. He didn't see why Alastair couldn't have told him to open the package and help himself to a dab now and then. If Alastair hadn't maintained, in brazen defiance of logic and circumstance, that it wasn't coke and if he hadn't humoured him.

He had run out of charlie, he was in trouble and friendship had limits. Payment in kind was in order whether Alastair sanctioned it or not. A few grams were nothing from a few kilos. He opened the freezer and tried to slide out the bottom tray, but gouts of ice welded it to the freezer's interior. After several wrenches he sheared the tray off. There it was, the package's virgin garb dissonant against ancient spillages, feculent mould, loose peas shrivelled and blackened by age and frost.

It was on the kitchen table, films of condensation scattering light from its shroud. He thought about how to open the wrapping in an undetectable way, before realising it was only a white plastic bag. Easier to replace the whole thing. He looked for a knife, he knew there was a kitchen knife here somewhere. There it was; he picked it out of the scrap on the work surface next to the cooker. The phone was ringing in the living room, he ignored it. The answerphone clicked in.

'Billy, are you there?' said Alastair.

He sprang back from the table, looked at the knife in his hand, threw it aside.

'Alastair,' he said.

'You must be low,' said Alastair. 'Come round.'

He replaced the package in the freezer.

*

Everyone around Becky is chattering away in Alastair's drawing room. It is like a manic coffee morning arranged by an unusually progressive vicar. Can is on the sound system and it is difficult for Becky to lose herself in its insistent and discordant repetitions.

She suggested ambient, Alastair derided it as commercial. He is wearing, sometimes, the way he makes every choice of entertainment an aesthetic issue.

Alastair has a new toy. He has made a crack pipe from an Evian bottle, a biro casing and some foil. He has the rocks to go with it, as well as some brown he chops into little lines, chasers to help everyone cope with the pipe and its volcanic effects. The brown sits there in small sand dunes on its own CD case. Becky supposes this was an inevitable development, as she declines both pipe and brown.

'Kevin Thorn is talking about having his next show in IS,' says Alastair.

'How has he the option?' says Erick. 'He's under contract to Linda Bloom.'

'Linda has to indulge him,' says Alastair, 'or he'll move on from Bloom's. He must be thinking of that anyway.'

'Why should he bother with IS?' says Tom.

'Why should IS be bothering with him?' says Erick.

'Kevin is under siege from the art establishment,' says Alastair, 'so he'd like to come back to IS for a one-off.'

'A most token gesture,' says Erick, 'he has made his choices.'

'It's a generous offer,' says Alastair, 'but I don't know if it will happen.'

Tom seems to possess all of his customary composure, meets Becky's eyes without any apparent difficulty. An escapologist triumphantly free of his bonds. She is the one fumbling, groping for ways to pretend everything between them is normal. She nods at his tracksuit.

'Is it new?'

As soon as she has said this she realises it isn't, but she felt compelled to say something, anything. His nose cants as he looks down at himself and fingers a worn patch on a sleeve.

'Does it look new? Lanchester's not paying me a wardrobe allowance, that's for sure.'

Futile to point out that his aplomb makes his clothing look immaculate even when beyond repair. It is a pity Tom is hung up over street culture, Becky thinks, because it stops him having more fun. His forbears in the last fin de siècle romped about in cloaks in the plush of the Café Royal, procured rare parchment to draw upon, ate hashish in rooms darkened by velvet drapes. Had themselves bound and whipped too.

'Money is not primary,' says Erick. 'It is the art that is mattering.'

'That's why you're so bothered about the rent rising on your studio, is it?' says Tom.

Becky is pondering whether Tom's over-sensitivity is a symptom of discomfort when the entry phone buzzes. Moments later Tania enters. Becky is surprised because normally Tania doesn't ascend to Alastair's studio, preferring to discuss the management of IS down in the gallery itself. Not that she has been in the gallery much lately. Becky has an idea that after she started seeing Alastair, Tania visited IS less frequently and ceased coming up here at all. She hopes that Tania wasn't involved with Alastair, though there is no sign of bad feeling from Tania towards her, at least no more than towards anyone else. Tania nods at a CD case loaded with sparkling mountain ranges of charlie, an adjunct to the main action.

'There should be warning posters saying, "If you take cocaine you will talk shit for hours and carry on like a bad chat show host".'

Alastair inverts his lighter over the pipe, sparks up and draws, and watches Tania stir in her seat.

She points at the pipe. Always Tania has to be centre stage, Becky thinks.

'And that, that will drive you crazy. It should come with a guarantee: "If you aren't a loop in a fortnight, contact customer services for a refund".'

'It gives us succour,' says Alastair.

'Whenever I say black, you say white.'

'No I do not.'

'You see. You have made bullshit your own. You make a profession out of going round saying things like, "People don't have heads!".'

She raises her voice for emphasis, and one or two members of her audience start.

'To come together in primal communion,' says Alastair, 'means to form a single, headless body.'

'Need I say more?'

Alastair raises his arms in a calming gesture.

'So much hostility,' he says.

'Black and white,' she says.

'Equals grey?' says Tom.

Tania's hair, Becky thinks, looks like the nose cone of a Soyuz space capsule painted revolutionary red.

'If I wasn't fucking angry,' says Tania, 'you would all stay in your own tiny little worlds, out of your tiny little minds.'

'Is that aimed at Erick in particular?' says Tom.

Erick sighs, draws upon his cigarette, a neat figurine in his workwear overalls. There is no paint on them, although he has come upstairs here from his studio. Becky guesses that these are his social overalls and that he has some more in his studio he wears exclusively for work. Tom breaks a long pause.

'Tania, you're being very aggressive and very unfair,' he says.

'It's time you left Linda Bloom alone,' she says.

'What the fuck are you talking about?' says Tom.

'A headless body,' says Erick, 'I like to be part of this headless body.'

'You little shit,' she says.

Tania's abuse lashes down like the hail which has begun bulleting up against the windows from the darkness outside. Becky finds that she has raised a protective finger up to her scar. Though she feels tied still by obligation to Tania (because Tania has been her first champion) there are some things she does not wish to learn from her.

Alastair attempts to remonstrate.

'Tania, I don't—'

'Are we getting a commission on the sale of Becky's installation?'

Becky is glad this question is addressed to Alastair and not to her, but he does not respond.

'He'll give us a third of the price, no problem, maybe even half. All you have to do is ask. Sorry Becky, but that's how things are done.'

'I am not asking anyone for anything,' he says.

'There is something evil about you, Alastair,' says Tania.

'There is no such thing as evil,' he replies. 'Although as a concept it has undeniable creative potential.'

Ccrr... www... HHHUUUUUUUPPPPPPPP

Tania hurls the door shut behind her with shattering percussion.

Soon the chattering starts up again and it is all like an animated coffee morning at the vicarage once more.

18

The Wriggling Flesh

Billy arrived at Bloom's early, charged with nervous expectancy. When he looked through the overcast, drizzling dawn into the gallery's enormous plate glass window, he saw a tall skinny ghoul staring back at him. He shifted his gaze away; he was not looking good. The scene around him made for scarcely better viewing. He watched pedestrians shunting through the porridge of filth on the pavement, imperilled by the edges and angles of vans rat-running down the narrow street. He listened to the screeches of drills and grinders, the moans of mixers, his palate fouled by a bitter curd of exhaust fumes. Half-past seven in the morning, an extraordinary time of day to be conscious. At this hour, he suspected, he would one day expire.

Tom had rung him the day before, told him Lanchester liked his article and that he wanted Billy to accompany them round a few shows, the first at Bloom's.

'Isn't that the last place you'd want to take him?'

'I'd rather poke out both eyes with a tent peg, but he's got it into his head he wants to go there.'

Linda had identified the City firm Lanchester worked for (through Becky, he suspected), before ringing his secretary and writing him an ingratiating letter of invitation. The visit had been fixed for this morning. It might generate copy, it might not; but he was here at Kevin Thorn's gallery about to meet his gallerist again and that could only help him get an interview. He paced back and forth along the pavement, and noticed he was generating two sets of footsteps, one more staccato than the other. Someone was walking alongside him in heels. Linda Bloom.

'I'm not late, am I?' she said.

A shudder of dislocated wood, a rush and sigh of air, as she wrenched the main gallery door open.

'There's no time left to get ready,' she said, as she vanished downstairs to the gallery area. 'Get a coffee and make yourself at home, darling.'

He looked around. His surroundings were not homely. To generate extra revenue Linda had set up a small café area above the gallery proper. With the geometry of its chrome chairs and tables undisturbed, the empty café presented an aseptic scene. The light from the chill counter showed off the food, in a series of pallid still lifes. Pitted olives stared sightlessly from their bowl, alongside a large container of penne and tomato salad resembling the aftermath of a disembowelling. He sat down and thought of making coffee, before dismissing it as too complicated. Linda re-emerged waving a buff envelope.

'Tom is being so naughty. The Inland Revenue want a ten-thousand-pound penalty from me.'

She stood there dangling the letter between finger and thumb to underscore its toxicity.

'That's harsh,' Billy said. 'I'm sorry. Fucking hell.'

Everyone knew Linda had been forced to appear before a tribunal because, it was said, Tom had grassed her for tax evasion.

'Language, sweetie. Maybe I should shop Tom to the Revenue,' she said. 'I can't imagine he's paying tax on the fees he gets from Lanchester.'

'What would you gain?' he said, eager to denounce denunciation.

'You're right,' she said, 'I'm not going to be a sneak.'

'Nice suit,' he said. He was always congratulating Linda on her suits, he realised.

'It's Jil Sander, the same one I wore to the party at Mother. Don't you remember?'

He recalled, instead, Linda telling him that when she was an art student, during her New Romantic phase she spent a week dressed as Elizabeth the First. Looking at her now, he found this unimaginable.

135

Tom and Lanchester arrived ten minutes later and that evening Tom told Billy what had happened to them en route. They met at Lanchester's office and it took them thirty minutes to drive over in his Audi (he was wary of using a more expensive car during working hours, for fear of alienating clients and subordinates). For much of this time the vehicle was stationary, part of a long chain of vehicles becalmed on the carriageway, glistening damply under sodium street lighting. Hoxton was no more than half a mile from the City, but congestion obviated proximity. It was an unfamiliar environment for Lanchester and Tom saw him frown as he observed battered warehouses, derelict industrial premises and what appeared to be, from its blacked-out windows and absence of identification, a porn cinema.

As they turned off Great Eastern Street a man wearing a hi-vis jacket over a white coat stepped into the road and flagged them down. Lanchester pulled in obediently. It looked like a check by a transport official; he carried a clipboard and there were pens clipped to his breast pocket. Lanchester pressed a button to roll down his nearside window and leaned out.

'Hunh huuu urrr... oorrrgh.'

'I beg your pardon?'

'Nnn hhhmmmffff... wtttiiiinn?'

There were unfocused eyes and a slack jaw above the white coat.

'Get away from my car!'

Lanchester closed the window swiftly and drove on, looking significantly less leonine

'Jesus Christ,' he said. 'What was that all about?'

'The poor chap is mentally ill, that's all.'

'Have you seen him before?'

'I might have. I'm not sure to be honest.'

'Just what sort of area is this?'

'I expect he's harmless, Henry.'

'Thank god we've got our own police force in the City to deal with this sort of thing.'

When Lanchester parked outside Bloom's Tom noticed that he looked around cautiously before climbing out of the car.

Linda and Billy met them at the main gallery entrance where Lanchester had regained enough of his customary ebullience to offset some of the gloom of the street. Tom greeted Linda without antipathy and showed no signs of disaffection, yet he looked pale. It was an unusual hour for him, too, to be about. Billy knew it was Lanchester who had requested this early morning visit and Tom hadn't liked that.

'Interesting space,' said Lanchester.

'Thank you,' said Linda.

'What was it before?'

'A clothing factory.'

Rick had much to say about sweatshops, but Billy liked the image of ranks of seamstresses stitching and cutting, modish apparel springing from nimble fingers.

'You've transformed it impressively,' said Lanchester.

'That's so kind of you to say. It was such an awful lot of work,' said Linda.

Tom was mute. In his tracksuit he looked, paradoxically, both smarter and more relaxed than his employer. Maybe it was dress-down day in Lanchester's office. He was wearing a taupe polo shirt and chinos. The preppy outfit looked incongruous below his elder statesman mane of hair.

'Your letter was flattering,' said Lanchester. 'Although I'm not sure that I am quite a major art world player just yet.'

His laughter shattered the gallery's austere calm. Tom winced, Linda smiled.

'I've heard about your purchase of Rebecca Edge's installation,' said Linda.

'There was publicity,' said Lanchester, winking at Billy.

'An exceptional work by such a talented young artist,' said Linda.

Billy shared eye-contact with Tom and saw the corners of his mouth turn down.

'Let's get down to it,' said Lanchester, 'to business I mean.'

Linda smiled again, and Tom looked more unhappy still. Linda had no problem with flirting if it helped business. They walked downstairs into the main gallery space, where half a dozen paintings and an installation comprised the show that was to open officially that evening.

'So you like Joshua Elam's work?' said Linda.

'Love it,' said Lanchester. 'I own some of it already.'

Elam was bruited as a precocious talent. Less than two years out of Goldsmiths', already his work commanded hefty fees. He painted in acrylics, often reproducing images from newspapers.

'He reminded me of Trevor Locke to start with,' continued Lanchester, 'but he's gone off and developed a tremendously punchy style all of his own.'

The paintings were on thick white blocks with a peculiar texture, similar to polystyrene. At first sight they were images of tabloid newspaper front pages. Billy saw Lanchester inspect the one in front of him more closely. Almost all of the type, or the representations of type, was out of focus, except for the word "MILLIONS", which could be made out in what must have been the main headline. An image next to this might have been a photo of a man's upper torso — again, it was too blurred to be sure. Underneath, were a couple of other stories with smaller headlines and a representation of what was probably a bikini-clad woman. But by now Lanchester had moved onto the second painting, where his attention was caught by a big headline: "NOTHING TO HAPPEN. OFFICIAL".

'Superb,' he said.

'Fabulous isn't it?' said Linda.

She delivered her lines with vim. Tom took a notepad from a pocket and cleared his throat, but Lanchester didn't notice; Linda had summoned an alchemy which rendered Tom superfluous. Every so often Lanchester made a positive exclamation, which was responded to in kind by Linda with shameless fidelity. He was making rapid progress, busy gazing at the third in the series of newspaper-like representations.

'I hope everything is to your satisfaction, Henry,' she said.

'Yes, very much. So considerate of you to open up early for us.'

'You are very welcome.'

Their exchanges were beginning to make Billy feel ill, or more ill, and he could only wonder at Tom's mental state.

'I enjoy collecting contemporary art so much,' said Lanchester, 'because I know that I'm always going to be near the beginning of it.'

'That's so interesting,' said Linda.

'Yes, there's none of that disappointment you get with old masters and prints and what have you, of realising early on that there's not much that's decent left out there.'

'That's such a fruitful strategic choice,' said Linda. 'So perceptive.'

He nodded at the works on the wall.

'These have grabbed me. What do you think of this one, Tom?' said Lanchester. 'Tom?'

This last was louder and Billy felt embarrassed. Rather than accompanying Lanchester, Tom's attention had wandered and he had started to stray, describing increasingly larger ellipses around his master. He hurried back from the far end of the gallery and opined.

'It's rather mannered. I think that... '

'Could you add it to the list please?'

'His best painting to date,' said Linda.

She remained the most willing of captive satellites, fixed at Lanchester's off-side to avoid eclipsing the art works. Linda was just as formidable as Tania, Billy thought, if less rambunctious — but he was sure Tania's brutality concealed a kind heart; it had to be hidden in there somewhere. As for Linda, increasingly it looked as if her camp affectations were there to modulate a predatory assertiveness.

Lanchester nodded before moving on again to stand next to Elam's final work, an installation entitled *Soft Handles*. It was a row of doors: front doors, interior doors and a wooden gate, all with handles which were life-size reproductions of human hands.

The hands were modelled in latex and complete with hair, wrinkles, liver spots, rings and nail polish.

'This really is disturbing, isn't it?' said Lanchester. 'Can I have it, please?'

Billy found the show reasonable. In his view Elam's work couldn't come close to Erick's, let alone Thorn's. Lanchester was of a different opinion. 'How many is that?' he asked.

'Four paintings, plus the installation,' said Linda.

'Not a bad morning's work,' said Lanchester.

Billy saw that Lanchester's eyes were wider and his gestures more extravagant. He was outside his customary habitat, but that hadn't restrained him. Was it the shock of the new, hunter-gatherer genes showing through, or simple greed? Whatever the causes, seeking out fresh works was intoxicating for collectors. Lanchester was high on art.

'All before the private view, too,' said Linda.

'We'll come back to you with a final decision,' said Tom, 'that will—'

'No, we'll take everything on the list,' said Lanchester, 'if you don't mind pre-selling them.'

'I'm sure we can come to an arrangement,' said Linda.

'I'll add fifteen per cent to each sale price and lend them you for the duration of the show.'

'How can I possibly refuse such a super offer?'

Lanchester turned to Tom.

'And you were so resolutely opposed to my visit.'

'Well, you see—'

Lanchester laughed again and Linda smiled more brightly still. She conducted them up to the main gallery door and the daylight, or what had to pass for daylight on a morning like this one.

'I am also extremely interested in Kevin Thorn,' said Lanchester.

'His next show is opening here very soon, I'm proud to say.'

They all shook hands and Linda's smile did not waver as Lanchester also kissed her cheek in farewell. Tom gave her a small nod, complete with a modest dip of his nose. Billy followed Linda back to her cramped office and watched as she keyed numbers into a calculator, before re-keying for certainty.

'How much?' he asked.

'Just between the two of us thirty thousand, give or take. That's sorted the tax problem. Fabbo.'

'Lanchester is your white knight.'

Linda allowed herself a smirk.

'Galloping to the rescue on Tom, his trusty unicorn,' she said.

19

My Arse is All Yours

Women are more friendly towards you. They are on your side. You've been used to girlfriends being on your side, at least to start with, and you know that here and there other women have upheld you and your cause. That has changed. There are women who are on your side before they meet you.

Many of them are from a higher social class than yours. From a class that has paid you little attention until recently. Many are extremely attractive, in the most conventional sense. Not women you stood a chance with before. But you have begun to realise that it isn't you that they like. It is their idea of you as an artist.

You understand that there are pressures on women to ally themselves with men higher up any social hierarchy. You think about survival, pair bonding for successful procreation. You know we are all big pink monkeys. However, you also know that sociobiological analyses are elastic and untestable.

Snobbery based on misconceptions is a simpler explanation. You are aware that your social status is undemocratic and dependent on the standing of your art. You know also that, ultimately, your art has nothing to do with you, because you are a conduit for your works and no more.

Which means two sets of false values are being projected onto you, but it is sensible to ignore this. You would be mad to turn these women down. Your talents could vanish at any time (you hope that, in this respect, they are not like your former girlfriends). You must take advantage of everything your art brings you while it lasts. At times you do wonder how long you want that to be, as you think about the cost of all of this to your mental health. You ask yourself whether you would be better off in a steady relationship before you remember what your steady relationships were like.

In the past, when you were at parties often you fantasised about charming a couple of the best-looking women there and fucking both of them together. Nowadays you can do this if you want to. You need a large quantity of charlie and a reasonable helping of discretion. You did it at Joshua Elam's private view and then during Angela Flaxman's housewarming at her studio in Leonard Street (Angela Flaxman might be no longer on speaking terms with you. It is hard to know; you haven't spoken since her party). Mostly you are less ambitious, but you do not stint yourself. Though you do have to be careful. You have noticed that some of the women who come on to you have their own mental health issues. You feel sorry for them, but you also worry about your safety.

*

Billy was with Erick for his eviction. His presence was not planned: it was not an event anyone would want to witness and Erick had not asked him to attend. They had been drinking and doing charlie all night in a couple of clubs with the others; after a while there were fewer of them and then only Erick and him were left. By now he wasn't going back home to the tower block very often. He had an idea that he was under observation by the police, and maybe by worse people too. So he was partying all night whenever he could, crashing on settees and floors, moving around to give the slip to anyone watching him. He told himself that he was on tour, and the chemicals helped with that, with many hours of excessively fine feelings to be had, especially towards dawn. They were on the way back to Erick's studio. Billy realised that entering the French Place building wasn't great for security, but at least he wasn't going to be up in Alastair's place.

Billy had heard that Erick was thinking of shifting his representation from Idiot Savant to a commercial West End gallery, Makin's. They didn't want him putting his best work on

143

display anywhere else in the meantime. So, as it turned out, his *Nothing* installation in the group show at IS was an also-ran, a work that was not rated highly by Erick and something Makin's didn't want to try to sell.

This was sobering for Billy. His judgement needed more tutoring; he had thought the work inspired, after all. And Erick's acquiescence with Makin's wasn't his finest moment, but Billy supposed he had bills to pay and couldn't remain loyal to Alastair indefinitely, especially when IS was slipping over the brink.

When they got inside Erick's studio more charlie fast forwarded everything, although the drinking was a brake of a kind. The raising and lowering of each glass started to provide a measured tempo for the passage of the final hours. Billy looked over at Erick in admiration. If his exact address wasn't Wisdom Palace, Excess Road, the postcode was similar. Yet no matter how much they ingested, they could not stop the session drawing to a close.

The edges of the blinds slashed into relief with the dawn, and the contents of Erick's studio sharpened into focus as he tried to sort it all into cartons. Erick liked to think of his studio as a laboratory but Billy could see that, of course, it was a wreck. Cigarette in hand, Erick was going through a mass of crumpled flyers, sketches, correspondence, leaflets, manuals, paint, brushes, clothing, bottles, cans and foodstuffs, thrusting some of it into the boxes for retention, the rest into bin bags for disposal. Billy could discern no criteria for his keeping or discarding. It all looked like an undifferentiated mass or, more accurately, indistinguishable mess.

Erick's complained incessantly. He had lost his definitive list of polymer paint compounds. He thought he had left it in the fridge, but when eventually they opened it — there were several bulky items in front of the door — the contents were limited to open cartons of milk of elderly vintages and a single small trainer (not in Erick's size). He had mislaid his prized pair of broken glasses, the work created from his mugging with much effort and persistence. (After the initial assault he had asked the mugger to

144

punch him in the face again, with more force, to make it easier for him to recapture the sensation later on. A lengthy walk to the nearest cash point had been necessary, he said, to cajole his perplexed assailant into additional violence.)

He could not find the special lard he had been storing for a sculpture he wanted to make of a human head. Whose head he didn't know; they discussed that again for a while without making progress. Ordinary lard would not hold its shape, and the special lard he had obtained at great expense through a small family butchers in Dalston had disappeared, all of it. He found an envelope full of undeposited cheques from an arts foundation that had awarded him a stipend (during all of which time he had grumbled bitterly about poverty and exploitation) and shoved it indifferently into his pocket. They hoisted bags and boxes outside, stacking them in the corridor (Erick the eighth of Snow White's dwarfs — Arty) and saw three men walking down the corridor towards them.

The bailiffs came first. They were larger than Jeevons the planning official, familiar from his previous visit and lagging a few paces behind, but they looked more amenable. The preliminaries were strained. The bailiffs introduced themselves as Colin and Trevor: perhaps they found informality made removing people from their homes easier, though they paraded their bulk in glossy suits. Billy wondered if anyone ever laid hands on them. The suits were their armour; severe retribution would follow if their sleek drape was violated. Jeevons wore the same brown jacket as last time.

Colin had a turnip-shaped head and small eyes, and he was chewing gum. This detracted from his formal attire while underlining his bored indifference. Trevor's features were striking. With his firm jaw, prominent ridges of cheekbone, quizzical eyebrows and the searching gaze he turned upon them, he was seriously miscast.

Erick nudged Billy. 'He is looking like someone famous,' he whispered. 'Do you know who? Somewhere from modern art history but I can't remember who this is.'

Billy shook his head. Erick raised his voice to speak to the bailiffs and the planning official.

'Almost all has been packed.'

'Need a hand with anything?' asked Trevor.

'I am managing, thank you.'

Erick sucked on his cigarette and addressed Jeevons.

'You are bringing some friends with you, aren't you?' he said, nodding towards the bailiffs.

Billy was reeling under the freshness of another day and trying to pull himself together, even as fatigue and a desire for an ending made their claims upon him. Even so, the stress of the situation was lending his perceptions acuity. Through Jeevons' overgrown beard he caught glimpses of his lips; the narrow lines of rosy tissue around his teeth made his mouth into an overgrown anus. Colin stopped chewing, removed the gum from his mouth between a finger and thumb, pressed it onto the corridor wall.

'We're not here to make trouble,' he said. 'As such.'

'You're lucky I have not decided to squat,' said Erick.

'That's what you've done, close enough,' said Jeevons. 'You've breached your lease by using the premises as a private residence.'

Colin took out a packet of Wrigley's, extracted a fresh wafer and offered round the remainder. Billy declined, nobody else accepted.

'Do you have a van coming?' Colin asked.

'Where are you expecting me to live?'

'We've got the address of the council's homeless unit,' said Trevor.

The lack of expression upon the poised symmetries of Trevor's face made it impossible to assess how helpful this was meant to be.

'You evict me so the owner can sell the building for an obscene profit.'

'I would rebut that, Mr Heckendorf. I am merely applying the law.'

'I hope your bribe is large.'

'It is your friends you should speak to about bribery, Mr Heckendorf, not me.'

'What are you meaning?'

Jeevons pushed a greasy forelock from his brow.

'My understanding is that an Alastair Given has been instrumental in resolving the dispute between you and the building's owners over the length of your lease. Mr Given has pointed out to the building's owners that you have breached your lease by living in your work space. That is why I am here today, not because of any illegal transactions between myself and your landlord.'

'I am not believing this,' said Erick.

Billy didn't believe it either. It didn't make any sense to him, given Alastair had so often paid Erick's rent for him. Through his shock he couldn't think of anything to say. Even the moral support of his presence was limited, given the disembodiment descending upon him.

'This isn't helping,' said Colin. 'Where's your van?'

He was well into his second piece of gum. Erick nudged Billy and whispered again, nodding towards Trevor.

'He is looking like Josef Beuys.'

Billy didn't know why Erick was under the delusion Trevor couldn't hear him.

'Josef who?' asked the latter.

'He was a genius,' said Erick.

'He was a famous artist,' said Billy, keen to establish they weren't winding up the bailiffs. Because it was true enough. Trevor looked uncannily like the German giant of conceptual art from yesteryear. There was a Beuys retrospective on at the Tate, Billy had seen it and so he knew Erick was right.

'I've been called worse,' said Trevor.

'A lot worse,' said Colin.

'I am going to do Josef Beuys's head in the lard,' said Erick. 'When I find it.'

Billy started to laugh. He didn't know why, but he couldn't help it. Everyone stood there and stared at him.

20

Don't Enjoy Yourself

The first thing Becky does with her fifty thousand pounds is to offer Alastair most of it. She takes him out to lunch to celebrate and does not invite any of the others, because she wants to talk to him alone. Becky doesn't want to eat locally. Hoxton is becoming claustrophobic; the intrusion of new businesses surfing off gentrification is oppressive. Canteloupe, the Fire Station and Home — Becky doesn't want to eat or drink in any of them.

Instead they meet in a new restaurant near Paddington. It has bleached floorboards and walls in earth tones which bear oversized mirrors in plain wooden frames. She could have chosen somewhere more central and famous (even this early on she knows the PR value of patronising institutions where photographers wait outside), but she doesn't want Alastair to think she's wasting money that could save the gallery.

Becky is early but finds that Alastair is earlier still, although he hasn't taken off his coat or scarf.

'Here's a little present for you,' she says, handing over a small, gift-wrapped package. He opens it, examines it briefly and stows it in a pocket.

'Thanks. That's kind of you, but you shouldn't have bothered.'

She expected less perfunctory gratitude yet ploughs on.

'So how about champagne? Let's celebrate.'

'Not for me thanks.'

He is sipping a flat mineral water and eyeing his surroundings with distaste. She orders herself a small glass of white wine. Her sudden affluence is coming between them. A bare week ago they would have been mocking the restaurant's lame concessions to minimalism. She raises her glass to him and he responds. There is a satisfactory clink.

'Congratulations,' he says.

'Thank you, Alastair.'

'I can't stay for too long. I've tried to shuffle things around—'

'That's fine. Don't worry.'

The reshuffle could be because of a meeting with a creditor, she thinks, or a criminal. It could be a visit to another gallery. It could be a coke binge. It could be another girlfriend, or a new girlfriend. Alastair has never explicitly renounced monogamy, but she knows he is faithful only to art. She cannot easily tackle him about other alliances, not least because of her ambiguous liaison with Tom.

Whatever the reason for his haste, she knows that to ask for explanations would be mistaken. There can never be any systematic audit of Alastair's life. Becky realises this is the first time she has ever seen him outside of Hoxton. Sometimes she thinks that he is a figment of their collective imagination. It is as if they all wanted someone like him to exist so much that they have conjured him up to come and join them, at least for the time being.

She tries a smile and receives no response. Their starters are served. Nouvelle is enjoying a renaissance. Becky admires discs and rectangles of brightly coloured animal and vegetable matter adrift on wide porcelain seas. Alastair remarks upon the modesty of the portions and she asks herself whether this is churlish, then remembers that he has no real interest in food. Once he made eggs Benedict in the middle of a party and another time he appeared at her studio with oysters and mixed black velvet to drink with them, but for him cuisine is no more than an occasional novelty.

Alastair's haste precludes any considered discussion. Their traffic is brief, and almost at an end before the arrival of their mains. She waves a fork about nervously, the light reflected from its tines spilling over the blank wastes of her plate. Throughout he remains unmoved by her words. He is, she thinks, such a formal creation.

'I know you said to Tania that you don't want Lanchester's money, but I think Idiot Savant should have it all. Without you and Tania my art would be going nowhere.'

Somewhere inside herself she knows what he is going to say. She dreads it, but also she is fascinated. There is no one else, there will never be anyone else, like the person sitting before her.

'I appreciate the gesture — of course I do — but the money has to be for you to keep.'

'Don't you want even some of it to keep the gallery going?'

'It wouldn't make any difference now.'

'You could pay off all the creditors with it, of course you could.'

'Money is meaningless when compared to making the art. You must use all of the money to buy yourself time to make your art. The art must go out there into the world. That is what Idiot Savant has been for, nothing else.'

Becky realises Alastair is using the past tense to refer to IS. She knows she must not cry as she tries to think of something to say. To start with nothing comes to mind worth uttering; her thoughts trickle away, unvoiced, down between the beech floorboards. She looks at him. He is a chimera frozen into a moment in time and she will never know him.

'For me you have always been art,' she says. 'And that is what you will always be.'

He looks at her in turn for a moment before he starts to laugh.

'Don't be so ridiculous.'

She has never seen him laugh so wholeheartedly and she begins to laugh too, in relief.

Alastair summons the waitress and requests the bill, still laughing, and he vanishes into a taxi before the plates are removed.

'Your friend was in a hurry,' smiles the waitress, 'but he seemed to be enjoying himself.'

'Yes,' replies Becky, still smiling. 'He was.'

There is a coda in two parts. The first of them concerns what has taken place inside the restaurant. Becky felt awkward as she handed Alastair his small present — a modest precursor, she hoped, of the bigger gift. She had an idea, she recognises in retrospect, of what Alastair thought of the ritual giving of gifts that are not needed, and of thoughts always counting. He had opened the box at the table, eased up its velvet lid to discover a golden wristwatch. He saw tiny dials full of recondite data and looked at a second hand sweeping around a circumference of sapphires. Becky watched him turn the timepiece over to see engraved initials on its base before he thanked her shortly and put it away.

The second part came as Alastair's taxi pulled away. Becky saw a hand emerge from a rear window and toss the box, a diminutive coffin, into a litter bin. When she left the restaurant Becky did not attempt to retrieve it.

*

Billy was looking into her eyes as he came back into consciousness. They weren't Becky's eyes. He had been thinking about Becky, but these eyes belonged to somebody else. He had blacked out again and there was a gap in his memory. Mind the gap. The charlie was bringing him back. He was drinking a glass of wine and talking about death with this woman, whoever she was. A mirror sat in front of him with a small pile of powder on it. Probably his. It had a depression at its peak so that it looked like the snowy cap of a volcano, Mount Fuji in miniature.

'... yeah,' she was saying, 'he's developing a big piece of performance art around the Hungerford massacre.'

Billy said something about fake blood and she gave a detailed response. He chopped and snorted a line to pull himself back more fully into consciousness and looked about at the decor. They were not alone, she and he. There were faces on the wall, impassive faces with closed eyes. Death masks. There was a glass jar on a plinth containing an object which looked like a skinned rabbit, but smaller. A foetus. He looked elsewhere and saw a severed head, its neck crusted with gore. The face's even curves and unpitted sheen gave it away: it was plastic, a customised mannequin. He felt disappointed, then relieved. She was talking about a play at the Roundhouse in Camden, a drama about Reginald Christie.

'The serial killer?'

'That's right'

His attention drifted. She talked of necrophilia, of orgasming over death, of dead people's pubic hairs in a matchbox. If he wasn't drunk and coked up he would be exiting the flat swiftly, running off down the street. She wanted him to go to the play with her.

'I don't think it's my kind of play. I'm not sure about the playwright.'

Besides being a bizarre drama to see on a first date.

'It's the sort of play Kevin would go to,' she said.

He remembered that she knew Kevin Thorn or had known him. She shared Thorn's fascination with death, but there were troubling differences. When Thorn used cadavers in his work the results were on display in public. He went all the way in his exploration of death, but that was solely for his art and not for any other reason. When he exhausted the aesthetic possibilities of death, he moved on. By contrast this was furtive and obsessive, the secret flowerings of a private neurosis.

He tried to recall where he had picked her up, failed. Probably a private view earlier that evening. If he wasn't so keen to avoid his own flat he wouldn't be here at all, he told himself, and then wondered if that was true. She was talking of her experiences when she was an embalmer. How she brought things home: glass eyes, other prosthetic devices. How disease lurked in the bodies.

'I caught flu from one of them. Kevin got it from me. He was really angry.'

It was maddening. He wanted to know how she knew Thorn but she must have told him already and he couldn't ask her again.

'Loved it to bits.'

Now she was talking about Thorn's art: the dead bodies, obviously. Then silence. She had talked herself out, charlie or no charlie, seemed bored by the subject of Thorn all of a sudden and wouldn't say anything more. They were climbing into bed, he heard a clanking noise.

'Don't worry,' she said. 'That's just my chains.'

At the end of each chain was a leather strap. His arms and legs were secured to the bedposts. The straps were snug. There was a question he had wanted to ask her, but he couldn't quite summon it back from memory. All at once it came to him.

'Are you going to kill me?'

'Lie as still as you can.'

Death was nothing to worry about because it was nothing. Transition from being, to non-being, was incidental because he was doing it for so much of the time anyway. His thoughts went elsewhere, settled into blankness. She sat on him with her back to him, rubbing the end of his penis against her perineum as though the organ was a cloth or sponge and she was working away at a recalcitrant stain. He doubted that she would get him hard, because he was drunk and the charlie had shrivelled him, but she was skilful and persistent in her manipulations. Soon there was a mushroom in her hands, a fungus from a dark, damp place of decay which stirred and filled out.

He had forgotten a condom, gave that thought up because it didn't matter. After a while she was riding him and he was bucking up into her, straining at his fetters. She was tight. Too tight. There was a smell emanating from the junction of their bodies, an odour of something intimate, yet dirty and undesirable. Foetus, faecal. A roiling miasma which made him understand he had been violated.

'You do remind me of Kevin,' she said. 'He liked this.'

Don't worry, he thought. All be dead soon.

*

Becky decides to visit Bloom's to see Joshua Elam's show. Her interest in his new work has been honed by Lanchester's acquisition of most of it. She wants to find out more about Lanchester's judgement, the judgement that has found so massively in her favour. Reminding Linda Bloom of her existence will be a bonus if she is in the gallery.

There are tangible similarities between Idiot Savant and Bloom's. Bloom's is part of another old factory building, its brick and timber also drenched in history, but Linda has taken up this legacy of commerce and transported it emphatically into the present. She made use of her artists' craft skills in the conversion, partly because it kept the costs down but also because she could exploit their perfectionism. The floorboards have been painstakingly sanded and varnished, the walls stripped back to brickwork and then sandblasted and dressed, and the result is transatlantic. It does not, Becky thinks, have much to do with Hoxton but it is impressive, nonetheless.

The most visible difference from Idiot Savant is Linda's expensive plate glass frontage with the gallery name etched into it. It is always spotlessly, gleamingly, clean (window cleaning is a significant percentage of Linda's monthly budget) because it is a huge shop window for the art displayed inside. When Becky looks into the glass usually she loses herself for a few moments, imagines she is staring down into a tropical lagoon with the gallery's shipwrecked treasures scattered about its pellucid depths.

It is different today. Later Becky will realise she must have turned up and seen Bloom's window no more than a few minutes after Tom fled, because the paint is still wet. She walks round the side of the building to where she can see Linda in her office, waves to get her attention.

'Come and look at this,' Becky shouts.

The street is busy. Couriers, white vans, a cab and some harassed looking pedestrians traverse her field of vision, all rushing onwards in ceaseless, mundane expenditure of energy. Becky sees that the bins to one side of the gallery entrance haven't been emptied and refuse is piling up. Rain spatters, boluses of icy damp by special delivery. A crow is cawing on a windowsill across the street. It cocks its head and regards her with an unblinking eye, a bedraggled gauleiter who decided to take her to task loudly before flying off.

Becky thinks about getting her Silk Cut out, decides to wait. Lighting up will appear unsupportive, although she needs nicotine to help her decide where her loyalties are in all this. Linda leaves her computer screen and comes to join Becky on the pavement. They stare at the glass, where the legend is sprayed in neat crimson letters four foot high:

ART + MONEY = SHIT!

'This has gone too, too far,' says Linda. 'I'm phoning Tania.'

21

The Two Strange Partners

Late one night towards the end of another long session, Tom and Billy were left talking together in Alastair's studio. Erick had lapsed into unconsciousness and Billy did not know where Alastair had got to. It was hard to believe he had retired early; as likely as not he was involved in another marathon binge somewhere in the vicinity, in the way an inveterate gambler plays a couple of roulette wheels simultaneously. As usual, Billy did not want to fight his way back through the numbing cold to his flat to wait there for whoever might wish to come calling. It was preferable to sit on until the numbing powder in front of him was all used up. He knew Alastair's place might be a target zone too, but at least he wasn't in there on his own. There was some safety in numbers, however small.

Small numbers. The group around Alastair and IS was fragmenting, despite all the support he had given them. It was like watching moves in a chess game, the way commercial logic meant his artists were being taken away one by one.

Was Becky and Erick's joint show the watershed? As well as Erick's palming off of inferior work on Alastair, it turned out that Tom too had weakened his links with IS over that show, and more severely still. Billy had heard Tom wouldn't participate at all for fear of harming his chances with a commercial gallery. He didn't want his work damned by association with Erick's second-rate offering. Or with Becky's installation, because at that point Becky was an absolute beginner.

Billy couldn't blame Tom because his work was so luminously remarkable. He looked over at him and registered his angular body and features, set off by that proud nose (surely the nose was created first, the rest of the body thrown in as an afterthought?), all of it untouched by doubt or indecision. Then Tom told him why he was losing interest in making art.

Alcohol reveals what is close to the mind's surface, while cocaine trawls up secrets from deeper and darker depths. The confessions come as the weariness of never feeling weary creeps in, from attempts to keep euphoria alive with ever more expansive revelation. Tom started by saying he was finding Lanchester's mockery of his attire oppressive.

'I wish he'd stop asking me if I've been out for a run. Or offering to buy me a whistle. I'm sure he wants me to wear a suit.'

'He's a pretty liberal employer though, isn't he?'

Billy had thought about Lanchester. The banter and that extrovert hair (extrovert for the city, at least) showed he enjoyed his wealth and power. But what he was, was a middle-aged man determined to have a small amount of fun collecting contemporary art, in between the deadening obligations of serving Mammon for most of his waking hours.

'He could be a lot worse. New money is brutal, all these spivvy upstarts — no offence, Billy.'

'It's not as if I'm upwardly mobile exactly, in fact it's starting to look—'

'He's sacked people from his firm once or twice, then rung them the next day and apologised, asked them to come back.'

'Not heartless, more indecisive, then—'

'The name, the name puzzles me. Henry's an old money name; he should be called Nigel or something. Not that any of it matters. Did you know I had decided to stop trying to produce art for a while, even before Linda Bloom rejected me? I'd been finding it impossible to make new work.'

Billy couldn't stop a sceptical expression crossing his face.

'You haven't heard anything about my time in Cologne have you?' said Tom.

'Alastair told me you were an artist's assistant there for a while, and he—'

'It's something you should know about, I suppose, given your support for my work.'

Lanchester was in the habit of talking over Tom, and Tom was talking over him. Billy did not take offence, because this was the coke speaking. Besides, he knew Tania was worse. (Who would have the last word if Tom, Lanchester and Tania got together? Tania, without a doubt.) Tom launched into his tale, a bobsledder plunging down into an icy, narcotic chute of recollection.

'When I left the Royal College of Art in 1988, I looked around and I heard that Martin Herrenberger needed a new assistant. I got in touch with him straight away because I admired his work a lot; I was still capable of looking up to people back then, and he was one of my idols. So I was amazed when he invited me over to Cologne, interviewed me and offered me the job.

'To start with I loved Cologne. It was like all German cities in that it was as if every building, old and new alike, together with the streets around them, the public transport systems, even the pedestrians, were minutely well designed and thought through, all manufactured somewhere else and then shipped in and unwrapped, fresh and clean from their packaging.

'It had a lot to offer me, because it was the centre of the German art world, sophisticated and cosmopolitan. I rented an apartment in Südstadt, the hippest part of town. My assistant's duties were not onerous and most days I didn't rise before noon. I mixed paint, went out and about and bought the materials for installations and sculptures. Some days I had to work late, into the early hours, but I didn't mind any of that. I couldn't believe I was working for Herrenberger, he was such a hero to me.

'He towered over the art scene in Cologne the same way the cathedral straddled the skyline. The other artists in town were doing well. The 1980s were motoring and there was money around. Everyone wore black and everyone was making grandiose, superficial works. Everything that they produced had some postmodern self-reflexivity in it somewhere. Often a get-out clause to excuse mediocrity, but at the time I wasn't too critical of it all. I knew Herrenberger was different. He addressed the same questions of the status of art and artworks. The difference was he did it with such wit and verve.'

Billy wondered whether to ask him about Erick, whether they encountered each other back then, but he knew that Erick had been based in Berlin. Besides, he wouldn't be able to interrupt Tom's flow.

'We would lock the studio each evening and set off on a night's drinking in Chlodwigplatz, so chic — and now I come to think about it so emblematic of the bourgeois world we affected to despise. Even before we left I would be drunk. *Bezoffen*, but not from alcohol. Instead I was intoxicated by Herrenberger's cool.

'He took a real interest in me, in my art. The turning point came one day when I was constructing an installation. It was a full-size model of a bus stop and I made a mistake, put some of the lettering in the wrong place. I pointed this out to Herrenberger, remarking that the overall effect of the changed signage was strangely pleasing. He stared at it, tapping the toe of his black cowboy boot. "It's an improvement," he said. "But it's more than that — it's genius." That's what he called the installation: "Genius". It was a success, and that was the beginning of my downfall. From then on each time we embarked upon a new work he asked me to ensure that I fucked something up in the production process.'

It was hard for Billy to imagine Tom making deliberate mistakes. He was so precise in his speech, his dress, everything.

'He was delighted with the results. The anarchy of the mistakes did help the work, I think. The discussions and exchanges between us over them opened the art up, made people engage with it more readily.

'That phase didn't last very long at all. Herrenberger began to brainstorm with me from the outset in order to enlarge the function of intervention in his work. I told him stories about my childhood, explained my favourite insights and ideas, and we made all of it into work. The concept was that the works were mainly mine — even though, naturally, he was the artist putting his name on them. In interviews he would explain exactly what we were about with this wholesale rejection of authenticity. Everyone would applaud his witty undermining of artistic identity. But by then I was no longer finding it so entertaining.'

Tom paused, and if they hadn't been doing coke Billy would have said he was collecting himself together before he could continue this painful exploration of his past. As it was, they were in no pain at all, so more likely he was simply grabbing fresh breath.

'For two years I supplied Herrenberger's entire artistic output: the initial concepts, the work, the titles, everything. He only saw the completed works at the openings.

'He came into the studio for an hour or two every week, discussed my ideas with me and then gave me the go-ahead to do whatever I wanted to do, never vetoed a single suggestion. The rest of the time he lazed about, stirring himself now and again to ring his gallery and see how much money he was earning.

'I complained to him, and he provided me with an assistant — an assistant's assistant. He suggested that I work with my assistant in the same way that he had worked with me. In due course, my assistant might have had his own assistant. We could have created a chain of exploitation linking everyone in Cologne.

'When eventually I escaped, I was creatively bankrupt. In art, to be candid, there are only so many ideas to go round. If an artist can come up with a few concepts that are special to him, then he milks them in the early part of his career for all he's worth. Let's face it, a lot of artists don't progress on from there, and Herrenberger got hold of all of my initial output.'

'What happened to Herrenberger?'

'He died of a heart attack a year later. I didn't think of it as justice — he was in his late fifties, so it's true he passed away a little young, but he died fulfilled at the end of a magical career. I can't deny I left myself open to it all and that the same sort of thing happens to lots of other artists, maybe less directly and blatantly, that's all. I turned to photography because I thought I had painted myself out and Alastair was a great help there, I have to say. Most recently he funded the triptych, the hire of the equipment and everything else, and I think that's worked out fine as far as it goes.'

'It's brilliant.'

'Thanks, but I don't know where to go now. I thought I'd try and get myself a proper gallery, because I couldn't progress anywhere further with IS. You know, with IS it's Alastair's vision for the gallery that's important and in some ways the art itself is secondary. Sometimes I can't help thinking it's as if he is the artist and we're all his assistants.'

Billy started to make noises of protest.

'It's true he's said all along all he wants is to help get the art out there,' Tom conceded. 'He's never asked for anything in return. But you could argue, too, that from his point of view it hardly matters who actually makes the work — although I'm not saying he's as bad as Herrenberger.'

'That would be hard.'

'Yeah, but all the same, it's not as if Alastair ever wants to sell any of the art. It's academic for me because I'm low on ideas now. Maybe Linda Bloom was right not to want to represent me. It's a good thing I've got this advisory role to support myself, even if Lanchester can be a plonker.'

'You'll get more ideas.'

Tom shrugged.

'In the end I suppose Alastair's right. The main issue is that the art gets made, regardless of who makes it. Even Herrenberger was right in some ways. The ideas are floating around out there, independent of any particular individual. Not that many are floating around me, but you see what I mean. No one can take the idea of the artist as some kind of special person seriously any more.'

Billy wondered how seriously Kevin Thorn took himself, as Tom took a drag on a joint and gazed into his past, with an expression like a surveyor observing a crack in a supporting wall.

'For what it's worth, producing art isn't all or nothing, whatever Alastair believes. Most of us have to do other things for a living. The reality is that most artists become art school lecturers and art teachers who make works in their spare time. Speaking of which, your writing has a lot of potential.'

'Thanks, thanks a lot.'

He sounded patronising, but Billy knew it was probably well meant. There was always this weighing up he went through with Alastair and the others. They knew stuff that he didn't, they could tell him things and give him insights he would not receive otherwise, and that was compensation for the ways, sometimes, they indulged themselves at his expense. Rick would say they were better informed and educated because of unwarranted privilege, but this was the world they were all in, and Billy wasn't going to let the politics of class exclude him from the best parts of it.

'I mean it,' said Tom. 'I agree with Alastair there. You should definitely go to art school, give yourself a solid background.'

'Yeah, well. I've no money or qualifications. Or a portfolio — it's not as if I want to be an artist as such.'

'Alastair will find a way around all that. You'll get your chance.'

Billy wasn't so sure. His complete ineligibility couldn't just be talked away. Alastair couldn't give him any financial assistance, whatever he said. There again, you never knew with Alastair; he could talk most people into most things. Billy thought about the package less than half a mile away in his flat, and then tried hard not to think about it.

They lapsed into silence. The cold tide of charlie was starting to recede, leaving Billy un-high and un-dry, saturated in the Stoly he had been digging into all the while. Insulation for the freezing street outside, as finally he made up his mind to leave.

He knew that even as a loser he could never win. Effortlessly, Tom could lay claim to being a much bigger failure than him, and he had more options to play with for the future than Billy. Even this downfall at the hands of Herrenberger might become rich material for Tom in due course, something to make more of his art from.

*

Outside and a man on the ground was stabbing a monstrous finger towards Billy. All remaining intoxication was snatched from his

162

brain as it shied from the sight. It was not a finger; it was far too large. It was a bone gleaming against the icy paving stones. A long gory shard sticking up and out from the bloody unplaited flesh of a leg. The other leg had shorter shards projecting out this way and that.

A paramedic in green overalls cutting trouser cloth away and the bone pulsing blue with the ambulance light. Billy crouching to vomit, the paramedic shoving him aside: 'Out of the way, fuck's sake.'

He looked round again to see eyes flickering, chest fluttering with shock. Life flowing away like drink from a toppled glass. Slid into the ambulance, the burgundy blanket not a good enough match for the blood. All over the paving slabs, soaking the cracks between them, everywhere.

22

An Attempt at Self Criticism

You've been moving around for most of tonight. By half-six you are at a party in Axel Beidermayer's place in Curtain Road. His posse are all there. Ellie Sachs who does those sound installations, Liam and Danny Sheehan and their Staffordshire bull terrier, Mary Carmichael and that Polish designer boyfriend of hers. You notice that almost everyone is wearing vintage trainers. Dennis Smythe arrives in drag for no obvious reason and no one pays him any attention. His last show was appallingly bad and you ponder the connections.

You last twenty minutes before realising you've had all the stimulus you are going to get and head to a spieler off Shoreditch High Street, where you meet a couple of gangsters. They can't be anything other than gangsters: the pecs, the tats, the schmutter. But mainly the attitude. The bouncer was very deferential when they walked in; you saw one of them reach round inside his coat and give a nipple a wrenching twist anyway. The bouncer tried to laugh it off, but you saw him hide a grimace of pain.

They know who you are and they give you the biggest wrap of charlie you've ever seen. You ask them what their favourite film is, and you know they're going to say *Get Carter*, and they know you know they're going to say that, and you all start laughing. There's none of that cold sneer or flat, impassive face stuff. They don't have to bother with all that. They say they like old Jags, you say you would have thought they drove BMWs, they say yeah, of course, but they have a soft spot for vintage British cars. You kind of knew they'd say that too.

You enjoy an open discussion. You are at the top end of your profession, they are at the top end of theirs. They say it's a cliché that it's all about respect in their line of work, but it's true enough. They tell you they had to break someone's legs with a tyre iron half an hour ago, and you receive this information in the matter-of-fact way that it is given. One of them says he bent the tyre iron; the other complains the blood ruined his suit. There's a knack with compound fractures, they say, like ripping telephone directories in half. Both legs in one go is a lot to deal with, so the punter might die of shock. They're not bothered about telling you this and you feel flattered they've confided in you.

They talk about Alastair Given taking liberties. There's some property of theirs he's got. You say you can't help them with that. You would if you could because it makes no odds to you. None to him either, because everyone knows he's got himself in the shit. You catch them looking at each other.

All you're bothered about is your art, you say. While you state this you're reminding yourself that your creativity ignores all boundaries, but you know full well your renegade status can never match theirs. Although they are not making any kind of statement about it. They're curious about you in the same way that you're curious about them, that's all. They want a bit of fun in just the same way as you do. But still. You look at them and you know there is no one over them, no one at all. One of them winks at you. The other fingers a stain on his suit and tuts.

*

It was late the following afternoon. From his desk in the back office, Billy witnessed another television interview in Idiot Savant. There was the same elaborately intense lighting as ever, making it seem as if he was outdoors in daylight (although by now it was pitch black outside), the same additional set within a set. Yet this time the interview was not the same.

'No, I think the art being produced around here is being grotesquely misappropriated and perverted,' Alastair was saying.

This interviewer was as groovy as all the others, but more seriously groovy still. Lips pursed enough for keys and loose change. A jacket of tweed thick enough for doormats. Temples carpet-bombed with grey, so that it was hard to pick out the silver arms of his spectacles. Though the grey was premature; he could have been all of thirty-five. Even so, Alastair needed all of his preternatural maturity in this company.

'Perverted?'

'Art is being exploited as an image by developers and businesses who have seen their chance to cash in.'

'Many of these artists use popular culture for subject matter.'

'There's no such thing as popular culture, only culture. And culture isn't overpriced flats and expensive restaurants and bars. The best art being produced anywhere in the world is coming from here, but the artists are being forced out.'

'You can't deny that Hoxton's really starting to blossom.'

'The flowers that were beginning to appear are dying off, and the media is helping to trample them. You're leaping on the bandwagon, cheapening art the way you cheapen everything else.'

'Cut.'

Billy saw the director step from behind the camera to break up the uneasy nexus. He was younger than the interviewer, seemed younger even than Alastair, though his clothing had something to do with this: flying jacket, string vest, combats, a facial piercing or two. His voice was the defining element — the inalienable tones of the home counties safeguarding the status quo.

'We mapped all of this out beforehand,' he said.

'I'm not interested in your map.'

'You're wasting our time.'

'You're wasting everyone's time, putting this trash out.'

*

He could see Becky's eyes in the mirror above the bar, those eyes of hers, between the mock Doric columns holding up the shelves of spirits. She was watching the two of them sitting at the table, before she paid for the drinks and ferried them over in a couple of trips (she could have managed it in one if it wasn't for the chaser of Bell's he requested with his Stella), setting them down carefully on the table.

Poked away down a side street, The Dragon was a traditional boozer and a good choice for a discreet meeting place. It was, however, a distinctive venue in its own way because its decor set it apart. It looked like someone had taken a colour chart and decided to make everything clash: red paisley carpet, stools covered in olive leatherette, an egg yolk ceiling, snot-hued wainscoting round the walls, pink lace curtains at the windows, violet and blue silk flowers on the window ledges. Office workers in distressed suits were scattered about, busy stupefying themselves with alcohol. In these surroundings Billy reflected, they needed it.

After re-seating herself Becky took out a Silk Cut and offered the packet to Rick, who declined politely before reaching for his Old Holborn and Rizlas. They watched as Billy helped himself to a drink. Leaning forward all the while to minimise upward forearm rotation, he tipped lager into his mouth, swapping glasses swiftly to charge it with whisky before it disappeared. His self-indulgent calisthenics over, he sat back.

'You want to cane it a bit,' said Rick.

'First one today.'

Becky and Rick were looking at him doubtfully. He knew he was not at his most impressive. He felt as if he had been dragged through a hedge backwards, and then forwards, many times. Before being left in the hedge for a week or two prior to a bonus session of prolonged dragging.

He stared back at Becky. In a way it was dreadful, how mesmerised he was by her. When she said she had something she wanted to discuss he came over straight away, and when he arrived the sight of her left him as confused as always.

Becky had her hair in pigtails, pigtails like small silken wings which emphasised her doe eyes, leaving only the scar as a reminder of more serious realities. For the first few moments tonight he had believed, in defiance of all that had passed between them, that she was here for him. Then he saw Rick. He knew Becky was with Alastair, so where did Rick fit in? The rational part of his mind knew Rick's presence simply meant they had business together and nothing else, but his grip on all things rational was not what it was.

'Rick's been handling my housing benefit claim,' she said. 'He was doing such a good job, but of course that's become unnecessary.'

Rick's smile loosened and widened, and Billy was not sure it stemmed entirely from her praise and the news of her windfall. He knew his infatuation with Becky meant his suspicions of Rick lusting after Becky were as unavoidable as they were, almost certainly, baseless.

Rick took a sip of his pint. 'Cheers,' he said. 'It ain't easy to sort things in there.'

'Let's hope the other claimants sell their art for astronomical prices in due course,' Billy said.

They smiled uneasily.

'No harm in hoping,' Rick said. 'Bit like my activism, as it goes.'

He could not believe Rick would stand a chance with her over Alastair. There again, there he was, sitting there with that mouth of his, and that mouth with its retro styling (Jagger, Gaz) would appeal to many women. More crucial was his good nature; he was the kind of person who always understood, and while that could be irritating (irritating to Billy, in particular, sitting there in competition against all of that selfless understanding), it was difficult to claim it was a negative trait.

'I won't ask for any details of that,' Billy said. 'I expect a lot of it's confidential, internal party matters and so on.'

He bulleted down his remaining whisky and eyed what was left of his beer mournfully.

'That's what we wanted to talk to you about,' Becky said, lowering her voice, 'Rick's political work. He's in an anti-fascist group—'

'I'm sure that's interesting,' Billy said. 'But why are we whispering?'

REM was on the jukebox. He listened to the lyrics. He was not going to try not to breathe, because he was restive and uncomfortable as it was and it wasn't all of it to do with feeling like a gooseberry around Becky and Rick, along with the knowledge that feeling that way was bonkers. Because the conversation was starting to unsettle him and already, regardless of Becky's presence, he wished to leave.

'Rick's involved with the *Searchlight* people,' said Becky. 'You know, the investigators who run the magazine that exposes fascists.'

'Don't think I've written for them,' he said. 'Do they have an arts section?'

'It's very sensitive work,' she said, her voice still low. 'Rick wants to get you to help him.'

'Right,' said Rick.

'I don't know any fascists,' Billy said.

Becky must have been wondering why Rick and him were friends, he thought. If they were still friends — the personal being political, and all. In the end, he thought, they were like Linda and Tania. What was there beyond shared history to explain their bond?

'Look,' she said, 'this is something bigger than the three of us.'

Three. Why not two? Billy was ignoring Rick but he continued to smile, his equanimity as admirable as it was awful.

'I understand where you're coming from,' she said. 'We've all got to earn a living.'

He said nothing, because now she had the option of taking a long break from earning a living. Maybe she assumed her entry into a much higher income bracket than his was the natural order of things.

'I've got quite a full diary,' he said. 'You should talk to my agent.'

'You haven't got an agent,' said Becky.

He shot her a hurt glance.

'We thought that maybe you would be in a position to help us,' she said. 'You're a journalist after all, used to investigating things, and you know Alastair.'

'Alastair? I thought you were going out with him. Surely you don't think he's a neo-Nazi?'

He had been drinking elsewhere before he arrived here, inevitably and despite telling them otherwise. His speech was beginning to slur. He was making declamatory gestures, clasping his pint glass like a chalice, an inebriated latter-day messiah.

'I'm not going out with him any more.'

He felt sick, felt like spewing the whisky and beer back up (though that would have been a terrible waste) as he registered that Alastair might truly have been supplanted by Rick, though he tried to continue undeflected.

'You are joking, aren't you? He runs an art gallery, not a fascist cult. There's nothing to investigate.'

'Some of the people he's in with are lairy,' said Rick.

The alcohol began to dissipate as Billy remembered his encounter with Harkness. Another silence. He tried not to look worried.

'Did you know that a guy got both legs broken outside IS, early this morning?' said Becky.

'He died of shock before they could get him to hospital,' said Rick. 'Poor bastard.'

'Yes, I do know and that was fucking horrible, but it can't have had anything to do with Alastair.'

The incident and its implications were an excellent reason to have a lot more to drink, he thought, if ever there was one.

'It ain't the drug dealing that bothers us,' said Rick. 'It's not that.'

By now the alcohol had almost vanished away from his system. There was no need to vomit.

'It's the people supplying him,' continued Rick. 'They're into worse.'

'Listen,' he said, 'count me out of whatever this is, I'm in enough trouble.'

'What do you mean?' asked Becky.

He paused, then back-pedalled clumsily.

'Work-related stuff. It's tough out there.'

'Billy,' said Rick. 'We're mates aren't we?'

He ignored this and he saw them look shocked. Instead he put his own question to Becky.

'So one minute you're going out with Alastair, and the next he's a neo-Nazi? Not an amicable split, then?'

It was desperately wrong she was not to be his soul mate, and maybe was now Rick's instead — though he knew within himself with whatever sense he had left that this imagined new liaison was not likely at all — yet if that was the way it was to be then she had no more power over him. As it was he resented the power she'd had unelected, unearned and unrequited. Becky's expression was pained, pain endured for the common good but pain nevertheless, as he turned to Rick.

'You're relying heavily on these imaginary fascists.'

Rick was starting to look disconsolate. Still a smile, but with less lip to spare it might be a grimace.

'Fascists do exist,' he said.

'I expect they're all around us.'

None of his digs seemed to faze Rick.

'Hoxton and Shoreditch are a couple of the most racist areas in the whole of the UK,' he said. 'The BNP had its headquarters right on Shoreditch High Street until recently before it moved to Welling. Remember when the London Apprentice was rammed with gay skinheads? Some of those were BNP.'

'Like Ernst Rohm and the Brownshirts?'

'Right.'

'History mate, all of it. Stick to raves.'

'What's happening round here isn't history,' said Becky, 'and it's only the activists who are dealing with it.'

'Get real. There's no activism any more. The Berlin Wall's down, Marxism's dead and Thatcher's handbagged socialism. This is just more retro shite, isn't it?'

'Billy—'

Rick started to respond, but he wasn't having any more of it.

'Good luck with your investigations,' he said. 'Let me know when your massed forces are ready to strike.'

As he rose he gestured to the rest of the pub and shouted, pointing at Rick:

'Watch out, he's in the Thought Police. I'd stop having forbidden notions if I were you.'

The adjacent tables watched him with mild interest.

*

There was a sombre atmosphere around the table in Alastair's studio, quiet drinking, muted snorting. Besides Alastair, only Tom and Billy were present. They were like one of those kitsch ornaments, a winter snow scene inside a plastic dome. Every so often their little bubble was shaken, and powder flew about, before everything settled into immobility once more. Except for Billy's mind, accelerating with wild swerves, trying to fathom the difference between utopia and dystopia.

'Hoxton and its denizens are rejecting us,' Alastair said. 'Soon we'll be history.'

'For god's sake change the record Alastair, just this fucking once,' said Tom. 'The truth is that this is already a place that rejects everything, but that's because of its geography, not due to any stand. The place people mostly call Hoxton is actually Shoreditch, and Shoreditch is really just one gigantic traffic island. It's a big triangle bounded by Great Eastern Street, Shoreditch High Street and Old Street. The traffic forms a metal wall round the perimeter, penning everyone in while they descend into atavism and insanity.'

Alastair laughed.

'That's all very J.G. Ballard, but I'm completely sane thanks.'

'So it's everyone else who has lost it?'

'Mad people do seem to end up here,' said Billy.

He was one of them, he thought. The crack pipe was out and circulating, he was smoking metal, heavy metal, a chemical orgasm took hold of his body, combusted his brain, exploded up through the top of his skull. As he took a chaser of brown to put out the flames he asked himself again where all this was going, whether it would be simpler to put a gun to his head and just to have done with it.

When Erick appeared it was almost a welcome distraction. The company set aside glasses and pipe to observe the spectacle. Alastair was wearing a white seersucker jacket with a Nehru collar; the effect was colonial. Erick stood before him in his overalls, an apprentice with a grievance.

'You have me evicted for a lousy couple of grand,' said Erick.

'That's not what happened,' said Alastair. 'You know I've been helping you out with your rent all these months. I just don't have access to any more money, that's all.'

Tom stirred himself, started to say something but thought better of it.

'Why didn't you ask me for the money?' said Erick. 'I would give this to you.'

He drew on his cigarette and grimaced as he exhaled and Billy looked at his teeth, rows of halved aspirins.

'You know you haven't got enough,' said Alastair. 'No one has enough.'

'I have lost all respect for you, Alastair.'

'You're not even the first person today to say that to me.'

23

Negative Degradation

He had five wraps left. A short time before there had been ten. If the wraps were fingers, he had lost a hand. He was in 333 and everyone was smoking heavily. Normally Billy liked smoke, the mysterious wraiths and tendrils, the life cycle of the cigarette. Cradle to grave in five minutes and then the butt, the dead end. Each cylinder an elegant metaphor for mortality, yet subservient to the smoker's whim.

Tonight his appreciation for cigarettes had reached its limit. The fumes in here were so thick the air-conditioning couldn't cope and his eyes stung. Mother, upstairs, would be better but he was with a large group of people and stuck fast amid their inertia. A skinny woman in a black tracksuit was talking to him. He'd seen her before, hanging round the Lux. She seemed to know him, but he wasn't sure who she was.

'Whose party is this?' she asked, nodding her bony head towards the rest of the group.

'It's not a party, just a few people who've come on from a private view round the corner.'

'Do you want an E?'

He considered briefly. Why not? She asked for, and was given, ten pounds. He necked the tablet straight away, crunching it up and washing away the bitterness with lager, trying to forget the touch of her fleshless fingers. The booze might swamp a lot of the MDMA, but what was left should cut down his craving for charlie. He thought about offering her a line, decided that there was no point. She was a collection of lines already, a stick woman, and anyway she was gone, lost to the murk.

A conversation was taking place around him. Words and phrases were buffeted about by gusts of music, intermittently spattering into him. There was no point cupping hands round ears and shouting requests for repetitions, because he wasn't that interested. Every so often he yelled something non-committal in a likely direction. The others were probably doing the same. It was peculiar, he knew that the music was KLF's *Chill Out*, but it had never sounded this way to him before, like a gale in full spate.

He finished his drink and looked into the glass in surprise, as surprised as he had been on looking into all of the other empty glasses he had seen in his life. A pint seemed such a lot to start with, but never lasted long. It was time for another line; the E wasn't having much effect.

The toilets were at the rear, round a corner. Long and low, dank and ill-lit, they were reminiscent of a pantry in an old country house. He stepped into a cubicle and, impatient, rammed the bolt across. It wouldn't go home, and the cubicle's walls and door juddered at the impact. Taking more care over alignment and docking, he managed it at the second attempt and started to dig out the plastic bag containing the wraps. It was oversized and its compression in his pocket meant that when he tugged, one fold emerged at a time. The process was like pulling out a parachute, but he stopped because he had become distracted.

The cubicle's walls were white plastic laminate, covered with a myriad of blue lines so fine as to be almost invisible. He wondered how many there were altogether: more than the grains of sand on a beach or less? Probably less, but still an incalculable number. They formed a measureless labyrinth: a tiny man or insect could start from one side and spend a lifetime navigating between them to reach the other. He stared at the lines and they hung in the air before him, diaphanous and shimmering. The E had kicked in, and it was far stronger than he had anticipated. He was tripping heavily.

Wall, floor, ceiling — which was which? His spatial coordinates had gone and the ability to discriminate at all within his visual field was receding. He couldn't feel his hands and feet.

They were becoming numb, solid, white. Hard and shiny. His torso, his torso was rapidly calcifying. He was turning into porcelain, part of the lavatory. Soon people would come in, and piss and shit all over him.

An uncertain amount of time later the rush wore off. He needed to get home at once, immediately. Everything would be more manageable in a place of safety. What a joke that was. His flat was the least safe place in all London for him, but there wasn't anywhere else to go in this state. How the fuck would he make it back there from here? He needed a sedative to bring himself down. Easy to say, to think. It would be very difficult to get hold of a Valium. Maybe one or two of the clubbers somewhere in here had some, but he would never be able to identify them.

The important thing, the most important thing of all, was not to panic. If he panicked he would make everything worse, much worse than it was. There would be sedatives in the nearest A&E department if he could get himself to it. Where was it? Guy's? No, it had to be the London Hospital down in Whitechapel. One of the bar staff could drive him down there, surely? But they'd refuse, laugh at him, even if he could get as far as the bar. That would be almost impossible, like trying to fly abroad after arriving at the airport naked and without a passport, all the while steadily turning into a lavatory pan.

A minicab, that was the answer. Somehow or other, he would have to get himself into a minicab and persuade the driver to take him to hospital. How? It couldn't be done; he knew that he would never make it to the club's entrance. He'd get lost and go round and round, trying to retrace his steps until he collapsed. They'd move him back to the toilet, plumb him in. If he told a stranger or one of the group he was with — though they were strangers as well, he did not know them at all — about his plight, begged them for assistance, would they help him? No, they'd be like the staff; they'd think he was mad, they'd disengage, mock him and walk away.

This wasn't E. It was acid, very strong acid. He should never, ever have taken that pill and he was never, ever going to take drugs again. Why hadn't he been alive to such obvious portents? The music was the tempest before the tragedy. The skeletal woman in the black tracksuit was death and she had scythed him down with her dodgy tab. He was dying, his life force slowly dwindling under a ferocious chemical assault.

The cubicle walls were pulsing in and out, giant bellows. Voices, he could hear voices. Some clubbers had entered and were going about their business. Thank God. The voices resolved themselves into two people immediately outside the cubicle, next to the washbasins. One of them sounded American, the other Scottish.

'...sure fancies himself, goddam it—'

'Ah ken, he's thinks he's the big banana... '

It was some of the group from the private view and they were talking about him. Should he draw attention to himself to stop them? No, he was too far off his head to be able to do that with any effectiveness. They wouldn't be around long, anyway; in a minute or two they'd be gone.

He waited and waited, but they didn't go and their jibes became more and more poisonous. They knew he was in here and they were taunting him, sensing that he was powerless to fight back.

'...always kinda thought—'

'Tae flash—'

'Awesome amounts of money—'

'Yir jokin, that fuckin waster.'

If he was in his right mind he'd go straight out there and confront them, tell them exactly what was what. For a start, it wasn't true that he had too much wedge. True, sometimes he might give the impression he had plenty to throw around, but he was just shuffling plastic to preserve an illusion of solvency. Why couldn't they lay off? One of them banged on the cubicle door, they were getting more aggressive.

'...dae ye ken whit's up wi' him—'

'So gross, thinks he's such a big noise—'

'Naewan wants to know any more—'

'Like a total embarrassment... '

He couldn't catch everything because they started the hand dryer in a mocking pretence that they didn't want him to hear what they were saying. The rushing air from the dryer was never-ending if it was the hand dryer and not an airliner passing overhead. How long had he been in here? It must have been more than an hour. He looked at his wristwatch. Two minutes had passed. Impossible, the watch must be broken. Unless his sense of time had gone completely. What if he was stuck here forever, living through an hour for every minute that went by in the real world? He would go mad, have to be locked up. Maybe he should start screaming at the top of his voice, get it all over with quickly.

Another rush slowed. His surroundings were at the same time so vivid and so dreamlike. When he turned his head everything left long, colourful contrails. He tried to stare at one thing alone, the top of the cistern, but it flexed and flowed and swam about like an enormous amoeba.

All this time the slagging outside the cubicle continued, venomous, unrelenting. They didn't know that he was in serious trouble in here. Or maybe they did and didn't care because they had him where they wanted him.

'...someone should dae something...'

'Time to kick ass—'

'It's oot ay order—'

'Sure sucks...'

If only he could get out of here, get himself somewhere he could be alone and drug free. He remembered the charlie. If he tried to go to A&E he'd be arrested, they'd find it on him, if he managed to get that far with it. Maybe those bastards by the hand dryer would take it off him, ignoring his ineffectual protests, before throwing him out of the toilets back into the bar area, to be pitched out into the street by the bouncers and complete his mental disintegration in public. Hell. He was in hell. The voices reached him again.

'...all that blow—'

'...polis—'

'Turn him in—'

'Barry solution…'

They were going to keep him in here, trapped, while they called the police and had him arrested. With all those wraps they'd charge him with dealing, search his flat. Get rid of the drugs. Get rid of them straight away.

He fumbled in his pockets for the plastic bag containing the wraps, it could have been in any one of them and they had all become vast, confusing caverns. The only feasible way to get hold of the bag was to disinter the entire contents of each pocket and to arrange all of it on top of the cistern, which continued to swim around. It took a long time, and painstakingly identifying and re-identifying everything took longer. It was impossible to work out what most of the items were without intense concentration, and once he'd settled one object to his satisfaction he'd forgotten the identity of the others and had to start again.

Eventually he found the plastic bag. It had been hanging half out of his pocket where he had left it, but he hadn't been able to differentiate it from the fabric of his trousers. He threw it into the toilet and tried to recall how to flush it away. After lengthy trial and error he wrenched the handle in the correct direction, and water rose up in a maelstrom which made him shrink back. When the force of the torrent was spent he was convinced he could see a solitary wrap left floating on the surface so he flushed a second time and the dam burst once more. They were all gone, he was sure of it.

They had nothing on him now, those evil fuckers outside. Let them malign him as much as they wanted with their slimy serpent tongues, he was out of here, hallucinating or not. He put everything else back in his pockets; that took a while but it was quicker than taking it all out — it reminded him of re-packing his bags at the end of a holiday and how much easier that was than the packing before setting off. Then he unlocked the door and walked out, striding boldly towards the wash basins.

The lavatory was empty except for a fair-haired youth in a striped T-shirt of blue and white hoops. He turned from washing his hands to stare at Billy, and then into the cubicle he had left.

179

'I thought there were a few of you in there, mate.'

Billy said nothing as he turned abruptly and made for the exit into the club. A terrifying realisation slammed into him. There had been no one slagging him off. He had been talking to himself inside the cubicle in different voices, thinking that they belonged to other people. He had gone completely crazy, but there was no time to think about that now. Home. He must get home.

An indeterminate period of time later — it could have been an hour, or a couple of weeks — he slammed his front door behind him. Identifying and inserting the key had been another agonisingly protracted process, and that had come after it had taken all of the personal resources he possessed to get himself the short distance back. Crossing the roads had been torture; he couldn't judge the speed of the vehicles. Thank god none of the block's other residents had been in the lift. Rick. Loopy lips Rick, looney tunes Rick. He couldn't have coped with Rick, couldn't have coped with anyone. Never again, he would never, ever take another pill. After fetching himself a glass of water he lay on the settee. He knew that anyone out there who wanted could smash through the door and come get him whenever they felt like it, and there was nothing at all he could do about it. He would have liked to have shut his eyes and slept, left it all behind regardless, but there was a white light burning inside his head and it was inextinguishable.

An hour or two later he crawled into the bedroom on his hands and knees, occasionally stopping to clutch his chest and moan. Dimly, a horrifying item of information brought itself to his attention. He'd thrown all that coke away for nothing. There was a package full of it a few metres away, but he couldn't touch it for fear of his life and now his own supply was completely gone. His answerphone was at his eyeline, and he noticed its light flashing. Perhaps, he thought, if he played back the message it would take his mind off his terminal stupidity. He reached over gingerly, hoping the motion would not induce a fresh bout of hallucinations, or a heart attack.

'Ah Billy, a quick ring about that article...'

He didn't recognise the confident voice booming out.

'...if you could phone me when you get this message... '

No hang on, it was that suit he'd interviewed, Lanchester, the one who'd paid fifty thousand for Becky's installation.

'...we must talk, I'm on... '

What was up with the bastard? How had he got his home phone number? He hadn't sounded amicable, he had sounded as if he was about to do something terrible to him. Billy knew that he must have libelled him inadvertently. He was going to be sued, ruined, broken. He lay there whimpering as the light inside his head blazed out into the night.

24

Discrete Entities Moving in Similar Directions in Search of Mutual Comprehension

Tom says he has a sniffle. Mucus is pearling at the rims of his nostrils. He dabs it away but it has spread to his upper lip, and he must renew his efforts there. He crumples his sopping linen handkerchief, transfers it back to the pocket of his tracksuit. Becky thinks he might as well have done with it and change a baby on his face. She is losing admiration for Tom's nose. When it is wet it is too much, a monstrous growth excreting snot, discoloured by rawness where he has been wiping and re-wiping.

No one can blow their nose so often and maintain decorum and, besides, public nose-blowing distresses her. It has nothing to do with her heritage, she thinks, because she found it distasteful from long before she became aware of Japanese sensitivities around it (it is interesting — nevertheless — the way her personal distaste ties in with all of that so neatly). She has always thought talk of big noses the crudest racism, but there is no denying their nastiness when one of them is dripping steadily in front of you, and there is no possibility of escape.

It might be coke prompting Tom's nasal excretions. They all do far too much of it and adverse consequences are unavoidable. Becky cannot see the point. Nothing can compare to the satisfaction of creating art, definitely not any transitory pleasure from an overpriced drug.

Everyone in the Bricklayers is jostling each other to get to the bar, cigarette smoke is lining the low ceiling and spilling downwards like leaking roof insulation. The weather has become much too cold for the drinkers to spread themselves out along the pavements outside as they did all through the summer. Although that is something Becky would never do anyway, perch on the kerb with her feet in the gutter alongside all the students and crusties.

Tom didn't want to meet here but she insisted because she likes the Bricklayers, despite the teenage clientele it is starting to attract, and it is a change from the Lux. The problem is that this Charlotte Road pub was only ever meant to be a small neighbourhood hostelry down a backstreet. Ongoing schisms between the artists who patronised it shrank the clientele further; not so long ago it closed at weekends for want of custom. Now it is rammed. Becky listens to the jukebox, tries to find refuge in the music from the thicket of encroaching elbows and from Tom's ministrations to his proboscis.

'Petty revenge doesn't interest me at all,' Tom is saying. 'That graffiti was nothing to do with me. My own flat was graffitied — don't you remember?'

'Yes,' she said. 'That sounded unpleasant.'

'It took me ages to scrub it off. Why would I do that to someone else?'

She remembers him complaining loudly that there was a spelling mistake in the graffiti, as though that was the worse aspect of it all. Linda says this was probably where he got the idea for spraying his abuse on her front window. He widens his eyes, touches her upper arm for emphasis and she almost believes in his innocence, before remembering he adopted the same body language when persuading her he hadn't alerted the council to the lack of fire escapes in Bloom's, or the Inland Revenue to Linda's tax irregularities.

Over her shoulder she sees a barman drying glasses. He smiles and waves his cloth at her in sport. It reminds her of Tom's handkerchief, and she doesn't smile back.

'What if it happens again?' she says.

'She can wash it off, can't she? Why is it such a big deal?'

This isn't a subject Becky wants to dwell upon. Oasis click into place on the juke box: the manager has got hold of a bootleg of their first single, prior to official release. The band's lachrymose grandiosity makes her smile. Tom looks startled as she nods towards a speaker in explanation.

'You don't like them, do you?' he says.

'Look at those caterpillar eyebrows. And what about the music? You can't argue with all that post-industrial passion.'

'Especially if it's northern. Does Tania like them too?'

'She wants to make love to them all, in a huge writhing mass, and cook them burgers and beans afterwards.'

'I expect she's already done that,' he says. He is beginning to grin. Then he sneezes again and the handkerchief appears.

'Do you think Henry Lanchester would like to see some more of my work soon?' she asks.

Tom looks less amused.

'You need to finish off some more of it first, don't you?'

'Lanchester rocks,' she says.

'Even more than Oasis?'

'A lot more.'

Lanchester has paid her work a huge compliment by investing in it so heavily. She has decided that with his middle-aged features and his mane of hair he looks like the Cowardly Lion from *The Wizard of Oz*. Though he is far from cowardly.

'He is so fucking alpha, that guy,' says Tom, as if echoing her thoughts.

'What's wrong with being bold?'

'It could be worse,' says Tom. 'He could be keen on vintage cars or antiques, like other slickers. It's hard to rein him in, that's all.'

Becky is heartened to hear of her benefactor's drive, but Tom is asking her something.

'I'm sorry?' she says.

'Is it possible that we could do it again?'

Polite, diffident, and a little anxious.

'Do what again?'

Then she understands, looks at him, takes in his dripping nose. Makes her decision and smiles at him. It is a confident smile.

*

Once or twice towards dawn he descended into fitful sleep but the acid lingered, continued to fill his mind with empty, blinding light. When it finally departed, its message remained — there was nowhere to hide, from himself or from anyone else. No one had come for him in the night, but he knew it wouldn't be long. There was nothing he could do about that, except to carry on staying away from the flat as much as he could.

And now there was another catastrophe to confront: he had to ring Lanchester back. He debated phoning *The Herald's* lawyers first, but that was impossible without knowing the details of his transgression. Ignoring the call would be idiotic, he was sure that would get him into even worse trouble.

A couple of lines were essential to restore himself, but there was no charlie. The bereavement tugged at his bowels and sent jolts through his nervous system. The knowledge came to him that flushing it all away was the stupidest thing he had ever done. He attempted to dismiss the memory of his crazed disposal as he held his head in both hands and considered what to do next. The obvious answer was to crawl into the bathroom and vomit. As he bent over the lavatory bowl, strands of bile hung from his lips and swung back and forth with his heaves.

It was possible that Lanchester had not rung at all, that the answerphone message was another delusion: last night had been a concatenation of hallucinations. He tried batting the wrack away from his mouth, gave up, raised himself un-precipitately and went to the answerphone. The message was still there.

He picked up the phone, a game warden trapping a venomous serpent. Laboriously, he poked Lanchester's number into the handset, trying to remember the right legal formula to ensure that the conversation wouldn't be resurrected in court. Was he meant to say that all discussion of the article was without prejudice? It was something like that.

'Ah, Billy. How nice of you to ring. I wanted to congratulate you on that marvellous piece you wrote.'

A short conversation ensued. After hanging up he lit a cigarette, by a supreme effort stopped himself retching again. Substance abuse was becoming his passport to ever-increasing psychosis, in which he placed the worst construction on every occurrence. Lanchester's praise had been fulsome, and the would-be king of the art jungle had asked his advice about a confidential matter. He phoned Tom straight away.

'He asked me about this story going around, that you're harassing Linda Bloom,' Billy said.

'It's nice to hear of my employer's confidence in me.'

'Not at all.'

'Have you heard Kevin Thorn's next show is going into IS?'

Billy was an inhabitant of a monochrome world, all colour drained from it by last night's psychoactive overload. Yet if his sensory perceptions were dulled, his emotions remained bared and acute. Alastair owed him; he should have had the news before Tom. He had heard rumours this might happen, dismissed them, since it seemed unlikely Thorn would interrupt his upward trajectory by bothering with IS any more. When he rang Alastair, he was either not answering or not at home, so Billy meandered over to French Place and went up to his studio, which did not contain him.

He ground his way through the afternoon in the IS office, trying to get hold of people who didn't want to talk to him, wondering all the while where he was going to find more coke. He considered whether to return home and try going to bed for a few days, before realising he couldn't do that safely. His back was hurting; it crossed his mind he should be seeing an osteopath, he realised he couldn't afford it.

Thank god Becky's installation would be removed from IS to make way for Thorn's work. The film was starting to drive him crazy — or even more crazy — a constant reminder of his guilt. That huge accusing face, the hammer descending again and again in retribution. Those flying geese: the last things he wanted to look at under the lingering influence of a mind-blowing psychedelic. If there was a shot gun in here he would seize it, load it up, go out there and blast away, blow holes right out through the centre of those features, shoot those fucking geese stone dead. He was preparing to leave when Alastair walked in, untroubled, unfazed. Billy knew he had to grasp the initiative.

'Can you get me an interview with Kevin Thorn? I've chased him for months.'

'His press agent's talking about using a higher profile writer.'

Soames, that slimy fucker Soames, but he was not to be diverted and he had leverage.

'How about telling Kevin the show's off unless he gives me the interview?'

'He doesn't need IS, he's reaching the point where he can do a show anywhere he likes.'

'All the same, if you could do your best to get me the interview I'd be grateful.'

'There's not much I can do.'

'Our arrangement's become very risky,' said Billy.

There was no need to spell it out. He felt ashamed about cornering Alastair like this, and yet he went ahead and did it.

'We can't do anything about it now,' said Alastair.

His message was unmistakable: Billy was no longer a free agent.

'So I'm lumbered?'

'Only for a couple more days.'

*

Sea change; see change. Hoxton made it into the mainstream media more and more often, saturation was reached and passed. The happening place, the place to be. Teens and twenties arriving, first at weekends and then in the week. Ones and twos, then in gangs and bands, and in strings and posses, threading their way through all the narrow, cobbled streets, braiding them together with their shining new faces.

The bars full of swarms of fresh flies: the Bricklayer's, the Barley Mow, the Lux, the Conqueror, the Macbeth, Charlie

Wright's, the Complex, the Foundry, Home, the Electricity Showrooms, Canteloupe, the Great Eastern, 333. Tomorrow's people looking for something, that something around the corner those others (Rimbaud, Kerouac, Camus, Dylan, De Beauvoir, Lennon, Reed, Warhol and all the rest) searched for and found. The Life.

Everyone wanting to get away with it the way the artists get away with it. Smoking and drinking, snorting and toking, fucking and fighting. Going out and having it large. Spending, spending, spending. Beer, wine and whisky. Flashing the cash. Coffee, cigs and kebabs. Pills and charlie, nightclubs and minicabs. Punting the plastic and downing deposits. Renting lofts and buying apartments. Furniture, clothes and cuisine.

The art? That was the thing about Hoxton, there were lots of artists around for a short while but very few galleries, so there was never much art to go and see. Not that the new kids on the block were bothered by any of that.

*

Billy lit another Silk Cut and dragged at it raggedly as he began to panic. His heartbeat, already tachycardic with comedown, accelerated. He had held himself together while he was tripping, more or less — all right, he hadn't, but at least he hadn't completely disintegrated, fractured into a thousand schizoid splinters. Now he had nothing left to deal with this. Alastair had as good as told him that he was trapped and must continue to court disaster.

He didn't know what to do. Without charlie he couldn't think straight. Whatever he did would be wrong. Yet he had to carry on and fuck up everything all the same, or the terrible panic would not go away.

He was starting to feel angry with Alastair. He knew some of that was self-righteousness. Really he was angry with himself for trying so disloyally to exploit Thorn's show at IS to his own advantage. But it was becoming clearer than ever to him that Alastair could never be — could never have been — any radical

188

alternative to the mainstream art world. Artists produced possessions for rich people, and nowadays when they claimed to be anything alternative — surrealists, situationists, communists, whatever — it could only ever be in ironic acquiescence, the same ironic acquiescence that had Warhol selling pictures of Mao. Alastair was play-acting in a different way to the rest of the art world, was all.

The others didn't support Alastair when it came down to it, so there was no reason why he should. Maybe they were all of them craven, but in the end their cravenness was simply common sense, and he hadn't had any of that.

There was no need for Alastair to put him through all this, to pull him under with him as he went down. He wanted to forget Alastair, forget the rest of them, walk away from this mess, but it was too late. He had so fervently wished to be a part of it all and now that he was, there was no escape. Except through betrayal. He was entitled to try at least to save himself. He dredged his trouser and jacket pockets — a disturbing reprise of his search in the toilet cubicle — found the piece of cardboard Harkness had given him and rang the number on it.

'That's you Billy, isn't it? You've got such a distinctive voice. I've been looking forward to your call.'

'Are you going to arrest me?'

Without a confidence boost from charlie this was excruciating.

'Is that what you'd like?'

'No.'

'Tell you what, there's something I'd like you to see tomorrow night.'

'Are you asking me out on a date or something?'

'No, attractive and engaging as you are, but meet me at Knightsbridge tube at half seven, just outside the exit for Harrods. Don't be late.'

25

Industrial
(Part II)

Another warehouse party, and Rick and Billy were hanging out behind the DJ and his mixing desk. Rick committed to partying, Billy getting in what might be a last burst before prison or worse. Rick didn't appear to hold the scene in The Griffin against him, must have realised Billy was drunk and out of control. You could say what you liked about Rick (and Billy did, if only to himself), but he never held a grudge. That didn't mean that Billy was about to subscribe to his conspiracy theories and if Rick started to give out (or Trot out), the party line on Alastair tonight, he would simply ignore it.

While he was musing about the loose-lipped hazard that was Rick, Rick took over the decks, acting captain of the spaceship because the DJ-proper wanted a break. Rick threw in some hardcore, mixed things up a bit. Electronic noise, sampled drum breaks, hyper-syncopated beats. The energy level rose as he switched in Energy Flash. Lots of pills in the house tonight, plenty of charlie too. No need for a chill-out room. Billy looked around at the dancers, at the surroundings and realised that tonight might be the one and only time that a group of people had ever had this much fun in this room, instead of being bored shitless year in and year out, piling crates or sewing shirts or whatever, for fuck all money.

The DJ-proper was being generous with his charlie and Billy's mental voltage was peaking, neurons fusing nicely, when he saw a disturbance near the door. He was tall enough to stare over the heads of the crowd, although there wasn't much light in here to see whatever was happening clearly. It didn't last long, a few seconds, before there was a parting of the Red Sea, the dancers springing aside as if a bus was bearing down on them. A couple of buses: two big geezers were surging through the throng. There was something familiar about their uncompromising progress, but he had no time to think about that. They were moving in a straight line towards him. It was time to pray; he tried to remember a prayer. God bless, nighty-night.

One of them ripped out the power cable to the sound system, and a golden arc of flame and sparks ripped over from socket to plug. Silence, a complete silence which was disorientating, deafening, after the aural avalanches of the past few hours.

In the dim light that was left both of them remained visible at the mixing desk a few feet away from him. The nearer of the pair wore a sleeveless T-shirt and his bare shoulder was at the centre of Billy's field of vision. It was mottled and bruised in mauves and blacks, the engrained colours the brandings on a joint in a butcher's display. After a moment the markings resolved themselves into a tattoo of what looked like a Viking helm with runes below it. The shoulder's contours were ridged by snaking veins. Above it a squat neck and hairless head formed itself into a single unyielding limb.

The neck and head turned to scan the crowd and Billy saw eyes that, for an instant, showed the uncertainty of the toddler who, in his solipsism, knows he is king and nothing can hold him back, and has to decide what he should do next.

His accomplice was larger still and dressed more formally, his pinstriped jacket retro-posh. He climbed onto the mixing desk and made a speech. There was a thespian quality to his delivery, rendering his bass reverberations statesmanlike: a young Churchill on steroids rallying the nation.

'We don't know most of you. And you don't know us.'

He raised a broad, heavy arm. Billy looked at the cloth covering it. A Neolithic image: chalk furrows in dark earth.

'But we do our very best to make you happy, to make all your lovely faces smiley.'

They had the committed attention of their audience; the speech was being monitored on a couple of hundred huge, empty pupils.

'We are real people, we have to live in the real world, we like it the way it is.'

He raised both arms to either side as if to encompass all of his world in his embrace. They were real enough, Billy thought, maybe the only reality there was in all of this, making everything else fantasy — the vapid claims of culture, society, law.

'We will do what we can, but we are facing an insidious enemy. If we are not careful it will get the better of us and we will go down once and for all, all of us. We hope it is not too late.'

A lengthy rhetorical pause.

'But this young man' — he pointed to Rick — 'is not with us.'

'Nah,' said Rick, 'I'm—'

His voice was almost inaudible, reedy thinness against the other's bedrock rumble, which drowned him out effortlessly.

'He is a loser. A loss to himself, a loss to you, a loss to us all.'

The denunciatory drama had been short, but the question remained of how serious it was. Any doubts were resolved swiftly. Rick stepped towards the mixing desk and started to remonstrate, he was swatted aside as they strode away. The human sea divided again and they were gone. Billy looked over at Rick, checking to see that he was all right. It hadn't seemed much of a blow from where he was standing. More of a tap.

He peered closer in the gloom and saw that the lower half of Rick's face had become a hole. Insides could be seen which were not meant to be seen. A mouth that was a gaping crater of shiny tissue, slimed with spurts and gobbets of blood, teeth in shattered disarray like a bulldozed picket fence. Dislocated jawbones held the void wide open in a fixed, silent scream.

There was talk of a knuckleduster and someone took Rick off in a car to A&E. It took an hour to put in new fuses and restore the sound system. The mixing desk had buckled under the weight of its temporary human load, but it was working. There was music once again, but there was no more happiness in the house.

Billy knew it was hysteria, but with a small, despicable part of himself he could not help noticing that what the gangsters had done to Rick captured the empty horror that Francis Bacon had aimed for in so many of his paintings, popes and all. At the centre of himself too, while he knew Rick was in a gruesome state, and however much he felt shamed by it, he could not help his relief over his own escape, because it was all-consuming, a glowing rush that grew and grew.

26

Chasing Unfeasible Situations for Evermore

You are standing in the centre of an empty studio acutely aware of the passage of time. Each moment diminishes the total store of moments available to you for the creation of your imminent show. Each moment has another function too, performed with an enviable, inexorable perfection. Each and every moment marks a perfect endpoint for all of the moments that have gone before.

The work which you must produce very soon has to mark another kind of endpoint. An endpoint for art. Not only that, this endpoint has to be different from all its predecessors — or supposed predecessors. You are starting to think the task is impossible, because there have been so many of them before.

None of the ideas you have had so far are any good; you know that much. You try to reassure yourself that the possibilities are infinite, that up to now you have demonstrated an ability to reach out fractionally further than anyone else and to pull in something new. Not only new. It has been art that is both original and archetypal, of the moment and timeless. Your work has always been special, always carried a feeling that it has been simply waiting for someone to bring it into material existence. It has made critics question why no one has done a particular work before, given untutored gallery goers the certainty that they have seen it or something very like it somewhere else.

You are wondering if there is anything left. You have had these doubts for months. You have become sensitive about your creative processes. Those processes that happen and that do not have to happen at all. You fear that they will vanish if you analyse them; you have become superstitious about them, phobic. You have never liked talking to journalists and you have cut that out for good. Those interviews. Saying the same things again and again. Things that should have remained unsaid. The damage that might have been done. That has been done.

You dismiss idea upon idea. You ask yourself whether you can rely on your instinct any more. Eventually something better comes to you, merges with you. You start to feel pleased with yourself. You stop yourself. The work still has to be given an independent physical existence, but it is time for a reward. You look around for your works, for the brown. That affords a different kind of ending.

*

Tom lies upon the bed, naked and secured, tied down on his front, his head to one side. A skydiver captured mid-dive. To start with Becky was flattered, even excited, that he had chosen her to enter his secret life. She was interested in his deviance, but it has become less engaging. The script locked into Tom's cortex takes him away from his failing art, from his disappointments, from all of his experience of being himself. She thinks of the escapism making her videos gives her, but they are life-enhancing for her and it is hard to look upon Tom's compulsive displacements of himself in the same way.

Becky does not enjoy seeing him like this, so vulnerable. Trussed, trust. She does not feel good about whatever is going to happen, yet it is too late to do anything about it. The doorbell. She leads in Tania and Linda. The hue of Tania's hair contrasts with Linda's formal business garb, different varieties of ominous impersonality. They place themselves where Tom can see them. No longer silent, he writhes and strains, makes noises through the gag.

Hhhhhheeeeeeeeuuuuuuuuuuurrrrrrrrrrrrrrrrrrrrrrrrrggggggghhh

Tania stands over him. He is trying to jerk his head under and round so that he doesn't have to face her. She rests a hand on his head. He stops moving.

195

'This isn't a super idea, darling,' says Linda.

'It's the only way,' says Tania.

Becky is anxious, she hopes Tom won't be injured. Tania takes a step back and unbelts and unbuttons her mac, before reaching down and pulling something up and upright. Becky exhales, almost takes a step back. The dildo looks like a zeppelin flying out from Tania's hips, held in place by thick leather straps.

Tom's eyes have widened. Tania discards her mac and snaps on latex gloves. She produces a tube of KY and moves round behind him. There are hollows on the outside of each of his thighs, where his gluteus maximi have contracted to clench his buttocks.

'The important thing is not to tense your muscles. If you do that you'll get hurt.'

phhhluuttt

phhhluuttt

Two sharp slaps on the bottom.

'If you don't relax this is going to damage you.'

Tania dollops the jelly into the crevice, folding and working it in. Spreads it onto the dildo. Climbs onto the bed. She has to put her hands around Tom's throat and squeeze for a few seconds to make him cooperate. Becky starts.

'Stop that,' she says. 'You mustn't hurt him.'

'Don't worry sweetie,' says Linda. 'She's done plenty of this before.'

'Stop,' says Becky. She starts to weep. 'I can't stand this.'

'This isn't a video you can put on pause,' says Tania.

'I'm sorry, darling,' says Linda. 'It's too late.'

Becky thinks of running out and phoning the police. As if she can hear Becky's thoughts, Linda stands in front of the studio's outside door.

'It will be over soon,' Linda says.

Tania has abandoned the giant dildo. She can't get anywhere with it, so she has selected another one that is less formidable. Even so, it is still difficult for her to get into Tom, but she applies more lubricant and then she manages it.

196

She is moving back and forth, powerful thrusts that make the bed legs skitter and judder about on the floor. Her head scores and re-scores a horizontal red streak in the air. Most of Tom is concealed beneath her, but patches of his pale skin rhythmically appear and disappear beneath her.

Becky is still weeping but she cannot help abstracting herself. Prompted by Tania's brutal dismissal, she compares this scene to her installations, with their domestic settings and violent sub-texts — but she stops herself because what she has initiated here is an abusive act which has gone beyond her control.

Tom's eyes are closed so tightly the lids are wrinkling. Even so, his own tears start to sprout and sprinkle. Flowers are blooming on either side of his thighs, dark red flowers, stippled and latticed with browns and yellows. His breathing is fast and choking. Linda makes Tania stop by pulling back on her hair, clutching its flame in her hand.

'Fucking hell. That's enough now.'

Becky has never heard Linda swear before. Tania clambers off, smoothing the back of her head.

'Careful. That fucking hurt.'

'Sorry, sweetie.'

Tania leans over and pats Tom on the shoulder.

'That was a good gallop, wasn't it?'

She goes to clean herself up in the bathroom, before departing with Linda. Becky unties Tom. Gasping, trembling, crying. He won't look at her, dresses himself and resorts to the bathroom in turn before staggering out. She stares at the sheet. It will have to be thrown away. The rope too, she won't need it any more. Tom utters a single sentence before leaving, gets the words out with difficulty. They will return to Becky repeatedly:

'It must have been Alastair, all of it.'

27

Childhood at an End

I was at a private view over in the West End, Pauline Collard's latest work. There was the usual acid wine, fatty canapés and poor acoustics — why is it that every single venue in the West End, be it a bar, gallery, restaurant or club, has such shitty acoustics? I don't think my hearing's falling off, not yet, because from the start I had to strain to catch conversation in all of these places.

The show was disappointing; it becomes more and more obvious that none of Collard's new work will ever match the art she made in the early 1990s. I saw Soames in the crowd, went over and greeted him. Why not? He didn't recognise me at first, needed reminding — irritating that, because he's a PR man after all. Presumably I didn't come across like a potential client; he must have clocked my tatty denim jacket and old Vans. He's doing well, represents several big galleries and a few wealthy institutes. No stopping him. The art market continues to grow as part of colossal general asset inflation, driven by all the cheap money and the dirty money. It's many times larger than it was three decades ago and Soames has risen with it.

He looked almost the same, hair nearly gone. He didn't seem all that interested in the art, but that's to be expected from a publicist. He was there either because he represented Collard or wanted to. A complacent baby-boomer, but then exuding well-being is the PR man's stock in trade. As well as not giving much away. I had ventured over in that spirit of, well, we're all grown up now so let's be more open and nicer with each other, but Soames was already all that he was to become back then and he was not going to be any different now. So we had our chat about nothing much, and then out of nowhere he asked me about Alastair. Which was odd, that he would have retained any interest in Alastair.

He asked if it was true that Alastair had a large family trust fund behind him. I said it was news to me if he had. There was never any sign of it at the time, and if it was true, things would have turned out very differently. Soames nodded, said he was curious, that was all. He'd been very impressed by Alastair but wondered how he could finance the whole set up. That was more or less the end of our exchange; I wanted to get over to Liverpool Street station and catch my train back to Essex. It was all amicable enough, although I could see Soames casting discreet glances over my shoulder to see if there was anyone nearby more worthy of schmoozing. It's not that he's a hollow man, he talked of his daughter starting university, and maybe I'm being naïve but I'm not sure you can be completely hollow and a family man.

Every few years I hear a rumour about Alastair. The last one was Arab money. They are invariably word of mouth, always come from someone unlikely. None of them ever make it into the press. Alastair didn't have much of a public profile even at the time, and there's nothing in the aftermath other than this occasional hearsay.

Except there are the dreams. Occasionally I have dreams about Alastair, even though I haven't seen him for more than thirty years. In some of these dreams I am trying to find my address book, then searching for his number, before trying to find the telephone and dialling directory enquiries. No matter how long and how hard I search, I can never discover his whereabouts.

Sometimes Alastair does make an appearance. I am mounting the stairs to his studio and I know that another marathon session is about to start, and that this time he will explain everything to me and it will all be fine. I get through the door and take my seat at the table alongside him and the others, see my troubled face reflected in a mirror on the table, a mirror on which rests a fantastical amount of powder before Alastair turns to me. Always the dream ends before he can speak to me and I awake sweating, disturbed, deeply troubled, before I can collect myself and remember that no explanations are ever needed from an old friend.

*

Tania and Erick were on the pavement outside Tania's studio in Bethnal Green. Tania made her art in Hoxton for a while, but the rent for her studio there trebled a couple of months back and for now this area was reliably cheap. Once inside the main door she checked her pigeonhole for mail before they ascended to her workspace on the first floor.

'What kind of building has this been?' asked Erick.

'Some sort of municipal office,' she said. 'Look at the glazed walls and these stone steps.'

The frenetic chaos of the street had gone, to be replaced by a frigid calm. No sounds were emanating from the other studios. All their doors were shut, most of them secured with padlocks.

'No one around,' said Erick.

'Fucking good when it's quiet like this,' she said.

Tania unlocked her door and they entered the studio. The air was dank and she opened a window. As the glass pivoted feeble sunlight quivered in it. A mass of cold air gushed in; swiftly she slammed it shut again.

'Tea?'

Erick didn't hear. He was staring at the installation.

The box was practically half built and already it dominated the space. Its sides rested on supports and it looked like a vessel in a dry dock: a ship to sail away in.

'My god, Tania.'

'It's going to be four metres by three by three when it's finished.'

Erick walked around it, staring. His hands moved towards his pockets.

'Don't light up in here.'

'I am sorry. Why is it becoming so big?'

'That's how it's come to me.'

'But there is nothing in it.'

'Well, yeah, I'm starting to think it is just a fucking heap of wood.'

Momentarily Erick was distracted by Tania's hairdo. Her hemispherical coiffure extended some way further upwards, so that it was as if she had an enormous strawberry upon her head. His attention returned to her installation and he busied himself with its technical details.

'What sort of wood has it?'

'Ash and oak. There's a sympathetic magic they carry.'

The wood was an oddly reassuring natural intrusion into the studio's artificial environment. It was new but its grain embodied immeasurable volumes of history and life.

'This has a powerful presence,' he said.

'I've become so involved,' she said, 'that I've stopped drinking and doing charlie.'

'That is not sounding good.'

Erick continued to stare at the box.

'Can I ask of you a straightforward question?'

'Go ahead.'

'Why do you bring me here?'

'To see what you make of it.'

Erick paced a little more, a clockwork soldier. The disparity in height between the pair was marked as they stood side by side looking at the box, which lay there waiting for them. Erick smiled with his tiny teeth.

'I am thinking,' he said, 'nothing.'

'Don't fucking rub it in.'

'I do not rub this in.'

*

As he closed his front door behind him something caught his eye. He turned back to look and was saturated by fear. There was a huge red 'X' painted crudely on his front door. It wasn't random vandalism. He knew it was a message: X marked the spot for imminent carnage. He'd thought he'd got away with it when Rick had been singled out instead of him, but he'd been wrong. He moaned, broke into a run down the corridor. He was going to be erased.

Freezing darkness had descended by the time he was making his way up to Alastair's flat, taking two and three steps at a time. Always he was aware of ascending these stairs with a mounting excitement. It was a ritual, an essential preliminary to doing awful amounts of charlie. Billy knew that the sight alone of their dealers gave some cokeheads erections, their bodies thrown into confusion by overwhelming anticipatory surges. That did not happen to him, but there was no doubt that ascending those stairs and knocking at that door stirred up his brain's pleasure centres.

This time it was different, with crucial elements in the ritual disrupted. It was only late afternoon, despite the absence of daylight, and he was uninvited. The front door was open, leaving an orifice that was forbidding and forbidden. Alastair made some concessions to discretion and security, and normally it was closed and locked.

In his desperation he could not see why any of this should make any difference. Alastair would sort him out; in his mind he was already lowering the end of a rolled banknote onto a big fat one. He ventured down between the dirty pine walls of the small hallway to see that the living room door also lay ajar. Greed propelled him onwards. He saw the empty chairs around the table and then Alastair, standing by the window. Alastair turned to him.

'Ah, it's great that you've made it. We have arrangements to finalise.'

'Arrangements?'

Alastair looked at him again, started.

'I'm sorry, Billy. I thought you were Kevin Thorn.'

There was a pause as Alastair gazed at him questioningly, appraised the situation, raised his arms wide.

'I'm right out. Please bear with me.'

28

Phantasm

Becky is in her bedsit. A cup of green tea is beside her, cold and untouched. Her clothing is crumpled and grubby, and her hair has an oily sheen because she hasn't washed it for a few days. She stands and walks around, returns to sit on her futon, looks downwards and becomes irritated by the fliers for private views and other events littering the threadbare carpet, each trying to crowd out the others with provocative images and lettering.

She thinks of friendship. Her peers at Goldsmiths' are fading away in the face of her coup at IS, one or two making noises about her selling out. The likelihood is that most of them will never get a start as artists, though that was always the deal. Her new friends are working artists, and yet to be an artist is to be in competition with all other artists. Alastair has held them together in temporary alliance only.

Her finger rises to touch her scar. Whether it is because of her childhood or her creative disposition, always she needs to step back from humanity and that stops her being fully part of it. Tom was as vulnerable in his difference as she in hers and she betrayed him. Whatever happens in her life from now on this shame will always be part of it.

Becky looks critically at the Helen Chadwick print on the wall in front of her. It no longer excites her and she decides to get rid of it. Her gaze traverses the bedsit again and she thinks that the sooner she moves out the better. She can afford to rent a live/work space now, or even a flat and a separate studio. The noisy dolt next door playing his atrocious music through the walls (it is very often Boney M). The mould in the bathroom. The stains over the ceilings, whole continents of damp submerging her self-esteem.

The tepid heating, which means she has to put her coat over her duvet at night. Hoxton. The most fashionable area of town and nothing more than a slum — it should be pulled down and something better put in its place, something bright and shining, but she knows that is not going to happen.

She realises that she needs a break, she will not be sorry to leave all this behind for a couple of months. Becky would like to go to Japan to see her father. She is sure she would have become an artist regardless of him but she does like his work, confrontational anti-art with roots in 1960s happenings and counter-culture politics. His life has been more engaged than hers. So far her life has consisted of skating over surfaces, like one of the flat stones men always pick up on beaches and bounce over waves.

Most of the time no one sees past her looks. She is an exotic companion who makes the people around her look cosmopolitan and cool. Cool. The mask of indifference African American jazz musicians cultivated on the road, bolstered by heroin addiction, because of their need to distance themselves from their oppression. Cool is meaningless for privileged British people. They are all rude for so much of the time, either aloof and dismissive, or talking over each other. So careless about face.

Becky decides she will wait for the announcement of the Shiraz Prize winners and depart after that, though she hasn't decided whether or what to enter for the award yet. Leaving London for a while is a welcome prospect. She has never paid enough attention to her other culture. On her rare visits to Tokyo as a teenager, every chance she got she was off to Shinjuku to drink in the latest in clothes, music and film. Mostly her father would approve half-heartedly, while her grandparents would point out patiently that so much of this was western or western inspired. They tried to direct her to her own traditions, encouraged her to improve her Japanese, but she was too young to listen. Occasionally her father looked thoughtful when she returned with her laden shopping bags or when she played rock music loudly in her room. Yet only occasionally: the shame his generation endured over their society's devastating fall from grace was almost terminally severe, and its members were left unwilling to question the west and its culture, to talk about the ways consumerism and materialism created spiritual voids, fostered nihilism. It is only now Becky is adult that she can start to sidestep this sustained self-deprecation.

Her early separations from her Japanese self mean that when she visits Tokyo always she feels like a tourist. This does bring benefits. Those first bows from the stewardess on the plane — Air Japan, no other airline will do — then landing at Narita. Buying herself a copy of Hanako and reading it on the train to Shibuya. Saying hello again to the Hachiko statue. Autumn in Yoyogi Park, the Gingko leaves in golden walkways beneath her feet. She will eat better food, wash in proper baths. Apologise wholeheartedly to her favourite city for leaving it behind for so long. Listen to the cicadas, smoke her first Seven Stars. The schoolboys in their Prussian jackets. Even the pachinko parlours — she never thought she would miss those.

Leaving Tokyo by bullet train, trying not to look through the window at the dizzying rush outside. The deep, deep green of the countryside. She will arrive at her grandparents' house. They struggle with her twin states of being, gaijin and non-gaijin, but they are kindly.

She will rest there and explore the yin and yang of her dual background in luxurious freedom from London and its claustrophobic winter. She will assimilate her Japanese heritage more thoroughly. Membership of a society which lays stress on the group instead of the individual. Where there is less jockeying for position, where everyone and everything has its accepted place in a universe empty of separate self.

Her eyes fill. The dirt on the outside of the window foxes the reflection of the interior into smeary blurs of light. As she squints through teared lids the blurs slide inwards, to coalesce into an image of Alastair, but white-haired and lined, smiling sadly. She blinks and the image melts away.

*

'It's about a quarter of a mile away,' said Harkness. 'Don't look like that — all we're going to do is stand in the street.'

What Billy was, was no longer a human being but an unstable mass of craving. He needed charlie, not a jaunt down the Piccadilly Line. They were outside the tube exit and he looked around. For him this was a blank section of the A to Z: he wasn't in the habit of venturing into Knightsbridge, he didn't shop at Harrods, he didn't go to royal garden parties.

He had deliberated long and hard before setting out. What was the point in assisting the police with their enquiries if they hadn't arrested you? He didn't see how he could benefit from co-operating with Harkness, but it was true that Harkness could cart him off any time he liked, and that a search of his flat would land him in prison for a long time. Ten years, maybe. He would be no different by the time he was released; there was not even that consolation. There were plenty of drugs on the in.

'Posh round here,' said Harkness.

It reeked money. There were no dilapidated industrial buildings. White cliffs of townhouses ran down each side of the street. They were flanked by trees, copses of them set into generous gardens and grounds. It was easy to see there had been little recent development round here. Bar a few low-rise apartment blocks it looked to Billy as if nothing new had been built for half a century. In and around the shops and apartments there was a moving mosaic of pedestrians and traffic, many humans clad in furs, many luxury vehicles made in Germany, and perhaps somewhere within it all there were artists partying and throwing down their challenges to life — but that seemed unlikely to him. Within another half a century Hoxton would be as arid as this, he thought, Alastair or no Alastair.

He didn't know of any artists or curators round here, but there would be collectors. He thought about Lanchester and where he might be living — probably somewhere even posher, Belgravia or Chelsea as befitted a plutocrat — before he wondered whether he was anywhere near the part of Kensington where Francis Bacon had his studio. A few streets further on Harkness halted on the corner of a small mews, checked his watch.

'What I want to do tonight is to get you to have a look at them. Keep your eyes on that house diagonally opposite.'

They stood and watched for a couple of minutes while nothing happened. This was torture. Billy considered Alastair's decision not to give him more coke; it was hard to believe that he had run out. He could think more clearly if he had a line or two. If Alastair had sorted him he wouldn't have resorted to this, could have phoned Harkness and fobbed him off with some excuse.

Nothing was still happening at the house opposite. This clod of a copper had dragged him all the way across London for no good reason. He should have got himself a solicitor instead, found out exactly where he stood legally before he remembered solicitors cost money and he didn't have any. His need intensified and overtook him. He touched Harkness's elbow.

'Can you sort me out?'

Harkness looked back at him.

'It's that bad is it?'

Billy nodded. It was pointless saying more. Harkness was the last person on earth he wanted to know about his craving.

'It doesn't usually get people this badly. There must be something else going on with you.'

He shrugged as he handed Billy a small plastic phial, an action both magical and sordid. Relief obliterated shame as he examined the container. It was half full of powder and when he unscrewed the top it came off with a tiny spoon attached to it, a miniature ladle with a vertical handle. Some powder was already on the spoon. He applied it to one nostril, fed another spoonful into the other.

'Cheers.'

He tried to hand it back.

'It's yours. Now watch closely.'

A Daimler pulled up to the pavement, followed by an Audi and a BMW, then a couple of large and opulent saloons of marques unknown to him. Men in dark suits climbed out, doors went home with weighty reports. The town house's front door opened and a maid in an elaborate uniform — she looked like a Filipina — admitted the visitors.

'They're very punctual; they always arrive together. Look up the street there.'

Harkness nudged him and nodded. Alastair was flanked by the thugs who had invaded the warehouse party. This time both of them, too, wore suits and there was seigneurship in their stride, as if all Kensington had laid itself out before them for ceremonial inspection. Billy had no time to scrutinise Alastair closely before the trio turned and vanished through the entrance.

'That's all we're going to see tonight.'

Harkness walked off in the direction of the tube. He followed.

'It looked like a funding meeting of some kind of arts organisation,' said Billy.

'It didn't strike you as odd in any way?'

He speculated aloud, careful not to let slip he recognised Alastair's companions.

'Alastair was being interviewed by a group of trustees, very likely. It's unusual for an arts board to be entirely composed of white men nowadays, I suppose. But then benefactors have to be wealthy and maybe there were some other board members inside anyway.'

'That building isn't any kind of official institution with trustees, Billy. There's no nameplate, it's a very discreet set up.'

'It's one of the board member's houses isn't it? Nothing very unusual about that. If you've got all that space you might as well use it.'

'Some of them are property developers who've invested heavily in Hoxton and Shoreditch over the past couple of years. The two big guys are enforcers. And several of them are members of an organisation called England Forward.

'Never heard of it. Is it something to do with football? '

'It's a far-right group with paramilitary ambitions. It doesn't have a public face.'

'Alastair can't possibly be mixed up with them.'

Harkness fell silent. In and around the rich swirls of coke shunting into his brain, it struck Billy that this was some sort of answer to the bewildering question of where Alastair's money came from. Property developers — that made sense. It explained the enforcers too, and it wasn't surprising they were involved in drugs as well. Why wouldn't they be? The far-right stuff, though, that was bonkers. He didn't see how the thugs, formidable though they were, could be more than hired muscle and coke dealers. More importantly, he knew he couldn't discuss any of this with Harkness.

They were nearing the tube station.

'How do I know that you're not making all of this up?'

'Why would I? Listen, England Forward fund their activities through donations from wealthy supporters, notably some of the gentlemen you saw this evening. They have links to other neo-Nazi groups in Europe. We believe they're planning a violent action.'

'Arrest them.'

'We haven't got enough evidence for that.'

'So you want me to do what, exactly?'

'Why don't you think some more about how you can help us? This is where I love you and leave you.'

Harkness walked off into the tube station, leaving him standing there on the pavement.

29

You Mustn't Touch This

Imagine the perfect video for The Fall's 1993 cover version of *Lost in Music*. The setting is a kitchen, not a well-appointed kitchen. The units are old, their veneer cracked and fissured and coated in grease. One cupboard door is angled down to make a diagonal across the recess behind, held askew by a single hinge. Another is gone altogether. A naked light bulb hangs from a flex furred with filth, below an eczemic ceiling. Through a dirty window the midriff of a dirty tower block is visible, indicating we are halfway up another dirty tower block.

Action begins with a lone figure opening a freezer and taking a shoebox-sized package from it. His movements are rapid and erratic, and he is charged with sweat. It drips from his forehead and large, dark patches of it are visible under his arms. He stares at the package for a few moments, then rolls a banknote into a tube which he lays to one side, ready. Trembling hands move towards the package. Then he starts, twitches in his seat. He has heard something.

He rises and exits, returning quickly with a second figure. A brief conversation ensues. The first figure is making a lot of elaborate arm gestures, perhaps in an attempt to defend himself against some unspecified charge. The second figure picks up the package and exits. The first figure sits slumped in his chair for a while. Then he starts upright again and stares round at something outside of our line of sight. Something which, given his expression of terror, he finds alarming.

Two new figures charge into the room. They are muscular and determined. Furniture is knocked over, kicked aside. The first figure is extracted from the chair and tossed from one to the other, like a parcel. He is held aloft, first upright and then upside down. The biggest intruder thrusts the chair through the window several times. The glass around the edges of the frame becomes angular shards, before mostly disappearing following further thrusts. The first figure is held out of the window by the biggest intruder. We get a rear view of him, and we see the stripes of a pin stripe jacket flicker and ripple.

Fortunately for the first figure this is not full-blown defenestration. The other intruder pulls a bulky portable phone from his pocket to take a call and moves over quickly to the biggest intruder, who yanks the first figure back in through the window. After his retraction he is left lying on his side on the kitchen floor. The remains of the chair are lying behind him, so that it looks as if he and it are all of a piece. We can see that, where it isn't concealed by food packaging, newspapers and other rubbish, the floor is slicked in grease and dirt. The two intruders leave swiftly and purposefully, but not triumphantly. The naked lightbulb shines down from the end of its furry flex. The first figure continues to lie on the floor on his side.

30

Unfaithfulness of the Image

Near the beginning of your career you meet young and inexperienced journalists. Sometimes in interviews they share material about themselves which relates in a direct or indirect way to something you are saying. You do not respond. You might actually talk over them, to get what you want to say across and to stop them deviating off into irrelevancies from their own lives. This isn't nice, but you are there to talk about your work and your concerns, and not about them.

Journalists who are older and more professional do not fall into the trap of dropping in personal confidences and leaving themselves exposed to this ignominious treatment. They know that the interview is not an equal exchange, but their awareness of this is also a problem. They might not be fully aware of the resentment it causes them, but they do resent it. They believe that they are talented creative people too, at least as talented as you are. Even though they have to sit there discussing you, and not them. The result is that, whether they are conscious of it or not, they will be out to get you.

You are vulnerable. The most significant aspect of your personality is that you have a massively overdeveloped ego. You could not be a successful artist otherwise. Your ego ensures that your art gets made and that it is put on display to reach as many people as possible. Unfortunately it doesn't stop there. Your ego dictates you are the most important person in your life and that your art comes before anything else. You must try to conceal this monstrousness from predatory interviewers.

You have practised at this a lot and it is no longer difficult. This enormous elision means that the interviews will have little or no meaningful content about you, but there is no fundamental deception or duplicity involved. Saying what you really think about yourself, and everyone else and your work and everything in general would not make your art any more or less explicable. Which is the crux. Interviews are hazardous because you risk putting your sociopathy on display, but they are also pointless because they are never any use for explaining the only important thing — the work. Because you cannot explain creativity. It is not a rational process and its irrationality is not accessible. What inspired you to do this? Where did you get that idea from? Shite, all of it.

*

'Any idea what the cricket score is, mate?' Soames asked.

'None at all,' he said.

They were seated in a small office in an anonymous block near Covent Garden. Thorn had not yet appeared, but Soames assured him he would be along soon. Billy could barely believe that Alastair had pulled this off for him.

The pain of the past few weeks was falling away. Armies of journalists out there would elbow him aside to be here in his place, but this wasn't only a supremely privileged opportunity to talk to Thorn about his art. Alastair had his agenda, which Billy supported of course, and it went beyond publicising Thorn's show in Idiot Savant. Of all the artists Alastair had brought together, Thorn was the one who most personified Alastair's vision for art. Billy hoped Thorn would give his own take on that vision and, if so, he would record it for posterity to the best of his ability. He could do no more than that for Alastair.

He noticed a photograph of an infant daughter on Soames' desk, all bunches and gums, her eyes as shiny as the metal frame around the picture. Soames caught his glance.

'Great smile, hey? She'd do well in this business.'

He grunted, the vision of an expanding tribe of Soameses was unattractive. His receding sandy hair, his Next off-the-peg, his uncritical acceptance of the role of public relations in art — the twenty minutes he had been in Soames's company seemed penally longer. He looked at the print on the wall opposite.

'That's a Miro, isn't it?'

'Is it? Can't say I know the first thing about art, to be honest. My business is dealing with people. I'm a people person.'

For want of anything better to do Billy began to flick through his file of cuttings on Kevin Thorn again. He started when he saw himself staring up from one of them, before realising that it was a picture of Thorn. There did seem to be a superficial resemblance between them. In his sole interview this year, with (bizarrely) a student magazine, Thorn was quoted as saying:

> Money and celebrity are utterly meaningless for me. My art is the only thing that matters to me. There will never be anything else in my life. I am my art and my art is me. There is never an hour during the day when I am not thinking of my art, wherever I am and whatever I'm doing. It is a slavering monster. It can never get its fill.

Billy had never come across anyone so possessed, but he had to accept, regardless of his ambitions to explore Thorn's relationship with art, there might be no real revelations to come. He wasn't naive. This encounter might give rise to an interesting piece of writing of passing interest, like his Bacon interview, and not necessarily much more. It was opportunity to stand at the edge of Thorn's inner world for three-quarters of an hour or so, looking over but unable to venture in.

None of this put him off. He couldn't wait to meet Thorn and put his questions to him. To start with *The Herald*'s arts editor hadn't been keen. He'd asked Billy to hold off for a couple of weeks, before he pointed out that he had an exclusive interview with the most exciting young artist in Britain. An initial invitation to write up the interview as a trial in return for an offer of some undefined further work with *The Herald* at an unspecified future date had been refused. After the commission was agreed in principle Billy demanded a heavyweight — not to say obese — fee, on the basis they both knew he could get more money elsewhere for the feature, and finally extracted begrudging assent for that too.

Silence. Silence was no good, because then he began to think, to think of how much he needed more coke. The phial Harkness had given him was long empty. The silence registered on Soames and, like a good PR man, he tried to fill it.

'I was delighted when Linda pushed this deal for press and publicity liaison my way,' he said. 'It looks as if Kevin is going to become bigger, much bigger.'

'We're agreed on that.'

'I should warn you that he can be kind of, well, challenging.'

'Yes, I do know.'

'I can't think why he bothers. A glass or two of wine's enough for me.'

'Do you believe he plays up to that image?'

'God knows. I couldn't do my job if I was bothered by questions like that, matey.'

'I see what you mean.'

'I'm sure he'll be here soon.'

Billy pondered the likely size of the monthly retainer Linda Bloom was paying Soames. It would be much more than the fee he would get for his feature for sure, obese or not. His attention wandered. He was trying not to grind his teeth, he had prided himself on not grinding away like a cokehead when he did charlie, and now he found his molars grating because he didn't have any.

He had been so close to opening the package and getting his hands on more charlie than he could ever snort, and it had all been taken from him and he had been left, instead, with a seriously extensive collection of cuts and bruises. It was fortunate there were none on his face, that all of the glass had been smashed out of the window before he was dangled from it, held and shaken a hundred feet up in the air, wailing like a baby freshly birthed from the tower block, poised to slip from the midwife's hands onto the concrete far below. The knowledge his assailants had been about to let him drop, that only a phone call alerting them to other business had stopped them — this had broken him. Soames cleared his throat but he got in first, reluctant to endure further patter.

'It would have been easier to interview Kevin in his studio.'

'Kevin was dead against that. He said it would be an unwarranted intrusion. This is his first interview for months and to start with he refused point blank.'

'He wants to sell his art, doesn't he?'

'He's busy finishing off his next show, so go easy on him. It opens in a couple of days.'

'Yes obviously I am aware of that, but it's not as if it's his first interview.'

'He has made it clear to me that he wants to avoid certain topics altogether.'

'Such as?'

'Specifically he doesn't want to talk about his current work, his previous shows, his views on contemporary art and the art scene generally, and anything related to his personal life.'

'What does that leave me to talk about? Precisely nothing.'

'There's no need to exaggerate.'

'What's left? Go on, tell me what's left.'

The photographer arrived. He was bearded with long hair, rancid and sticky looking, and he was wearing a biker's leather jacket with many straps, buckles and metal trimmings. Perhaps he was a biker, thought Billy. He was assertive enough to be a biker.

'Look, how long have I got for the shot? You've got to give me a decent amount of time.'

'Kevin's very busy,' said Soames, 'would ten minutes at the end of the interview be all right?'

'You must be joking. It's not been worth my while coming down for that. I'll need three quarters of an hour, minimum.'

Billy did not bother intervening and arguing on the snapper's behalf; he didn't give a shit how long he needed to take his pictures. There were library shots of Thorn which could be used. Granted, a new image would brighten up the spread, but his mind was burdened enough without worrying about pictures. Thorn might not turn up at all. What a sinful waste of time, time he could be using to get hold of a dealer to sell him more charlie.

The snapper and the agent wrangled. Eventually they agreed that the snapper would start setting his equipment up and do the shoot while he conducted the interview. Billy did not think much of this; Thorn would probably be a tough interviewee and he would need his full attention. Yet there was nothing he could do. The snapper unpacked his bags and cases methodically, extracting umbrellas, reflectors, cables, meters and rods.

Billy's thoughts turned to the trip to Knightsbridge. He had done some research on England Forward and as far as he could see it was a nebulous organisation if it really existed at all. It seemed to be a kind of honey pot, a long running trap set up by the Special Branch and the security services to attract far right sympathisers. Anti-Nazi activists got drawn in along with them and the organisation appeared to be a focus for attempts to discredit them too. What Alastair and the gangsters had been doing in Knightsbridge remained obscure. Most likely it hadn't been an England Forward meeting at all; why would it have been?

None of what he had seen showed that Alastair was mixed up with Nazis. Harkness might want him to believe that for reasons of his own, though god knows what they would be. Most likely what they had witnessed was simply a meeting of property developers. Why Alastair was there was unclear unless he was asking them for money. Or maybe they were trying to get him to give them money back or demanding that he vacate the French Place building. Nothing was straightforward or verifiable. But whatever it was all about, he didn't want to know.

Harkness had rung him a couple of days afterwards and left a long message on the answerphone but he wiped it. He was too paranoid to listen and he wasn't going to tell Harkness anything — not after the gangsters' visit to his flat. Besides, he had nothing to tell anyway. He didn't have the package any more.

After the first half hour they all ran out of tasks to occupy themselves. Soames tried ringing Thorn and got no response. The photographer made noises about the other job he had to go to. They all knew that he would stay because the pictures would be lucrative. Soames' personal assistant, a trustafarian with received pronunciation to bely her dreadlocks, fetched them tea and coffee and managed to get all of the orders wrong. Billy thought it looked as if snow was starting to fall outside the windows, but he didn't say anything in case it was some sort of flashback from the acid.

'What made you decide to get offices out here?' he asked Soames.

'The firm's been based here for a long time. We would never set up in Hoxton; that's not the sort of image we're looking for.'

'Hoxton's on the way up.'

'Yeah, but it looks deprived. We've got a lot of international clients, and I'm not sure what they'd think about traipsing over there and seeing all that.'

Conversation died once more. There was a tension between wanting to leave in disgust and the desire to wait around so as not to miss anything. Thorn was exercising remote control over them. He was more important than they were so they had to hang on. Yet it wasn't simply a power dynamic, Billy reflected. Thorn had a sense of drama, and like a rock star he knew enough to turn up as late as possible, to keep his audience guessing.

Thorn arrived an hour later. He was tall and stooped, pale and gangling inside a long black leather coat, a larva undulating in a decaying cocoon. Billy noted that his gait was unsteady and his eyes unfocussed. He wondered why, there was no smell of alcohol. Instead he detected another odour, which he struggled to recognise. Soames was on his feet.

'Kevin, so good to see you. Thanks for coming in, let me introduce you—'

'I haven't got time for this.

'It'll only take a few minutes,' said Soames.

Billy had died many deaths while waiting for Thorn and now he experienced another, swifter demise. He needed more than a few minutes; he required up to an hour, maybe a couple of hours, to get enough material for any kind of adequate piece. Surely Thorn would understand that?

'I'm too busy. I came over simply to explain that.'

Thorn was addressing himself exclusively to Soames.

'Come on Kevin, give it a go,' said Soames. 'You've made it over here.'

'All right, but I can't spend too long over it. I have to get back.'

Billy asked himself how much work Thorn was going to be able to do, off his head and smelling foully. Soames nodded at him, and he addressed Thorn.

'So what's your new show going to be about?'

Thorn glanced in his direction and then looked over at Soames, who intervened.

'No, he's said he can't talk about that.'

'How do you think it represents a departure from your last show?'

'I'm not discussing anything to do with my current show. I've always been independent of the media in my career and I don't owe you people anything.'

Thorn stood there, rubbing his back with one hand, making no move to sit down. He appeared determined not to do anything which might demonstrate any commitment to the interview.

'How about starting at the other end, then? What made you decide to become an artist?'

'What a silly fucking question.'

'Some of the people who read this feature might be thinking of becoming artists. You could help them.'

For a bare second it struck him that Thorn could give him some advice about going to art school if he could be steered that way. Thorn was one of his own, after all. Although it was becoming obvious that he didn't have a working-class Essex accent, whatever the likes of Linda Bloom said.

'What a load of shit,' said Thorn. 'They can ask their teachers for help, can't they? They'd be in real trouble if they made career decisions based on something someone said in a fucking newspaper.'

He looked over at Soames again, jerked a thumb at Billy.

'Who is this tosser?'

He did not know what to do. Thorn had not recognised him or had pretended not to recognise him. The photographer was arranging his equipment, and a tripod leg struck Thorn's shin.

'You, fuckwit,' he said.

'Accident, mate.'

This was thrown back by the photographer, who was bent over his gear. Thorn cuffed the back of his head. It was not a heavy blow but the photographer turned and squared up to him, began to deliver punches to his face with the application of a hungry man devouring his dinner, flicking aside Thorn's attempts to retaliate with practised ease. Soames tried to restrain the photographer from behind before an elbow caught him in the mouth and he screamed and fell back.

The violence wrested a paradigm for itself within which everything seemed simultaneously faster and slower than normal. By now Thorn was on the carpet with the photographer staring down at him unblinkingly.

'You tosser, wasting my fucking time and hitting me.'

THU-WAKK

A kick with the sound of a carpet being beaten. The photographer was shod in boots which, like his jacket, were decorated with studs and chains. Thorn was lucky to be wearing a heavy coat, Billy thought.

'Do you want some more?'

'... —...'

THUM-K

Straight to the belly, the boot's silver side chains momentarily lost to view in Thorn.

Billy did not move, he could not save Thorn and the photographer might give him a kicking too.

Soames watched, blood globbing on his mouth, but did not venture into the mêlée again. Instead he picked up a phone with a shaky arm.

'Is that security? Sorry, I'll redial.'

'Do you want some more?' repeated the photographer.

'No.'

A weary negative of regret and resignation.

'And you should take a bath, you dirty bastard.'

CHU-WAK

Are you going to have a bath?'

CUWU-AK

'Yes.'

Barely audible, the timorous assent of an infant.

The photographer strolled to one of his hold-alls, lifted out an SLR and took a few shots of Thorn reclining on the carpet. The flashes threw the room into stark relief, parting lightning bolts from a Zeus who had chastised a refractory mortal. He packed up his equipment methodically. The interview was over.

Uuuuuuuuuunnnnnnnnnnnnnnnnnnnnnnnnn

Thorn started to moan. Soames was still on the phone.

'What do you mean it's his lunch break? Lunch was hours ago. What kind of security service are we paying for?'

The photographer and Billy left. Soames followed them to the door.

'We'll sue you for assault.'

The photographer turned, and Soames shrank back.

'No you won't. He hit me first.'

He nodded back towards Thorn.

'Anyway, the smelly bastard deserved a spank.'

They walked through the door and out, unimpeded. As he threaded his way through an unseasonal crowd of tourists on his way to the tube Billy threw a pound coin into a living statue's hat, aware that things had changed in a way that would take him a while to catch up with. Alastair was in the gallery office to greet him on his return.

'How did it go?'

'Very well.'

The phone rang in the rear of the gallery. Billy picked it up, recognised Soames' voice and switched on the tape recorder that was hardwired into his landline.

'You mustn't write anything about this.'

'But I must.'

'Then you'll never interview any of my clients again.'

'You haven't exactly been offering them up to me on a plate, have you?'

'We'll sue. Your photographer assaulted our client.'

'The photographer was entitled to defend himself.'

'If you print something that upsets Kevin it might affect his work.'

'He wasn't going to do much work in that condition was he? He's on smack isn't he? I could see his pupils.'

'Look, whatever you do, don't publish anything about that. Between you and me, I thought he was over the heroin, but the pressure of the new show's got to him.'

'What about the smell?'

'I don't know with any certainty, but I think when he's on it he forgets about hygiene — that's definitely off the record.'

'Ed, thanks very much for telling me all that. I am definitely going to use it. And you'll be interested to know that I've got the whole of this conversation on tape.'

Brief silence, before:

'You can't use it without my permission.'

'Yes I can. You'll find that's perfectly legal. It's sometimes illegal to tape or reproduce telephone conversations between third parties but none of that applies here.'

For want of an effective rejoinder, Soames hung up. Why had he let slip confirmation of Thorn's habit? Presumably seeing Thorn getting a kicking had made him distraught, skewed his judgement. He would probably lose his client but that wasn't Billy's concern, which was to deliver the feature as quickly as possible and then to source some drugs of his own.

*

Alastair had long gone, he was finalising the text, when the back-office door was wrenched open. Tania placed a foot up on his desk and stared at him. He gazed at her footwear, a large white trainer with its laces tied into an emphatically neat bow, and then looked up at her, smiled weakly.

'Well, hi, Tania, I—'

'I thought you'd be skulking around in here.'

'Not skulking—'

'What the fuck have you been up to?'

'I'm sorry?'

Her lipstick matched her hair and her nails perfectly, he saw, all of them a raw bloody red.

'You are going to be sorry. Becky's told me you're involved in whatever it is that's going on.'

'Becky—'

'Don't even think of bothering her again. Tell me what you've done or I'm really going to fuck you up.'

'Nothing, there's absolutely nothing—'

'You can stop that right now, you wanker, I've been burgled.'

'You can't blame me for that. Everyone burgles everyone else all the time round here.'

'Fucking funny aren't you? I just know it's something to do with you. My place was wrecked, but nothing was missing. They were looking for something and you know what it is, don't you?'

'I don't know. Really. That's the truth.'

Tania took her foot off the desk, leant over and gripped his upper arm, pulled him up to face her. A long-lost sister of Harkness. He had been manhandled by him, and now he was being woman-handled by her. He got a whiff of aniseed, maybe the base note of her perfume, more likely she had been drinking Pernod. There was a temptation to throw himself upon her mercy, to confess everything on her bosom in a sorrowful pietà — but there had never been any real sign of any mercy there. Woman-handled: there was a possibility she might be intending to shag him. Slight, yet it was there. He wondered how he felt about that. She must have caught his expression.

'I might as well tell you here and now Billy, I've never liked you. So forget it, you sick shit. Not even as a charity fuck.'

223

She continued to grip his arm while poking a carmine-tipped finger at him.

'Whatever happens to Alastair happens, that's his choice. But you've let yourself get dragged into something you can't handle.'

'That's not true—'

She waved her long bloody finger more violently, and suddenly, terrifyingly, he had a flash of the wretch with the compound leg fractures. Tania was enunciating slowly, with aggressive care, and it was as if she could read his mind.

'You're going to end up slaughtered.'

'Tania, I don't—'

'But I don't care about any of that. I want to know what you've been up to.'

She shoved her face more closely into his.

'And you're fucking well going to tell me.'

'There's honestly nothing to tell. Nothing.'

31

The Fold

I don't know what it is about public libraries that makes me unsettled. It might be the librarians. They are there to help, but at the same time they are authority figures too. Perhaps more so in Essex where books are associated with an obscure and dubious magic, which ensures that in the main they are shunned. My local library is under-used and they might close it soon, but in the meantime here it is: an impressive Edwardian building, finely weathered sandstone, art nouveau architraves and all. They've gutted most of the old interior (of course they have) and, in that signature note for municipal vandalism, installed ranks of fluorescent tubes on the ceiling. I find their radiance mildly hallucinatory and that doesn't help with my unease.

Derek's behind the counter today. He's in early middle-age, receding hairline making an open face more open still, weather-beaten. While there is some weather around here, almost certainly that roughened and reddened complexion means he is a drinker, because that is the main recreational activity hereabouts. What of it? He can do what he likes after work and I've never seen him drunk in here, or even smelt alcohol on his breath. He possesses the discipline so many others lack, myself included. Derek's reached the point, I imagine, where he doesn't need a lot of stimulus from his occupation, though he might need a few drinks after a shift. The job is quiet and undemanding, except on those occasions when he has to throw out drunks and the mentally ill, and I have to sit there thinking about whether and when that is going to happen to me. Now and again we have a conversation that goes beyond titles, reservations and fines; we might discuss football or the weather, or the library's lack of borrowers, or its underfunding. But I know his name only from the security badge on the ribbon round his neck; I recall him looking at me doubtfully when I leant in towards him so I could read it. However much I think I have more in common with Derek than I have differences, he is authority.

Yes, I still have this tendency to project myself onto the people around me. I looked down on Jeevons the planning officer and Soames the PR man because I feared ending up in an occupation which I would hate, not realising their work most probably suited them well enough.

Back then I didn't need a library because Alastair had all the art books I ever needed for reference, the gallery office was full of them. But I never made it to art school. Once Alastair wasn't around to help, any plans for my higher education fell apart. Not that they had ever been very solid. He could have put a word in with admissions tutors he knew, I guess, to get round my lack of everything that is normally required, and maybe it would have worked if there'd been the money to pay for it all. Instead I've had to rely on reading widely about art and that has helped me to become some sort of writer, now and again. Though what I really do nowadays, mostly, is claim benefits.

I don't have the same view of art as before. These days I am not sure the phrase "flickering brilliance" should be used beyond those artists who have a transcendental grasp of colour, say Rothko, and further away, Caravaggio and Titian. And yet maybe it does catch the way so many of those works I saw round Hoxton and Shoreditch set my mind alight. It's true that I had been doing a lot of E before I got into art, but even so I don't think that had anything to do with it. All of that art took place in one of those moments, a trippy historical lacuna all of its own that lent a lambency to so many of those works. As time passed that has started to leak away, but some of the art has lasted. Thorn's work has and even now a few of the others can fuel that instant, explosive recognition in me.

If my life options have narrowed, art itself retains an infinity of possibilities. Even after everything that has happened I still believe that to compare art to life is to cheapen the art. What great art is, often consists in the questions it poses and those questions remain unanswerable, despite being the only questions worth asking.

Even that second video of Becky's. Those endless repetitions dominated by her image, the whole making me want to take a gun to it and blast away. Art that hollows viewers out, forces them to think about the whole act of looking at it within that moment of time. Forces them to experience being. Twentieth century video art can be like Zen, not to everyone's taste and not to mine at the time, but it performs its function with a sombre intensity nothing else can match.

Derek hands me the new book about Thorn. It came out a few months ago to coincide with his last show, which is still in transit between global cultural capitals. Forty quid it would have cost me. I remain very interested in his art and sometimes, still, I wonder what it must be like to be Thorn. To have achieved everything you want. To have had no limits placed on ambition and aspiration. To reach the point where money is completely irrelevant. The sale prices must have meant almost nothing to him for a very long time now, not even as a way of keeping score, because he's left his competitors so far behind. The ballooning art market must mean very little to him either. If his work's a series of capital investments, then he would say that's got nothing to do with why he made it. He was often accused of being as much of an entrepreneur as an artist, but it was Alastair who promoted him so successfully at the start. Everyone's forgotten about that.

I made the mistake of thinking there was a direct connection between Thorn and me because he was from round here. He had, I believed, the same sort of background. I'd heard he spoke like me and that he looked like me, and he even had lower back pain like I had (and still have). It isn't surprising he began to represent my hopes for my own creative ambitions. Recently I found out that he attended a public school called Haycroft, not too far away from here. Their current fees are more than twice the national minimum wage. There are a few scholarships but Thorn didn't need one of those because his father was a doctor, a chest consultant who did a lot of private work.

*

They are walking down a badly lit street and intermittently Becky stumbles on cobbles which are slippery with slush. There are a few of these cobbled side streets left in the area and sometimes, late at night when she is a little out of it like this, gazing down on the cobbles makes her think that an army of tortoises is busy filing its way through Shoreditch, drawn by persistent rumours of enormous hidden caches of lettuce leaves.

The image cheers Becky for a moment or two; as she leaves the miniature hillocks behind and turns into Commercial Street with Alastair and some of the others (Tom is absent and so, thankfully, is Billy) she is wondering if she should have come along tonight. When Alastair asked to see her it would have been churlish to refuse and she is concerned for his welfare, but it is puzzling why Tania and Erick should be here after all of the rowing, and the expedition has an atmosphere that is making her uneasy. Tania has been polite to them all evening; that is a sure sign that something is going on.

Alastair halts outside the warehouse that is their destination. The entry mechanism buzzes and releases the latch, and they walk up a tiled staircase. Becky glances down at the tiles, cracked and shattered, each crevice an estuary silted with filth, the whole set into a stairwell of splintered and rotten deal. When they reach the top they emerge into a cavernous storage area which looks strangely like a ballroom. At the far end a DJ is funnelling solid noise into the space. Alastair bends to Becky's ear.

'An art collective lives here,' he says. 'They might be squatting. I think they had a short-term licence or something, but they're about to be evicted. This is their moving out party.'

He looks pale and unwell, maybe anaemic, but he hasn't responded in any informative way to her enquiries about his health. Once inside he wants to chop out lines for everyone. First they go to the toilets, but the queue is too long. They have a short debate about slabbing the coke out on a nearby table.

'There's all sorts of people here; this is virtually a public place,' says Alastair. 'It's never a good idea to do it where people can see you.'

'In case one of them's a plainclothes policeman?' asks Becky.

'No, because they always want some as well.'

They return to the main room.

'We can go behind that screen,' says Alastair, pointing to the far end of the room.

They walk over to an old freestanding office partition and behind it find a piece of abandoned machinery, from its wide, squat vent possibly obsolete air-conditioning plant. It has a flat surface, but it is dirty. Erick wipes it down with a paper tissue and the tissue comes up black. He makes another attempt, with better results.

'That's okay,' says Alastair.

He strews charlie over the surface, arranges it into lines and they snort it. Then they move to the bar, which is in a series of rooms off the main area. For some reason, maybe related to the licensing laws or perhaps to someone's idea of fun, it is necessary to buy a piece of a jigsaw puzzle and then exchange it for a drink.

'This is so seventies,' says Becky. 'Those ceiling tiles, that beige carpet, the veneer panelling. Look, on that TV over there, they're playing a video of *The Saint*.'

'But we are sinners,' says Erick.

Tania and Erick are becoming skittish. They whisper and giggle like conspirators, Tania leaning into Erick like an indulgent mother fussing over a child. Though they do not look so ill-matched as usual. The lighting is dim, making Tania's hair unobtrusive, and their disparity in height has lessened. Erick is wearing a pair of ankle boots with four-inch platforms, a departure from his customary trainers. They are black and bold, chunky and cheeky, and have been remarked upon by the others. Erick smiles, gives nothing away.

'The world of the Saint doesn't age,' says Alastair. 'When you watch it you are back in the same time you experienced when you first saw it.'

'Everything always has to be so fucking significant for you, doesn't it?' says Tania.

Tania has stopped being nice, Becky notes, and in some ways this is a relief.

'There is no past on that screen,' says Alastair. 'No future, either.'

'The past,' says Erick, 'is history.'

'And history,' says Tania, 'is so fucking over.'

Erick drops his cigarette butt to the floor, and his boot descends onto it like a small anvil.

'We will not be its playthings,' he says.

He starts to kick at the nearest wall. His shiny boots are miniature wrecking balls smashing into the planking. Tania joins him, booting away alongside him with relentless determination. The wall begins to alter, but not to yield or give way, not to splinter,

break or snap. It sta**rts** to r**i**p**p**le... and w**ave**.

'No one's pulling at our fucking strings any more,' Tania shouts.

'We are not puppets,' yells Erick, his feet swinging back and forth like destructive metronomes.

The wall is b**eco*m*i**n**g... *fluid*... and...

fl**eX**i**b**le. Tania and Erick start to stamp an**d** jump on the

floor and it b-e-**g-i-**ns... t-o... s-**h**-a-**k**-e.

'We're breaking through,' Tania screams.

The warehouse around them starts to... *fol*... *d*... and then to... *flicker*... and... *fade*...

and everyone flees, with shouts and shrieks fuelled by varying measures of panic and elation.

32

The Anti-Christ

You aren't wearing a watch (it would get coated) but you must have been doing this for what — nine, ten hours? It is best to keep moving in here because it is freezing. It has to be, or it would be unbearable. Two air conditioners are going full blast and the cold is getting to you. You would have worn more layers of clothing, if you hadn't known that you'd have to throw them all away afterwards.

Making the work is becoming easier. The basic idea is simple, but the realisation is not. It is messy, there is no doubt about it (this is easily the messiest material you have worked with) but you don't want it to end. There is something deeply satisfying about it all, more satisfying than the execution of any of your other works.

Mostly your ideas develop through the process of production. You literally work them out. Sometimes you have to strain to get them out. You can no longer comprehend how you did some of your earlier works. The details of their creation have become obscured. This one is unusual. It has been separate from the start, given to you almost whole.

It is the coup de grâce to the competition. You believe Hoxton should be a breeding ground for artistic talent. But in the mood that possesses you as you look at your work you cannot help thinking that — with the sole exception of yourself — this is hypothetical. You have a couple of dozen direct competitors within a quarter mile radius, at least in theory. There is Mary Carmichael and her chewing gum sculptures, Dominic Pearson and his reworkings of Dali, Strickland & Jessop and their architectural models, Dennis Smythe and his self-harming performances, Robyn Blackman and her faked family photographs, Denise

O'Donoghue and her supermarket trolleys, Tania Russell-Smith and her sex addict video, Edie Sachs and her sound installations, Joshua Elam and his newspaper paintings, Angela Flaxman and all her glass vessels, the Sheehan brothers and their granite jet aircraft, Gerry Locke and his prison cell doors, Peter Blacksmith and his small latex cars, Quentin Seymour and his copper leeks and kohlrabi, Raj Jaffrey and his big butane cylinders, Stewart MacKenzie and his plastic extrusions, Pauline Collard and her loofahs and soap dishes, Erick Heckendorf and his installations about nothing, Fleur Debries and her legions of doll men, Max Pirbright and his unfocussed hallucinatory paintings, Veronica Greenwood and her fat angry women, John Rowntree and his multiple garden sheds, and Coco Patel and her walk in the desert.

You know with coruscating certainty that all of this work is shite. That all of your so-called fellow artists are lifestyle merchant, part-time hobbyist, pathetic excuses for artists who are simply wasting ruinous amounts of their time.

No one has ever done what you are doing now, and no one will ever do it again. You are the first, the first to create the final work. The critics can say what they like, but they will be unable to deny that this is the end. You are going right back to the beginning and before the beginning of art to complete the circle. A circle which is shrinking and collapsing into itself, a singularity which will leave nothing behind it.

Your back is acting up, your eyes are tired. You are frayed and you are exhausted; it is time for a break. You look down at yourself. There is no point in washing until it is all over, but it is sensible to at least clean your hands before getting out the gear and the works.

*

'Tom, the art world is waiting upon our clarion call.'

It was half past eight in the morning and Lanchester was on the phone to his young lieutenant.

'I'll sort through the material I've received on new shows and make some calls, and get back to—'

'What about Kevin Thorn? It sounds as if he's got an incredible show coming up: there's an intriguing article about it in *The Times*.'

'Billy McCrory was interviewing him in *The Herald*, but—'

'No, *The Times*. The feature I'm talking about is in *The Times*.'

'Let me get hold of a copy and ring you, I'll—'

'Don't take too long over it, there's a good chap. I've a meeting at ten.'

*

He awoke and for a moment was happy without knowing why, then remembered. The Thorn feature was a triumph. There had been few moments to savour in his career recently, which made this one all the more enjoyable. When you had material as good as this the feature almost wrote itself. He started with the story of the interview and Thorn's beating by the snapper, used it to tease out the self-destructive patterns in his life and work to date, before speculating about the direction the new show might take. The sub-editors put a great headline on it: "Trashed".

The sublime moment passed as the memory of yesterday evening pounced. The first part was clear enough. For some reason, he couldn't remember why, he went into Soho to celebrate and much fun ensued in the French House and The Colony Room. Flagons of mead were raised to him around high tables by his fellow freelance knights to toast his success in battle. To ensure the forces of darkness were held at bay for the duration of the festivities he took potions, pills — 'I am thinking they're Es,' said Sir Erick, lyttle and valiant and ever possessed of a burning torch (in the fullness of day, as well as of night), 'but there might be some K in them, I'm not sure.' 'That's cool, the alcohol will swamp them anyway' — followed by magical powders — 'it's good coke, basically, but it's been cut with some speed. Here, wash it down with whisky'.

The potions did not render him invulnerable to his foes as Sir Erick, short of sword arm but wyse in alchemical lore, had claimed. A varlet suggested riding to an after private view party round the corner, in what seemed to be either a small club or a large castle, where all was well to start with and many more goblets were raised to his valour. He hoped his chivalry would help him to win the favour of the valiant knights and fair maidens accompanying him. Where were they? They had vanished. He woke from a deep trance in a shady glade of the club and went in search of them, to regale them with his adventures. A trusty squire and a maiden with flaxen locks were screaming. He knew he must rescue them. 'Get him away from us.' 'Who is he?' He was in a forest, a magical forest of human hands and arms which supported him, conveying him to a portal wreathed in mist and mystery.

*

'Henry? Yes, I've read *The Times*'s piece about Kevin Thorn,' said Tom. 'The show sounds interesting; I've heard a few rumours.'

'You don't sound impressed,' said Lanchester, 'but I know you're not keen on him. Can you arrange a special preview? I'd love to get in before Saatchi. It wouldn't surprise me if he tried to buy the whole show before it opened. I must have got him going by sneaking away Rebecca Edge's installation right under his nose.'

'I'll get straight onto it, I'll just—'

'This is the finest new art there is and I want to spend money on it.'

'I'm sure everyone will respect you for that, Henry.'

*

The memories unrolled with horrible vividness. After crossing the sacred threshold, gliding over it, because the gods had decreed that it was not fitting for him to walk the Earth as other mortals do, he entered Valhalla. His initiation by the immortal ones was hard. He was thrown onto an immense, smooth sacrificial slab and roaring salamanders with burning eyes poised themselves to rend him. He knew that he had been laid out here in this black, freezing

235

void as a test, that he had to lie still, but he was weak and could not stop himself rolling off the slab away from the beasts. It was terribly hard for him to follow in the ways of the immortal ones. He had failed and would have to return to the castle, to try once again to rescue the trusty squire and his fair maiden. His sword had gone, so he armed himself with an empty goblet and charged. The drawbridge was down but his foes had sprung a trap and were waiting.

*

As Becky nears Bloom's she sees faint traces of graffiti lingering on the gallery's glass frontage. It has become easier to believe that Alastair was behind the graffiti rather than Tom, but there is no way to settle the matter. She doesn't feel up to tackling Alastair on the subject, and communication with Tom has ceased.

There is a vagrant urinating in one of the doorways and he turns towards her so she can see his appendage, a battered faucet of gristle from which ropes of yellow urine play as he jerks it around derisively. He has a thick beard, each twisted hair a reinforcement of his disdain for everyone around him, and a long red nose — almost as long as Tom's, but unpleasantly thin. It is hard to say how old he is. The beard is still black but his skin is leathery, except for the nose which burst capillaries and impetigo have rendered raw and tumescent, making it more obscene than the penis on gleeful display below. Becky turns away, considers all the men who believe they are free to play games with the world without consequences.

None of this undermines her mood and she is confident as she makes her way out of the weak sunshine into the gallery, because she has an idea why Linda has invited her over. She hovers in the café area just as Linda appears at the top of the steps up from the gallery proper.

'That's such a nice jacket,' says Becky.

It is plum coloured, with a rich sheen. Becky admires Linda's mature poise, thinks about whether she will herself become so soignée in due course.

'Nicole Farhi. Do come down and we'll have a chat.'

Linda is keen that she joins her roster of artists and praises her work at embarrassing length. They are in the small office at the rear of the gallery area and today Linda has another visitor, an African grey parrot sitting on his perch in a large brass cage which hangs down from the ceiling, dominating the room.

'This is Crispin,' says Linda. 'He usually lives at home but lately I've been bringing him into the gallery, because he's decided he doesn't like to be left on his own for more than an hour or two.'

Becky has been hoping to meet Crispin and she looks at the savage red slash of his tail feathers, at the finer feathers scalloped around his head and neck like silken grey lace. For the rest of her visit Becky's attention switches between gallerist and parrot. She tries to keep her mind on management of her career, but that is not easy in this disorienting to and fro.

Crispin sidles towards her, rocking gently as he shifts his weight from claw to claw; Becky sees those claws are outsize, like collections of bendy twigs. He comes up close against the gleaming bars of his prison and regards her with intense curiosity through eyes that are big, black full stops.

'Does he talk?' she asks.

'Oh, lots sweetie, but he doesn't need to at the moment because you're giving him all the attention he wants. Look, he's entranced.'

Crispin stares at her, his head cocked on one side. For an instant Becky worries that he will start to screech a detailed deposition of all her crimes.

'I'm glad he approves of you,' Linda says. 'He's particular.'

Linda holds an almond out to him, leans over to kiss the top of his beak after he removes it from her fingers.

'And onto business,' says Linda. 'Idiot Savant can't give you all the help I can.'

'Alastair has been good to me.'

'I'm not saying he hasn't, but his pretence of being outside the art world isn't helpful.'

'What do you mean, "pretence"?'

'He's not outside it, whatever he says. Artists have always shown in spaces outside the art establishment, especially at the start of their careers. It's an entire tradition. The original anti-gallery was the Salon des Refusés in Paris during the nineteenth century.'

'This is new to me.'

'I wrote part of my dissertation on it, darling. Lots of artists showed there who couldn't get into the main institutions. The fact that Alastair doesn't pay his rent on his space doesn't mean he's especially alternative or anything. In fact, when I started off I squatted a couple of warehouse spaces before I secured proper backing.'

Becky doesn't want to listen to a lecture on art history or think much about any of this.

'I will have to consider your terms,' she says.

She remains angry over Tania and Linda dragging her into their vendetta with Tom, encouraging her to lure him to their trap. It makes her unwilling to sign with Bloom's but, in spite of Lanchester's patronage, so far no one else has approached her with a formal offer like this. No one with Linda's drive and ambition, anyway.

'Think it over, darling. I support my artists very actively, because I know how difficult it can be coming up with new work. I don't want to deal with any of that, thank you very much — I'd run screaming from a blank canvas. Running the gallery is far easier, believe me.'

Becky finds it hard to imagine being scared of making art, but she has found out that Linda began a fine art course, then dropped out precipitately and studied art history at the Courtauld before abandoning that too and starting her gallery a couple of years ago. She wonders if the wreckage that was Linda's father's private life put her off becoming an artist. As for Leon Bloom himself, maybe the pressure on him to produce work was what made him so wayward.

Sccreeeeooooooooooooooouuuuuccccccccccccch

Becky starts; Crispin is still staring at her. He plumps up the feathers round his neck and shoulders and starts to sing *The Ugly Duckling* in a smooth baritone. Becky catches glimpses of a swivelling black slug of tongue behind his beak. After the song's opening lyrics he stops abruptly.

'He likes his Danny Kaye CD,' says Linda. 'You see, they want unlimited attention. They're like small children, almost as needy as my artists.'

'Doesn't he get lonely without any other parrots around?'

'Parrots like people most of all, but it's true that they enjoy meeting other birds too. When I let Crispin out in the gallery he goes right up against the window and a crow from outside comes flying up. They have a little visit with each other.'

Linda rises and feeds Crispin another almond. Becky is enchanted, wrenches her attention back towards the issue of commercial representation with difficulty.

'I'll send you over a draft contract,' Linda continues. 'One of the first things I'd love to do is to enter your latest installation for the Shiraz prize. The closing date is next Wednesday.'

'Are you going to Kevin Thorn's private view?' Becky asks.

'Yes of course, sweetie. I'm not happy it's in Idiot Savant. It's such a pity there isn't a thing I can do about that, but there it is.'

'Alastair doesn't want me to go.'

'Why ever not? It's in his own gallery, for heaven's sake.'

Crispin eyes Becky again, makes a briefer interjection. *Sccreeeeoouuucccch*

*

It was pointless ringing the club and apologising. He had no memory at all of what had happened after he tried to force his way back in. Could be serious, could be trivial. He'd never know. They probably had no idea who he was. He seemed to remember Erick leaving before the trouble started. What was it he said? 'For god's sake, don't start in here.' Or maybe that had been someone else.

He fingered his face. Part of it was tender, above the left cheekbone. A new injury, not part of the gangsters' legacy. He was fortunate to get away with such a minor wound. His left knee abraded the sheet, sent in a message of more severe damage, and he expressed pain and regret by moaning aloud.

How had he got home? He didn't know. Best to be thankful that he had made it more or less in one piece. At least he hadn't got a proper kicking. His head moved slightly and pain needled into several widely separated points in his brain. He realised he had used chemicals to administer his own kicking, and he whimpered in contrition.

It became clear that he was fully dressed, though his left trouser leg was ripped through at the knee. His head swirled with dizziness and his vision was clouded by a frieze of fine dots, as well as whorls and lines. His brain was disintegrating, sloshing heavily against the paper-thin container of his skull, which could crack open at any moment. Glutinous grey tissue was about to slough out through his nose and ears, down his throat. Supposing the drugs he had taken last night hadn't worn off? He would lose all sense of who he was; he'd have to be institutionalised. His heart started to beat faster and louder, a drum machine looping up into one continuous blurring thud.

He tried to raise himself from the mattress and stopped. A new pain, massive and solid, as though someone had hit him over the head with a length of piping, crunching its way from his head down through his entire body. Persevere — he had to persevere. He clawed at the bedding for support, a man scrabbling at the turf on a cliff edge, dragged himself away from the abyss and over into a crouch. Something was striking the outside of his skull again and again, relentlessly, pitilessly. It felt like the edge of a steel ruler, but he registered that it was the telephone ringing in the other room.

The phone wouldn't stop. Why wouldn't whoever it was give up and leave him alone? He couldn't ignore its excoriating noise.

It had to be terminated. It seemed to have been ringing for a couple of hours already, but his sense of time must have been distorted by lingering chemicals. He tried to suppress the thought. Why wasn't his answerphone working? He was forced to leave off holding his forehead with both hands, in order to open the living room door against the resistance of a compost of soiled clothing and refuse, whereupon his brain shunted into his skull again.

As he neared the shrill harbinger of doom its clamour became agonising. He glimpsed a black oval moving from a fold in a garment, sliding across the room and under another pile of rubbish. A cockroach, or another hallucination?

'What a tremendous feature,' said Alastair.

'I'm sorry Kevin got stomped.'

'It's great publicity. I hope you'll be at the private view?'

'I'm not too well.'

'I would love to see you if you can make it.'

'I'll try.'

'But please arrive early, that's crucial.'

He saw that he was standing in a penumbra of ash and Silk Cut butts from an upended ashtray. He looked over to the broken window, clumsily taped over with cardboard, like something from a shanty town. The memory of being thrust out of the window came back. Another one to suppress — he'd never get over that; thank god he didn't have the package any more. Then he remembered Tania. He'd fobbed her off by claiming he didn't know anything, but she was bound to confront him again soon. His hangover reasserted itself, and as fresh images and horrors seized upon him, he knew that being arrested could not be worse than any of this.

33

Sight Unseen

'Henry? It's Tom. Kevin Thorn's show is strictly under wraps until the private view this evening. No special previews, I'm afraid. They say it's because—'

'Are you sure Saatchi hasn't set up one for himself?'

'I'm positive. Alastair assures me nobody is to know anything about the work beforehand. Everyone involved in the show, even the lorry driver transporting the pieces over from Thorn's studio, has been made to sign non-disclosure agreements.'

'If that's the way it is, we'll have to go along with it.'

'We can make offers for anything you like at the private view; I'm sure you'll come away with something substantial. I'll speak to—'

'Everything in sight will be bought up by then.'

*

He knew he needed to hide for a while. It was fortunate that there was no necessity to drag himself into his workspace at IS; he'd earn enough money from the Thorn interview to keep himself afloat for a few weeks. He could wait until everything blew over.

He staggered back to his sickbed, where he spent the rest of the day suspended between wakefulness and sleep, threshing about in the sheets, sometimes dozing for a few moments. Complete repose was impossible; his mind accelerated through the previous evening in horrid vertiginous rushes. There was no escaping from himself — the realisation was stark. Drugs were an alibi, concealing the ghastly void at the centre of his being.

Tania was ten minutes early. She was waiting for Erick in Cantaloupe, the restaurant near the junction of Charlotte Road and Great Eastern Street. The long wooden tables were refectory-like. Fashionable so often meant uncomfortable. Tania ordered a Moscow Mule, ensuring that she articulated extra clearly so that the waiter could understand. It was hard to make out anything anyone said in here. Patrons seated opposite each other found that speech floated off, to hover under the high ceiling in and around the exposed pipework, or to drown in the aural surf from nearby tables. It was fortunate the cocktails were superior, so that after a couple of them audibility was not an issue. Erick was exactly on time, as she'd anticipated.

'What would you like to drink?' she asked.

'Oh do not worry, I get one myself.'

While Erick was at the bar Tania greeted one or two acquaintances. There were several suits, too, looking askance at her crimson beehive. They were everywhere and their advance could not be halted, but Erick was a different and more welcome variety of worker ant. When he returned he perched himself on the bench opposite her.

'It's good to get outside of the fucking studio for once,' she said.

'It is true that this studio is intense.'

'Have you found anywhere else to live?'

'Not yet thank you' — he waved his cigarette back and forth — 'I hop from settee to settee.'

'Why don't you come and stay at my place for a while?'

'Thanks. You know, I am becoming interested in the way people will add themselves to one another, combine their thoughts and emotions, then sometimes create extra people.'

'I'm only offering to put you up temporarily, you fucking little weirdo.'

Erick's smile was a lower-case crescent of lips and teeth.

'Will you go to Thorn's private view tonight?' he asked.

'I suppose so,' she said. 'Can't ignore the dickhead, however much I'd like to.'

'Our experiment the other evening went extremely well.'

'I should have told you right away. We've been short listed for the Shiraz.'

'Are you bothered?'

'It doesn't matter, does it? Given the nature of the work.'

'I discover that "box" to British people also means "vagina".'

'Our work is a kind of birth,' she said. 'Or anti-birth.'

'This is the most exciting art I work on since I come here.'

'I've never found out why you moved to London,' said Tania. 'All I heard was that you had problems in Germany.'

'Ah yes, this is my *Art Bus* project. What I get into when the Wall came down. I obtain four old East German buses, large vehicles, and a group of us tour round Europe putting on shows, encouraging people to join in. We stage performances, we have music and poetry readings, and a fantastic light show. It is a huge success. In the East, especially, the people are ready — this is the right time.'

'What was the problem then?'

'Money, as usual. A couple of arts institutions say they will pay for the buses, so I put my name down on the purchase agreements. Then they back out and the vehicles have mechanical problems. The repairs cost a lot, I borrow more money, then most of the buses break down altogether after eighteen months or so and my creditors make me bankrupt. So I run away to London. I'm heavily in debt over there, even today.'

'That was a good time for an artist to arrive here, you must admit.'

'My work was reborn. Most of all, I was lucky to meet Alastair.'

'You're not serious?'

Erick lit a fresh cigarette and reflected.

'I remember once our art bus convoy draws up in a small hamlet in Prussia. It is one of those villages where the roofs look like giant witches' hats. There are one or two storks flying overhead; you could imagine them delivering babies to the villagers. We have painted the buses in bright colours, big swirls of Day-Glo. I suppose they look something like the subway trains in New York. We halt in the village square. A couple of the inhabitants walk up to look. Then there is a small crowd. "They're spaceships," someone shouted — he was drunk: there isn't much to do in these places besides drink.'

'Unlike here?' said Tania, sipping her Mule.

'Some of them touch the paint on the buses cautiously, to see if it will come off on their hands. We are the first visitation of any significance from the outside world for decades, a sign of momentous change. That evening we put on a multimedia show in the church hall. It is packed; every single resident is there, even the very old and the sick. We bring colour back into their lives.

'Afterwards, after all of the noise and the light, it is so peaceful. There is a stillness in the village and the countryside around it. Eerie. Almost uncanny: no birdsong, even. Later we hear that the Nazis set up a concentration camp for women nearby, which the communists take from them and enlarge. The next morning we pack up our equipment and prepare to leave. As we are about to drive off, finally, a teenager — he is a skinhead with a spider's web tattoo across all his face — walks up and says to me, "You're not coming back, are you?". I lie to him, tell him that, yes, we will return. Of course, we do not. We depart. We travel off, snatching away the new life we show them over a day and a half. They are probably still there trapped in their monochrome existence, waiting for late capitalism to rescue them.

'And you know, Tania, sometimes I feel that what we are to those villagers is what Alastair is to us. He gives us new life, expands our vision, not every time in an altogether beneficial or promising way, but he helps so to show us a new world.'

'If Alastair hadn't been around, your art would have developed and taken off anyway.'

'He is a benefactor for me, a benefactor for us all.'

'If that was ever true, it's ended now.'

'Yes, this beginning for our lives, this dreaming of all of the different kinds of futures we can have while we party and work on our art, soon it will all be over.'

*

He couldn't lie there in a prone position indefinitely. He could go abroad somewhere, start afresh. Completely teetotal and drug-free. Work hard at getting accepted into a community in say, Scotland. Perth. No: Perth, Australia. Attend Sunday services and play an active role in local charities. Help mentally handicapped children, join the Round Table... O god, the Round Table.

*

'If they won't give us a special preview we'll make an offer beforehand, regardless.'

'Is that sensible, Henry? We don't know for certain what's in the show, and I—'

'It's time for a gamble. I want you to make a few discreet enquiries to see if we can make a bid for part of the show. Why not say that we want to bid for the largest work on offer?'

'How much did you have in mind?'

'Let's say a quarter of a million.'

'Are you sure? It's very—'

'I want to make a big splash. The money is simply a way of making everyone realise that an important collector has arrived on the scene. There will be a bonus because we'll acquire a landmark work.'

'The biggest work in the show won't necessarily be the best.'

'What other way is there to choose?'

*

As daylight faded he rose and dressed, a process protracted by severe pain in his lower back. He thought he might have chipped a vertebra; this was much worse than his usual back pain. He smoked a couple of cigarettes and snorted a line of adulterated coke — the remnants of last night's binge — listened to the echolalia of the television as he searched for trousers that were not too putrid. An explosive sneeze. He wiped the discharge off his nose, looked into the fat comma of fluid in his palm, at the nebulae of blood and snot spiralling out within it.

This had to be the last time. He loved oblivion — it blanked everything out — but it all had to stop. The alcohol guided him to the edge and always he jumped. The coke was a detail; it allowed him to dally on the brink before the plunge. He'd had his final warning. At least he still had the flat and he didn't have to worry about intruders and their attacks any more. The worst that could happen had happened.

The phone rang again and when he picked it up there came a voice with a deep rasp.

'We're coming to see you. Stay right where you are.'

He hung up and then jerked the handset from its socket, before staring at it as it sat on the floor, a grenade with the pin out. He wondered if that call had been real; it must have been real. He had to leave immediately. It was not safe in here as it was. He looked over to the shattered front door — those bastards hadn't rung the bell or knocked when they'd come calling, and now it was secured with a clumsily attached padlock like a garden shed. That wouldn't keep anyone out.

The street and its battering surf of traffic, the screech of shearing metal and the driving piles of the building sites, the phalanxes of pedestrians striding out on the pavements. He wanted to retreat back inside but he knew that he couldn't, that Alastair and the others would be expecting him. He felt sicker still when he remembered Tania and her insistent threats; she was waiting to have another go at him too. If she turned up at the private view he could only hope Alastair would keep her from him. He tried to pare down his experiential field, stare downwards, breathe deeply, take one step at a time, keep placing one foot in front of the other.

He managed the short distance to French Place reasonably successfully. A beggar approached him for change, examined him more closely and backed off because it became obvious that it was Billy who needed change, a change from all of this. He collided with a pedestrian, but that wasn't his fault because it was a business boy babbling into his oversized portable phone and not paying any attention to anyone else. The parking meter's painful impact could not be explained away so easily, and it would leave another bruise. He rounded the last corner, taking it on the inside to husband his energy and slowing further to avoid additional accidents, before seeing the crowd outside IS.

*

'Henry? It's Tom. Sorry I couldn't get back to you before. I've made an offer of £250,000 for the largest work in the show, which has been accepted.'

'That's great news. Good lad.'

'They're insisting that you confirm in writing and transfer the funds straight away.'

'A detail. I'll do that now. We've arrived, Tom.'

'I'm sure we have, Henry.'

*

Kevin Thorn's opening was an event. Despite the cold the crowd densely thicketed the area around the entrance, spilling over into the street. They were drinking furiously and plumes and furls of cigarette smoke and frozen breath skirled upwards into the dank, matt night. Billy saw door staff hooking and unhooking a velvet rope from shiny brass poles as guests were vetted. He had never been to a private view before at which anyone bothered checking names.

Most of the crowd standing outside the entrance had been excluded. Nevertheless, their presence was necessary (an event requires an audience) and to keep them in place three black refuse bins had been placed on the pavement on the other side of the road, full of lager and ice — although whether the ice was necessary in this temperature was doubtful. In their beanies and ski hats, the personnel dispensing the beer were distinguishable from the rest of the crowd only by the bottle openers they wielded with redundant panache.

It was a cruel moment of definition. Billy noticed people staring from the windows of the gallery with what looked like glasses of champagne in their hands and with what could have been complacent expressions on their faces. There was something odd about those expressions, though he couldn't quite make out what it was. He was a little distance away, still, and his lingering dizziness meant that he was having difficulty focusing.

34

Beige I – VII

'Okáy, we've sorted the strategy and methodology so let's get on with it.'

This was an internal meeting with no clients present. None of the other partners were here either, so Lanchester could finish proceedings brusquely. He hurried to his office and rang Tom.

'I want to go down to the private view to see what I've got for my quarter mill.'

'Right you are. I'll be inside waiting for you.'

Lanchester packed everything into his briefcase methodically, made sure that his desk was completely empty, in all of its intimidating walnut expanse, and moved doorwards. His portable phone chirruped. He let his briefcase settle into the carpet as he retrieved the phone from his jacket. It was Booth, the firm's senior tax partner.

'Henry, the Benson bid is coming off.'

'I thought nothing was going to happen there for another week.'

'It's going to be an all-nighter, I'm afraid.'

'I'll meet you in the lobby.'

Manfully, Lanchester picked up his briefcase again and advanced towards the lifts.

*

The bodies at the entrance buffeted and manhandled each other, refused to merge smoothly in order to pass through the narrow aperture. Billy was sensitive to physical contact and he suffered. He noticed a camera crew in attendance, directed by a youth in a

Gucci baseball cap. It looked like an independent film company; a television news team would have been middle-aged, badly dressed. He reached a burly security man, further burlified by a puffer jacket of a volume to make the Michelin man envious. He eyed Billy disdainfully, checked his name on the list, grunted into his headphone and speaker set and admitted him. Billy walked into the foyer slowly and carefully, pausing every few steps for a rest. The floor possessed a slight inclination he had not noticed before. Sweating freely, he saw Erick, a foothill to the human peaks beyond. As Erick caught sight of him his mouth tightened and he exhaled cigarette smoke dismissively before walking away, shaking his head.

Billy halted, wondered whether to retreat or whether to hurry after Erick and apologise, though he knew he was incapable of hurrying. He tried to feel angry with Erick. It was his fault, handing over those dodgy drugs. Erick went so crazy so often himself, who was he to pass judgement? But he had always known that different laws applied to Erick. Erick was small and lovable, and he was not. More crucially, Erick was an artist of outstanding talent and he was not.

He became aware of a cloacal odour. The charlie had diminished his olfactory capacity, yet he knew that the smell must be coming from him. As well as being morally repellent, therefore, he stank. There was no point in begging forgiveness from Erick if he stank. He saw nauseated faces all the way round the gallery. Surely he couldn't be that bad? Alastair walked up to him, betraying no signs of disgust. With a pleasant smile on his face, in fact. The smell couldn't be coming from him, then — although given his disloyalty to Alastair perhaps it should have.

'Ah Billy, we've been wanting to congratulate you on your feature. Are you feeling better?

'Recovering.'

'Do come and join us.'

Alastair led him over to the others at the bar, which had been set up near the gallery's entrance.

'A glass of champagne will stand you up.'

'I'm not drinking at the moment.'

'Not drinking?' said Tom.

Outwardly Tom was the same as ever in his tracksuit. Lazarus in his cerements: Billy had heard of his encounter with Tania and Linda.

'I've decided to give up alcohol and drugs,' said Billy.

Tom laughed softly. 'What's brought that on?'

'It's something I've been considering for a while.'

'Nothing to do with a couple of incidents in Soho last night?'

Tom smiled at Alastair. Billy said nothing, stared downwards.

He noted that Tom and Erick remained on speaking terms with Alastair. Egos. They couldn't accept that anyone would do to them what Alastair had done, if truly he was behind their misfortunes. Or they didn't want to miss what might be the last private view at IS, even if it was Kevin Thorn's.

'Have a glass of champagne,' insisted Alastair.

One glass wouldn't make any difference. He could give up after that. It was medicine and it would help his hangover like nothing else could.

'Thanks.'

He accepted a flute, sipped. Bubbles scraped his throat, threatened to creep up his nose. The fluid prickled down. Instantly he started to feel better, cleansed and healed. Tania was nowhere to be seen; that was something.

Medicine. Already he was aware the flute was half empty and that he needed another drink. He nodded to Becky, gazed at her. If she got rid of the scar she could be a supermodel or movie star. Surely her natural habitat was a magazine cover?

'My,' she said, 'what red eyes you've got.'

Her smile was prophylactic.

'I'm a little under the weather.'

'Erick told me what you did last night.'

'Right.'

'I hope they arrest you this time.'

He avoided her stare and looked over at the gallery walls, saw what looked like a series of canvases covered in brown smears. He discarded his empty flute and fetched a bottle of Sapporo. Tom was wrinkling his nose, an unmissable signal of distaste. Again Billy wondered about the smell, the odour he had noticed at the entrance to the gallery, and whether it was coming from him.

'Where is Kevin Thorn?' he said.

'He hasn't turned up,' said Alastair.

It seemed Thorn couldn't be bothered with his own private view. Linda Bloom had arrived, but then left again precipitately as soon as she realised Thorn wasn't going to be coming. Erick joined the group and stared up at Billy.

'Do the police catch you yet?' he asked.

The police, Harkness.

'What do you mean?'

'The club should press charges.'

'Which club?'

Erick looked up levelly, chessman moving to mate. 'You are knowing which club.'

Alastair intervened. 'Billy wrote that remarkable piece on Kevin that I showed you.'

Becky and Erick exchanged glances.

'And you, Becky, you are now the great hope for us all,' said Alastair. 'The news you have joined Linda Bloom causes me distress, but I shall continue to support your work to the best of my ability.'

'Thanks.'

Becky's response was inappropriately brief, Billy thought. None of them stood a chance with her, even Alastair. Something bigger than Alastair, or Tom, or Rick was looking her up and down, preparing to make her its own. From now on her strongest bonds would be with the masses who went to see her shows and read about her in the media. Her public.

'I thought it might be interesting,' continued Alastair, 'for Billy to do a longer piece on you for *The Herald*.'

'I'm busy at the moment,' she said.

Memories of their last encounter came back to Billy.

'What's Rick up to these days?' he asked her. 'Did you hear from him after the attack?'

'He's recovering. He wants to get involved in environmental campaigning.'

'The trees need organising, do they?' he said.

Something was impinging on him, the odour had intensified. He looked from Becky to Alastair.

'What is that smell?'

Becky winced.

'It's making me feel sick. Can we go outside?'

Alastair was momentarily taken aback.

'In a moment. Billy hasn't had a chance to look at Kevin's work.'

He recognised the odour for what it was now and, feeling as he did, his gorge rose. In an effort to fight the reflex he closed his eyes for a long moment. He opened them and looked around at the canvases, all streaked with magnolia and coffee-coloured smears. Excrement, larded about in generous wedges, gouache in faecal matter, moulded into some sort of lettering. Stiffened into waves. An aspect of the way in which the private view goers — the ones, that is, who hadn't already left in a steady trickling away which, he realised, had been continuing all the while — had arranged themselves struck him more forcibly. They were all in the centre of the space as far away from the canvases as possible. Nothing unusual about that, but they were positively huddled together, smoking heavily and leaning inwards as if bounded by an invisible pentacle against supernatural horrors. He looked at Alastair enquiringly.

'Kevin's new work is challenging. As challenging as anything he's done.'

'Painting in shit, you mean?'

'That's right. Painting in shit as you so graphically put it, but isn't he simply reducing art to its bare essentials? This is revolutionary.'

'He's not the first artist to make use of human waste,' said Billy.

'He's the first to use it in a completely naked and unashamed way.'

'But no one can go anywhere near this.'

'Kevin has issues around authenticity,' said Alastair, 'and shit is the most authentic medium there is. Excretion is inextricable from being. It's our original spoor or mark, outside of any social hierarchy, beyond any cultural norm. It is the primary creative medium. It's the summary of our existence, the proof that we are alive. It is what all art is. If there's a better material to work with, I'd like to know what it is. Tell me.'

'How about paint?' said Tom.

Billy held his breath and took a closer look at the nearest piece of the work. "Kevin Thorn" could be made out in large smears of beige, though the clusters of flies and bluebottles feeding off the ordure were blurring the lettering.

'Why does he not grow up?' said Erick.

'Look who's talking,' said Tom.

Erick made a gesture of impatience. 'This is *épater la bourgeoisie*, isn't it?'

'And what's wrong with that?' said Alastair. 'Doesn't redefining what art is, or rather re-emphasising its original definition, involve confrontation? However, there's much more to Kevin's latest work than that.'

'Oh really,' said Erick.

'You will see that some of the canvases have very few insects feeding off them, while others are a boiling, buzzing mass. Consider the difference. Some of the works are tastier to the flies. Once a few of them settle on a surface others see them and are attracted, in turn, so that the process becomes self-generating. It is like any dynamic bio-feedback system. Like the art world in general. And Hoxton and Shoreditch in particular.'

'So I see,' said Erick. 'Now I go out for fresh air.'

'I'll have to go too,' Billy said.

'And me,' said Becky.

Tom broke in. 'Don't disappear Billy. I want to tell you about Lanchester's latest initiative.'

While Tom was speaking to him outside, he looked back. He saw two belated visitors to the show walk up to the security man who was standing there alone with his clipboard. There was an unsettling resoluteness in their gait. Billy recognised them and started; they didn't seem to be looking over in his direction but he moved quickly so that Tom obscured their line of vision to him. There was an altercation with the security man, the clipboard whirled up and off into the air like a misshapen frisbee, and they disappeared inside.

It was Alastair who was in their sights this time, he thought. It must be Alastair. Although they couldn't do anything to him in public, so that was a relief. He would get away with it, the way he got away with everything. Then a dreadful realisation took him over, so that he could barely hear what Tom was saying to him any more. This was not a public place any more, there was hardly anyone left around at all. The bins of drink on the pavement were empty, the ice in them turned to slush, and the crowd had dispersed. Almost all of the select group allowed admittance had gone too and the security guard had retreated.

There was nothing he could do short of calling the police, and there wasn't enough time left for any of that. He hoped Alastair would not be harmed, that everything would be all right, but part of him knew that wasn't how it would be.

It was freezing and damp out there. There were a few lights still on in the building, but it looked deserted. He felt like a survivor who'd jumped for it and was looking back to watch his ship finally founder, as an overwhelming emptiness started to flow all around him and through him.

35

Man Abandoned by Time

Back in the early 1970s there was a tragedy in Glasgow at Ibrox football stadium which has been largely forgotten. Hundreds of supporters fell down a long flight of steps and over each other. Dozens of them were crushed and suffocated. One prescient fan, alarmed by the surges of the crowd, stepped aside and in so doing moved altogether outside of the catastrophe's time and space. He managed to pull himself up onto the roof of a maintenance hut to one side of the steps. He sat and watched the disaster unfold itself beside him. You have read and re-read these details with morbid fascination.

When cultures shift it happens that a few people become focal points for the changes that take place. You have been affected by exactly the same social and cultural forces as your contemporaries, but it is you only who has come to exemplify them.

You might be the best artist around, though at times you are uncertain. What you do know is that you are different, not just because you have been immersed in this special creative moment, but because you have also conserved a distance from it. You have retained an ability to look back in at it from the outside world, and then to act as a bridge from one to the other.

You wonder whether an artist has to have entrepreneurial gifts. If there is no ability to get the art out into the world it follows that, in practical terms, there is no art. There are artists around who are gifted but who do not have this ability. You know who they are, other artists know who they are, but hardly anyone else does. You question whether, if your gifts were purely creative, you would be a better artist, more focussed. A genius. But these other gifted artists, the ones without much of a public presence, are not geniuses. Their inability to market themselves has not benefited their work. So there has not been a trade-off, a price you have paid.

That price, and it is a high price, is being paid by others. You have become concerned by what is happening to the art around here. Hoxton should be a breeding ground for artistic talent but whatever creative potential the area has is receding. There are always commercial aspects to art because there is no art without money, but when commerce arrives and dominates an area there is no longer any room for artists. You are not that fan at the stadium that day. Instead you know that you are the long, steep flight of stairs. Or a bridge. You are a bridge, a swaying, precarious bridge, for thousand upon thousand rushing people who are trampling on the art and over each other.

*

Fifteen men and one woman high up in the sky around a long oval table of French-polished oak, dotted with crystal decanters of mineral water, all willing to work late into the night for more money that none of them needed or knew what to do with. Except for Lanchester. An hour or so later, during a coffee break, features drooping with fatigue, he strode from the building and hailed a taxi.

'Take me to the Idiot Savant gallery in French Place.'

The takeover was being masterminded from the lead investment bank's City headquarters which were not far away from Hoxton. It was a short cab ride, swift at this time of night when there was little traffic left to clot the streets. The taxi forged ahead.

'If you step on it I'll make it worth your while.'

'Can't flog it more than this, mate.'

It took another five minutes or so to reach their destination, or almost reach it. They were no more than a hundred metres from IS when a figure in a hi-vis jacket stepped out into the road and flagged them down. Lanchester leant forward and tapped on the dividing window.

'Drive on, it's just a mentally ill chap masquerading as some sort of official. He's done this to me before.'

'It's a policeman.'

They came to a halt in front of red and white striped tape blocking off the roadway. The cab driver leaned from his window towards the constable.

'I'm afraid you can't go any further, sir.'

Lanchester wound his window down, poked his head out in turn.

'What's happened?'

'There's been an incident.'

'What do you mean, an incident?'

'The whole of the area around French Place is being sealed off.'

Lanchester instructed the driver to take him back to the bank.

'That's a funny smell,' said the driver, as he U-turned. 'Like a gas main's blown and taken a couple of drains with it.'

36

Where Does It All Stop?

Billy heard the explosion but did not witness it, because he had gone with Tom to the Bricklayers for more drinks. They were standing near the bar when it came, a flat retort cutting across the jukebox for several long seconds. No one reacted for a few moments, and then one or two people came running into the pub, shouting about a bomb round the corner. He didn't feel much surprise because he had been aware something was going to happen, that something had to happen, even if he didn't know what form it would take.

They hurried round the corner back to IS. Flames were rampaging around the ground floor, more than holding their own against the billows of sooty smoke pouring from the windows. Every so often pieces of burning debris fizzed into the air, leaving corkscrewing trails of sparks to float above the flames. The emergency services arrived in force, armed with trolleys, ladders, breathing apparatus and foam. There was an inappropriate eagerness to their activity. A bomb was a big event for them and they had received a lot of training they'd been waiting to put to the test.

There was nothing anyone else could do to help and as Billy watched he felt remote from the scene in front of him. It had something of Guy Fawkes night about it, despite lacking in any kind of festive atmosphere. There was that small despicable part of him, the same muted voice that had compared Rick's ruined mouth to a Bacon painting, saying that the explosion and its aftermath were excessively stylised and stage-managed — too much like an art video. That the bomb was an extension of the show and might as well have been part of the private view. He supposed these delusions could have been due to shock.

Eventually they were pushed away by the police, busy winding tape between lamp posts to seal off the area, and they returned to the pub for what turned out to be the beginnings of a wake. Next morning came the official casualty list. There were three fatalities: Alastair Given and two men who remained unidentified. Several other private view goers were injured, a couple of them seriously. Impregnation with excrement worsened many wounds. The casualties would have been worse, but the gallery's noxious contents had driven out nearly all of the guests before the explosion and most of the crowd outside had dispersed.

Speculation about the blast came in a further explosion, this time in the media. How the explosives got into the gallery was a mystery, as was the motivation for the bombing. Suddenly Kevin Thorn and his work were at the centre of more intense international attention than he had received so far, of a kind he had never anticipated. Various conjectures were abroad. It was a jealous rival of Thorn's. Or it was animal rights protesters who anticipated that the show would feature dead animals. Or it was an atrocity committed by an extreme right-wing group for unspecified reasons.

There was other news, in and around the stark facts of deaths and injuries. Soames announced that Thorn had admitted himself into a private clinic, citing stress caused by overwork. The details of his behaviour in his interview with Billy immediately before the show were re-analysed and there was conjecture about a nervous breakdown. Billy filed a couple of features, based on the bombing itself and his scoop of Lanchester's abortive purchase. He made play with the fact that Lanchester had placed an advance order and paid for a work without seeing it, a work that was unsellable.

He discussed the use of shit by other artists in their work and the ways they had sanitised it. Piero Manzoni, the pioneer in the field, sealed his shit inside airtight cans. Much more recently Chris Ofili had started to work with elephant dung on his canvases which he sealed away behind lacquer. Billy quoted experts on what possibilities there might have been of displaying Thorn's work in vitrines filled with inert gas or of sealing the excrement onto his own canvases with resin. The consensus was that there was no reason why not in either case, though his technicians would have needed to be meticulous with sealants and gaskets for the vitrines. His disdain for any hermetic barriers lent weight to theories that the artwork was simply a provocation and never seriously intended for display, and further fuelled gossip about mental health problems.

It was academic, in any case, because the work had been destroyed in the blast. By that point funds had changed hands and no insurance cover arranged, so it was unlikely that Lanchester would see his money refunded. Billy rang up Lanchester's firm and asked for a comment about their lead corporate finance partner's financial acumen. The firm said that it was Lanchester's affair and that he was unavailable for comment.

*

Lanchester sat at a conference table, round this time, with the managing partner and senior partner. The managing partner was thickset, a bulldog in pinstripes, his pink shirt setting off features ruddied by blood pressure. The senior partner had silver hair and long, slender hands which he steepled against his chest as he spoke.

'Thank you so much for coming in to see us at such short notice.'

'Not at all.'

'Would you like a drink of some sort?'

'No thank you.'

They had all been on the same management courses; when you were letting staff go it was important to offer them a beverage beforehand. No one knew why, but they all did it religiously.

'Henry, we can't go on like this.'

'Excuse me?'

'Your forays into the art market have brought the firm into disrepute.'

'I haven't breached any part of the partnership agreement.'

'We are becoming a laughing stock because you bought a pile of ordure.'

'Then why not laugh it off?'

'We'd like to settle this amicably. We want you to resign.'

'In that case, you can go and get fucked.'

The senior partner exhaled, an ageing parson dealing with a truculent choirboy. The managing director leaned forward.

'We can vote you out of the partnership.'

'You'll have to buy me out. You know that full well, and I won't settle for less than nine million.'

Lanchester rose.

'My solicitors will be in touch.'

*

He unfurled his legs onto the tabletop in front of him while his eyes drifted from the paper towards his living room window. Behind the tower blocks crowding out the horizon the sunset was purple and leaden with pollution, as if reflected from an oily puddle. Then he looked lower down and saw the line of trees at the edge of his estate where the dying winter light was turning them into silvery archways, diaphanous portals to the future.

In front of him was *The Herald*'s headline: "Bomb Blast At Thorn Show". It wasn't completely perfect because he didn't have the by-line to himself; a couple of *The Herald*'s news reporters had elbowed their way in and contributed bits and pieces. Even so it couldn't be ignored, there it was — his story was screaming from the front page: the bomb, the show and the shit painting sold for a quarter of a million pounds.

He tried to tell himself that his writing was now on a sure footing but part of him knew, even at this moment, that this might be more or less as far as it was going to go. Without Alastair's mentoring his career, such as it was, was looking precarious. All he could do was to make the most of what came his way while it lasted. He had neglected his diary for the past couple of weeks and it needed updating, because there was now no doubt that all the events around Idiot Savant were worth chronicling. But that task could wait a little longer, he wasn't going to let anything faze him for the time being.

He drew on his Silk Cut in celebration as his eyes descended to the wreckage strewn room. He wondered if he could afford to get a cleaner in to sort all this out. Perhaps he should ask one of those specialist cleaning firms to give the place a going over, since a normal cleaner might not take on a job like this. Too expensive, probably. The money *The Herald* would give him wasn't going to last long. He could ask them to raise his payment rate, but unless there were more scoops he knew they wouldn't wear it. His lower back ached and he wondered about seeing an osteopath before he looked around the room again. Whether he could afford it or not, maybe it was time to move to a better flat. He couldn't stomach living in this one any more anyway, not after what the gangsters had done to him in here. Public housing was dirt cheap, but it came with bargain bonuses of squalor and stress. He would look elsewhere. Prices were falling in the private sector and he could have a lodger in to help pay the mortgage. He wouldn't need to earn much.

He might move away from Hoxton. Hoxton was different without Alastair in it. His death had killed off any remaining spirit the area could muster, his warnings had come to pass and it really was all over. Increasing numbers of artists were packing up and shifting further east where space was cheaper, fleeing the theme park for youth the culturepreneurs were establishing in Hoxton, where everyone was a unit in everyone else's business plan.

He realised that he felt like a drink. Oh yes, the drinking. He toyed with the idea of booking himself into one of those expensive clinics, the Priory or similar, but there wasn't much point in blowing cash on that when AA was available free. It wasn't a problem, it could be sorted. He might allow himself a couple of final benders. The coke wasn't a big deal, he wasn't addicted — he could give it up any time he wanted, shortly he would chop himself out a couple of lines to prove the point. Finding another dealer hadn't been that hard.

Moments of unalloyed success in his occupation were few and he meant to make the most of this one. He stretched his arms up luxuriantly, before linking his hands behind his head and leaning back to enjoy the sunset. He was missing Alastair. Alastair had helped him with his work, he'd got his articles out there into the world just like he'd got his artists' work out there. Billy thought about his alleged infamies, but not deeply or for long. If he'd had an interest in the aesthetics of evil then that was no better and no worse than the aesthetics of anything else in the art of the twentieth century. From beginning to end it was the art that had mattered for Alastair.

He believed the bomb was deliberate. Big bang, big art. Alastair had gone out in a glorious blast, given his final and definitive judgment upon the art establishment, and taken a couple of evil bastards with him as a bonus. Not for him a life of meaningless toil and tawdry compromise. A visionary, a prankster. The best friend anybody could ever have.

Preparations were underway for the funeral. It was to be at St Leonard's in Shoreditch, and Becky and Erick were hand painting a coffin. All of the others would be there and this time he would be with them as an equal. Death had placed them all on the same level.

His thoughts were interrupted by the doorbell. He uncoiled his legs from the tabletop and slowly rose, thanking god that most of his callers were more civilised than the gangsters. They had probably shifted all that coke by now. It was a sorry consolation that Alastair wouldn't be approaching him for any more favours. He strolled to the door.

'We've got a few questions to ask you, Billy.'

Harkness, as ever looking like an unusually serious youth worker, a couple of other policemen with him. His colleagues were in plain clothes too but they were definitely policemen. Billy's new-found confidence upped and fled. Maybe the nightclub had made

265

a complaint, pressed charges, or it could be something to do with that visit to Kensington, long since dismissed from his mind. Whatever it was, it was trouble. They walked into the living room.

'Do you mind if I shift some of this?'

'Be my guest.'

Harkness tipped a chair forward, dislodged a pile of rubbish onto the floor, and sat. The others eyed the brimming settee, elected to lean against the walls and stare down at him instead.

'We want to know about the package Alastair Given gave you to mind recently,' said Harkness.

'What package?'

He knew he had to deny everything.

'The package of Semtex.'

'I have no idea at all what you're talking about.'

'The Semtex used in the explosion at the gallery. The bomb which killed three people and seriously injured several others. Two are in intensive care. Did you know that?'

'I know about the bomb, obviously — I've written about the explosion. Otherwise I've no idea what you're talking about.'

'You remember our chat about Alastair?'

'Of course I remember. What do you think I am, some sort of imbecile?'

'I don't think that's a fair question to put to the inspector,' intervened one of the other detectives, notable for an eyebrow piercing at odds with his plump features. He sneered at Billy and addressed Harkness. 'Let's take him in.'

Harkness held up a hand.

'You remember the meeting I took you to, the briefing I left on your answerphone?'

'Yes, I remember it all, I've said that.'

'That wasn't enough for you?'

'I didn't see what any of it had to do with me.'

'The fact that those gangsters had links to neo-fascists and got hold of explosives didn't concern you?'

'I don't know anything about any of that.'

'We had them under surveillance. We think they were planning to bomb the Bangladeshi community in Brick Lane. They got Alastair Given to mind the explosives for them. We searched his studio discreetly a couple of times, but he unloaded the Semtex to someone else. Then, as you know full well, he blew himself up along with the gangsters.'

'There's no way I'd keep explosives for him or for anyone else. I'm a journalist, not a terrorist.'

Harkness leaned closer. His eyes were brown, Billy saw, but not completely brown, he could see the irises were flecked with fine filaments of yellow.

'You're making it worse for yourself, Billy. We're talking about conspiracy to commit murder. A life sentence.'

He sat forward on the edge of his chair, did his best to meet Harkness's gaze.

'It's a tragedy Alastair's dead. I've no idea whether he blew himself up deliberately, or what happened.'

Nothing had changed. There was nothing to gain from volunteering information. The police couldn't do anything for him except take him away and lock him up.

'Do you want us to take you into custody under the Prevention of Terrorism Act?'

'I can't stop you doing that if that's what you want to do, but it would just waste everyone's time. I don't know anything of any use to you.'

Harkness sighed heavily.

'Do you think the law doesn't apply to you?'

'Do you want me to write about this in the press?'

'Is that meant to scare us?'

After they slammed the door behind them, he heard a parting comment from the corridor outside:

'The state of the place.'

He sat there hoping there was nothing they could get on him. At least Alastair wasn't going to give him away.

37

Dead Ends Expire Unexplained

It wasn't a long journey, only a few stops along the Central Line to Leyton but Billy didn't like looking out of the tube carriage windows at the daylight. Even though this was still East London at this distance from the centre it was starting to become suburban. If all of the streets in the middle of town were a gigantic sieve that occasionally caught a fleck of human gold in the endless dross and grime, then outside of them were the endless semis, homes for lives half lived. But a short walk away from the station there was something happening.

Bundled in overcoat and scarf, he sat in the middle of the street with Rick. Rick was wearing a complicated brace round the lower half of his face: steel rods, grommets and pinions. Billy thought of Tinguely, but mainly of Meccano. The brace was a miniature echo of the watchtower he could see on top of one of the houses behind Rick, a spindly edifice of planks with long legs of scaffolding, like one of the aliens from *The War of the Worlds*.

Rick stretched, let himself drop back into the settee they were sitting on. It had been dragged from a derelict house, a battered remnant of domesticity. The upholstery was stained, one of the base cushions was missing and both arms were badly slashed, but it was comfortable. Rick appeared oblivious to the cold, perhaps the result of a few hours labour helping to finish off the tower.

'Never worked with scaffolding before,' he said.

He showed off his hands. Scorings and scrapings, a couple of fluid-filled blobs forming. He started to build a spliff.

'We've already housed more homeless here than they did in that housing department.'

'Is that what all this is about?'

'You know what this is all about but you never want to get involved, do you? You coulda helped us stop that bombing.'

Billy sat more upright, folded his arms.

'I don't see how.'

'You knew something, I know you did.'

Rick was licking down a cigarette, opening it over a mosaic of Rizlas.

'Alastair blew up those racists or whatever they were,' Billy said. 'That was the end of it.'

'What about those other people who were injured?'

Rick touched the steel frame round the lower half of his face.

'Is this why you've dragged me all the way out here,' Billy said, 'to go through it all again?'

'No, to publicise what we're about. You're the only journo I know from the national media.'

'I don't have any clout there, you know that.'

'Sound more up for it, can't you? We want everyone to know what's coming on top here. It's all out in the open this time. That's the way things are gonna be for me from now on. No more undercover shit.'

It was amazing that they remained on speaking terms after everything that had happened. For a fleeting moment or two, as ever with Rick, he felt guilty. Rick was twisting round the end of his spliff, lighting it.

'We're gonna see action up here. That tower up there' — he drew deeply — 'that's proper art, and we're going to make more of it. Loads more of us are gonna come down here.'

If there was no brace round his face Rick would have smiled one of his wide and generous smiles, Billy was sure. He was happier out here like this, with everything laid out for him in straightforward ways. Rick took another toke, passed the spliff to him.

'The bypass ain't coming through here without a fight,' he said. 'We're putting Leyton on the map. Claremont Road is gonna be massive. We've got to stop all this mad roadbuilding. Protecting the environment is gonna be what politics is all about soon.'

'Rick, this is the East End. The environment round here's always been fucked.'

'There you go again.'

Rick laughed, then winced as his facial sinews pulled against his brace and coughed out smoke.

*

'My name's Marie and I'm an alcoholic.'

'Hello, Marie,' said everyone. The greeting was loud, as if to make up for its mechanical quality but, momentarily, this energetic coordination made him optimistic about the meeting's abilities to distil sobriety. Marie's face was the texture of orange peel. She talked at length about her teenage son's ecstasy binges, her inability to intervene because of her own problems with wine.

'Thank you, Marie,' came the chorus at the end of her offering.

Billy's attention wandered. He was in no position to think himself superior to anyone here yet it had been frustrating to be stuck at the meeting for more than two hours, hearing these stories which were tailored to the blueprint of addiction. There should be special AA meetings for creative artists, he thought, although he knew that if there were, there was no reason to think he would be admitted to them. Nevertheless it was a pleasing fantasy to float off on while he sat there. There could be a committee to assess levels of substance abuse against artistic achievement. An annual membership, waivable for artists of talent in reduced circumstances.

Even if anyone could come to this meeting, there were still some good stories to be had. One of the men told them about picking a woman up in a nightclub, and then waking up the following morning back at her place and realising he'd pissed the bed, before slinking off in shame. Billy couldn't help thinking that he should have told her she'd done it. Yes, he was very much part of this sordid shambles, alongside them all in the gutter, and there was no point claiming he was the one looking up at the stars.

Everyone in here saw stars when they were guttered, the same way he did

Twelve steppers stepped in and out, fetching tea from an urn in the hallway or using the lavatory. He wondered whether to exit under the pretext of using these facilities. Narcotics Anonymous was the alternative, but he knew it would be mostly junkies whining on in their phlegmy, smacked-out voices, complemented by a scattering of crackheads on the verge of meltdown. He wasn't going to sit there with that lot, worrying whether his wallet was safe.

This was no more than a religious service, the twelve steps were the creed and the confessions one long sermon, but the ways things were going, he knew this wouldn't be his last visit. He couldn't pretend there was an alternative; he couldn't afford the Priory. The proceedings ended with everyone rattling off a litany: 'God grant me the grace to accept the things...' He realised he needed a couple of drinks and a few lines. It was a blurred truth the lengthy meeting had brought into sharper focus.

*

Thorn said he would give him a proper interview, said he would help him with a book. Alastair's death had unsettled him, Billy thought, or unsettled him further. He had a couple of sessions with Thorn, but it didn't work. Thorn ranted over him, wouldn't listen to any of his questions. He ended up with a few fragments, raw and unpolished, whether they were nuggets or turds was hard to say, and that was all.

*

Though it was spotless with a freshly waxed floor and newly laundered drapes at its tall windows, the hotel's function room had the Miss Haversham's parlour air of all function rooms, of a deep stillness only briefly disturbed. But if its current occupants were sensitive to such nuance there was no sign of it. The evening had

271

begun at half-past six, it was now eight and the flimsy canapés on offer did little to soak up the champagne.

There was a lot of the latter because the brewing and distilling conglomerate which owned the marque was one of the award's sponsors. Nearly everybody was tipsy and Billy was swaying on his feet, periodically lunging through the crush towards trays of champagne, which now and again would be swung out of his reach. The staff were forming their view about him.

The Shiraz prize was awarded for the most innovative artworks during the preceding year by artists under thirty. It was prestigious, not as prestigious as the Turner or the Jerwood, yet all the same it was a noteworthy validation because it marked the point where the art establishment started to formally recognise and reward achievement. This year the short list featured some of the artists Alistair had assisted — Tania and Erick were on it, Becky too. There was a general feeling that it was a strong list; the critics said it had been a bumper year for works by younger artists.

Billy had blagged his way onto the guest-list for the ceremony by using *The Herald's* name, despite the fact they hadn't commissioned him to write anything about the awards. So what — he didn't see why he should be excluded. For him this was all about Alastair, about what he had done to help all of his artists, and Billy knew he was a part of that too. He gave up trying to get himself another drink, spotted Tom and made his way over to him.

'Congratulations,' he said. The Arts Council had appointed Tom as an adviser in its fine art department.

'Thanks. They were so flattering that I decided to give it a try.'

He knew Tom had scouted around collectors and galleries for another advisory position to no avail. His name wasn't mentioned in any of the media coverage, but everyone in the art world knew who Lanchester's adviser had been. Everyone except the Arts Council, that was; the existence of somnolent bureaucracies wasn't always to the bad.

'How's it working out?

'I've become the man with the cheque book.'

He looked at Tom's newly acquired suit, supposed there was a touch of the Lanchesters about him now. He considered asking after Tom's own artwork but decided that wasn't worth pursuing. He glanced around and saw Erick, busy drawing on a cigarette. Erick saw him and started slightly, stared about as if he wanted to lose himself in the crowd. Once he had been a friend and now he was avoiding Billy. The chill of rejection — a preparation, perhaps, for the day he would die, expelled from the world for good. He thought of the woman he had encountered who was infatuated with death, and of Kevin Thorn because she had been obsessed with him, and he thought of Alastair.

Already he was beginning to suspect that memories of Alastair would fade quickly. He was not an artist, after all, and his vision would end with him. He let his momentum carry him over to Erick, pretended he hadn't seen that Erick didn't want to know him any more.

'How's Tania?' he said. 'I haven't seen either of you since the funeral.'

'We are fine both of us, thank you.'

'I hear she's expecting.'

'Yes, that is correct.

It was hard to imagine, but anything that distracted her from action against him was welcome.

'Big change, eh?'

'There are quite a number of big changes recently. Ah, I see Tania waving to me; excuse me.'

Billy weaved over to talk to Linda and Becky. Becky's flute was brimming with sparkling spring water. Alongside her, Linda was holding a glass of champagne, because she believed a small amount of social lubricant helped her to network more effectively on these occasions. Linda air-kissed him.

Muuuwah, muuuwah.

'That's a nice dress,' he said. It was purple and velvet.

'Rifat Ozbek, darling.'

Becky was in a little black dress, the breath caught in his throat as he looked at her.

*

Becky moves back a step, retreating from his appraisal. His borrowed jacket does nothing to disguise his seediness and she hopes he will not try to kiss her.

'Waiting with bated breath, I expect Becky?'

'Exactly how does one bate one's breath?'

'Bate is a truncation of abate, isn't it?'

'You're so good with words.'

Linda cuts in. 'Billy, I'm dying to read your take on the short list. You're ever such a good writer, sweetie.'

'Thanks, that's kind of you to say so. Is it true that you were at the Slade with one of the judges, if you don't mind me asking?'

'That's right — Tim Lerwick. But there's no story about conflict of interest there, darling. He would have absented himself when Becky's work was discussed. Actually one of the other judges, Susan Jeffers, bought one of Becky's works recently—'

He burps — he cannot stop himself — and raises a hand to his mouth. Becky does not hide a look of disgust.

'...for rather a lot of money. She took a distinct shine to Becky. That's right isn't it?'

She turns to her protégée, who raises her chin. Billy notices her erect posture, as if for the first time, unless she had lately taken up Alexander technique or yoga. Yet it appears to come naturally to her, this confident carriage of someone of standing.

'I can't keep track of all these collectors,' Becky says. 'I'm not interested in the business side of things.'

'You see how idealistic my artists are, Billy. Bloom's is the acme of anti-capitalism.'

'If you say so.'

'You must pop into our new gallery in the West End soon.'

'I'd love to. And Crispin, where is Crispin tonight?'

'Back at home where he belongs. Did you expect me to come here like Long John Silver with him perched on my shoulder?'

'Birds of a feather and all that.'

'So I'm a bird now am I, darling?

For a moment Becky looks startled but says nothing.

'Here I was thinking I was an up-and-coming player in the creative industries.'

Linda folds her arms, stares him down, smiling all the while.

'Not as such, I meant...'

As he took his leave from them he made a false start, wobbling as if trying to move off in two directions at once, and caught Becky and Linda looking at each other. The chairman of the judges — a knight of commerce and one of the sponsor's directors — was starting his speech.

'Ladies and gentlemen, part of the reason London is now acquiring a new-found international reputation for the quality of its culture is, indubitably, due to its younger artists. This year has seen a particularly outstanding series of innovative works by the capital's youthful creative talents, which means that my fellow judges and I have had an onerous — though of course enjoyable — task in selecting a shortlist...'

On he went. If this guy was good at manufacturing washing machines and ovens, Billy thought, public speaking was not his forte. He had a disturbing intimation that the mediocrity of the rhetoric would be accompanied by a deficit in the judging panel's discrimination. The lack of independence there was also ominous.

The chairman extracted an envelope from an inside breast pocket and donned a pair of reading glasses.

'Without more ado, I'll reveal the names of the two runners-up followed by the winner.'

He untucked the flap of the envelope.

'Third, Tania Russell Smith and Erick Heckendorf for *Box*.'

A spatter of applause as the pair mounted the stage to collect the cheque. Tania was resplendent in a magenta dress to match the triumphal torch of her hair, Erick a compact acolyte at her side.

'Second, Stewart MacKenzie for *Doubtful Rhapsody*.'

This time the clapping was more widespread and vigorous. In and around it came muted cheers as the wayward Caledonian sculptor strode up the steps in industrial footwear.

'And this year's winner of the Shiraz prize is Rebecca Edge for her installation *In Between*.'

Strong, sustained applause as Becky walked on stage, exchanged kisses with the chairman and smiled carefully into the camera flashes.

Epilogue

Where Does It All Stop?

'Is everyone ready?' asked Tania. She was standing next to Erick, who was holding a crowbar in one hand, drawing on a cigarette with the other. They were both dressed in shifts of shiny fabric and looking over at us.

We were all there: Tom; Becky; Rick; Lanchester; Linda Bloom; DC Harkness and his two plainclothes colleagues; Kevin Thorn; Soames; a trustafarian PA; a man without a tongue (amid a corona of pale light); the skinny drug dealer from 333 and the Lux; fifty or so ravers; a clubber in a striped T-shirt; the bailiffs Colin and Trevor; Jeevons the council planning officer; a goth barmaid; a paramedic: several property developers in suits; a Filipina maid; the photographer; *The Herald*'s arts editor; two television interviewers and a TV director; a bouncer; a security guard; the waitress from the Bean café; a newspaper seller; a vagrant; a man in a lab coat with mental health issues; a policeman; a librarian in Essex called Derek; Booth, the senior tax partner from Millhouse Durrant; the senior partner and the managing partner of Millhouse Durrant; a knight of commerce; Stewart MacKenzie; a contingent of twenty-five other artists from Hoxton and Shoreditch plus a Polish designer boyfriend and a Staffordshire Bull Terrier; a man with two broken legs (also with a corona of pale light); Crispin the African grey parrot; the two gangsters (edged by coronas); Alastair (with his own corona); and I.

Everyone was ready, or at least no one said that they weren't ready, so Erick began to prise the lid from the box.

Acknowledgements

I would like to thank all of the staff and contributors of *Mute* magazine who were largely instrumental in introducing me to the art world. For help with the manuscript and for feedback I'd like to thank Philip Jennings, Nicholas Royle, James Flint, James Lever, Olivia Stewart-Liberty, Tom McCarthy and Hari Kunzru. I would also like to thank my agents Jonny Pegg and Shaheeda Sabir for their strenuous efforts in representing me at Curtis Brown. I'd like to express my gratitude to Vicky Olliver for her assiduous proof reading. Finally I would like to thank all of the staff at Pegasus Publishing.

Peter Carty is an award-winning writer and journalist who writes about art and culture for publications including the Guardian, the Independent and the Financial Times. His short fiction is on English literature syllabuses. He lives in London. This is his first novel.